Virginia Eviline Spencer

Alliteration in Spenser's poetry discussed and compared with the alliteration as employed by Drayton and Daniel

Virginia Eviline Spencer

Alliteration in Spenser's poetry discussed and compared with the alliteration as employed by Drayton and Daniel

ISBN/EAN: 9783337282011

Printed in Europe, USA, Canada, Australia, Japan

Cover: Foto ©Andreas Hilbeck / pixelio.de

More available books at **www.hansebooks.com**

ALLITERATION IN SPENSER'S POETRY

DISCUSSED AND COMPARED WITH THE ALLITERATION AS EMPLOYED BY DRAYTON AND DANIEL.

A DISSERTATION PRESENTED TO THE PHILOSOPHICAL FACULTY (I. SEET.) OF THE UNIVERSITY OF ZURICH, FOR THE ACQUISITION OF THE DEGREE OF DOCTOR OF PHILOSOPHY.

PART I.

--BY-

VIRGINIA EVILINE SPENCER.

APPROVED BY PROF. TH. VETTER.

1898.

CONTENTS.

PART I.

PART II.

LITERATURE.

1. McClumpha: The Alliteration of Chaucer; Leipzig 1888.

2. Petzold: Ueber die Alliteration in den Werken Chaucers, mit Ausschluss der Canterbury Tales; Marburg 1889.

3. Hoefer: Alliteration bei Gower, Leipzig-Reudnitz 1890.

4. Willert: Alliterierende Bindungen in der neuenglischen Bibeluebersetzung; Berlin 1897.

—4—

5. Seitz: Zur Alliteration im Neuenglischen; Itzehoe, (first part) 1883, (second part) 1884.

6. Zeuner: Die Alliteration bei Neuenglischen Ditchtern; **Halle,** 1880.

7. Opitz: Die Stabreimenden Wortbindungen in den Dichtungen Walter Scotts I: Trebnitz, i. Schl. 1893.

8. Ten Brink: Chaucer's Sprache und Verskunst; Leipzig, 1884.

9. Schipper: Englische Metrik; Bonn, 1881.

10. Saintsbury: Elizabethan Literature.; London 1887.

TEXTS.

Spenser: The Poetical Works of Edmund Spenser (5 vols.), London, William Pickering, 1839.

Drayton: The works of Michael Drayton, Esq.: London, printed by J. Hughs, near Loncoln's-Inn-Fields, 1743.

Daniel: The complete works in verse and prose of Samuel Daniel, by the Rev. Alexander B. Grosart, in five volumes. **Printed for Spenser Society,** vols. I, II. III, 1885; vols. IV, V, 1896.

ABBREVIATIONS.

SPENSER.

F. Q. Fairy Queen.
C. C. H. Colin Clouts Come Home Again
V. G. Virgils Gnat.
S. C. Shepheards' Calendar.
H. L. An Hymne in Honour of Love.
H. B. An Hymne in Honour of Beautie.
H. H. L. An Hymne in Honour of Heavenly Love.
H. H. B. An Hymne in Honour of Heavenly Beautie.
V. P. The Visions of Petrarch.
V. B. The Visions sof Bellay.
V. W. V. Visions of the World's Vanitie.
M. H. T. Prosopopoia; or Mother Hubbard's Tale.
Proth. Prothalamion.
Epith. Epthilamion.
Am. Amoretti; or Sonnets.
Daph. Daphnaida: (an Elegie).
Ast. Astrophel. (A Pastoral Eligie.)
El. An Elegie.
Ep. (I). An Epitaph.
Ep. (II). An Epitaph.
T. M. The Teares of the Muses.
R. R. The Ruines of Rome.
R. T. The Ruines of Time.
Muiop. Muiopotmos.
B. I. Brittain's Ida.

DRAYTON.

B. A. The Battle of Agincourt.
B. W. The Barons Wars.
H. E. England's Heroical Epistles.

1. R. H. Rosamond to King Henry II.
2. H. R. Henry to Rosamond.
3. J. M. King John to Matilda.
4. M. J. Matilda to King John.
5. I. Mor. Queen Isabel to Mortimer.
6. Mor. I. Mortimer to Queen Isabel.
7. E. A. Edward, the Black Prince, to Alice, Countess of Salisbury.
8. A. E. Alice, Countess of Salisbury, to the Black Prince.
9. I. R. Queen Isabel to Richard the Second.
10. R. I. Richard II to Queen Isabel.
11. C. O. T. Queen Catherine to Owen Tudor.
12. O. T. C. Owen Tudor to Queen Catherine.
13. E. C. H. Elenor Cobham to Duke Humphry.
14. H. E. C. Duke Humphry to Elenor Cobham.
15. W. M. William de la Pool, Duke of Suffolk, to Queen Margaret.
16. M. W. Queen Margaret to William de la Pool, Duke of Suffolk.
17. E. S. Edward IV to Mistress Shore.
18. S. E. Mrs. Shore to Edward IV.
19. M. C. B. Mary, the French Queen, to Charles Brandon, Duke of Suffolk.
20. C. B. M. Charles Brandon, Duke of Suffolk, to Mary, the French Queen.
21. H. H. L. Ger. Henry Howard, Earl of Surrey, to the Lady Geraldine.
22. L. Ger. H. H. Lady Geraldine to Henry Howard, Earl of Surrey.
23. J. G. G. D. The Lady Jane Gray to the Lord Gilford Dudley.
24. G. D. J. G. Gilford Dudley to the Lady Jane Gray.
M. M. The Miseries of Queen Margaret.
Nym. Nymphidia; or the Court of Fairy.
M.-C. The Moon-Calf.
I. R. N. The Legend of Robert, Duke of Normandy.
II. Mat. F. The Legend of Matilda the Fair.
III. P. G. The Legend of Pierce Gaveston.
IV. Crom. The Legend of Tho. Cromwell, E. of Essex.
Q. C. The Quest of Cynthia.
S. S. The Shepherd's Sirena.
Pol. Poly-Olbion.
Elgs. Eligies.

1. L. L. Of his Lady's not coming to London.
2. G. S. To Master George Sandys.
3. W. B. To my noble friend Master William Brown.
4. L. S. Upon the three sons of the Lord Sheffield.
5. L. I. S. To the noble Lady, the Laetis I. S. of worldly crosses.
6. P. C. An Alegy upon the death of the Lady Penelope Clifton.
7. L. A. Upon the noble Lady Aston's departure from Spain.
8. H. R. To my dearly loved Friend Henry Reynolds, Esq., of Poets and Poesy.

Ids. Ideas.

Owl.

Mn. Mn. The Man in the Moon.

Ods. Odes.
1. To Himself and the Harp.
2. To the New Year.
3. To His Valentine.
4. The Heart.
5. The Sacrifice to Apollo.
6. To Cupid.
7. The Amouret Anacreontick.
8. Love's Conquest.
9. To the Virginian Voyage.
10. An Ode written in the Peak.
11. His Defense Against the Idle Critic.
12. To His Rival.
13. A Skeltonian.
14. The Cryer.
15. To His Coy Love.
16. An Hymn.
17. Bal. A. His Balad of Agincourt.

Eclogs. Eclogues.

M. E. The Muses Elysium.

N. F. Noah's Flood.

M. B. M. Moses, His Birth and Miracles.

DANIEL.

S. D. Sonnets to Delia.
C. R. The Complaint of Rosamond.
O. M. A. A Letter from Octavia to Marcus Antonius.

Pau.   A Panegyrike Congratulatorie to James I.

F. D.   A Funerall Poeme upon the death of the Earl of Devonshire.

Eps.   Epistles.

1. T. E.   To Sir Thomas Egerton.

2. H. H.   To Lord Henrie Howard.

3. L. M.   To Lady Margaret, Countess of Cumberland.

4. L. L.   To Lady Lucie, Countess of Bedford.

5. L. A.   To the Lady Annie Clifford.

6. H. W.   To Henry Wriothesly, Earle of Southampton.

Mus.   Musophilies.

Ode.   An Ode.

Past.   A Pastorall.

P. S.   To Sir Phillip Sidney.

U. S.   Ulisess and the Syren.

E. S.   To Edward Seymour, Earle of Hertford

W. J.   Of William Jones, His Nennio 1595.

P. C.   Penelope's Complaint.

C. E.   To my friend Clement Edmonds.

Q. A. W. W.   Queen Anna's New World of Worlds.

J. F.   John Florio's 1613 edition of his "Done Into English."

B. W.   James Montague, Bishop of Winchester.

C. W.   The Civile Wars.

Cleo.   Cleopatra.

Phil.   Philotas.

V. G.   Vision of Twelve Goddesses.

Q. A.   Queen's Arcadia.

T. F.   Thety's Festivall.

H. T.   Hymen's Triumph.

Quality of Rhyming Letter.

Spenser's alliteration, in regard to the rhyming letters, is on the whole, exact and in accordance with the rules for the rhyming letters of alliterative poetry. There are however a few instances which deserve special notice. The combinations sp and st alliterate with s; as: save or spill; sword and speare; shield and spear; and: cloudie storme and bitter showre; streightway sent, shortly it restored; saddle, steed.

Such alliteration, however is comparatively seldom; another manner of alliterating, the combinations sp and st, though not more frequent than the one just noticed, is more unusual in character. The second letters of the combinations have the power to alliterate, when occupying emphatic positions in the verse, and when standing in close connection with other emphatic words with which they alliterate; as for sp:

Substantiative and modifying adj: (examples from F. Q.).

Spirituale repast, F. Q. 1-10-48; spoyleful Picts, F. Q. II-10-63; pitteous spoyle, F. Q. II-12-19; poynant speare, F. Q. 1-7-19; pittifull spectacle, II-1-10; spacious plaine, II-12-50; speedy pace, II-12-16; reproachfull spight, III-2-8; pretious spycery, III-6-16; imperious speach, III-10-25; purchast spoile, IV-9-12.

Substantives in coordinate construction or connected by a preposition:

Sportes and, pastime, 1-6-27; spot or pride, 1-12-22; point of, speare, III-1-9; spight of, prides, IV-1-42; sport and play, IV-4-13; spoile of peoples, V-2-27; push of pointed speare, 1-11-9.

Verb with object or modifier:

Spent his perlous store, II-11-27; prince espyde, II-11-24; pricks with spurs, II-5-38; praises speake, II-10-40; pride does spight, 1-4-14; price that he, spilt, 1-5-26; reproaches spoke, 1-5-50; powres, disperse, 1-9-18; pretious blood which, was, spilt, 1-10-57; pounces, spend, 1-11-19; spightfull poison spues, 1-4-32; repaired, her tackles, spent, 1-12-42; privy spyals plast, II-1-1; spare his payne, II-1-5; disperst with puff, III-1-16; respect of person or of port, III-11-16; of, puissaunce, spent,

III-2-3; spend her pining heart, III-2-41; spredd, prayse, III-3-3; with prophecy inspir'd, III-1-25; impressed in, spright, III-4-19; spare, with reproch my paine. III-6-22; employ, speare. III-10-28; pricke with, speede, IV-6-2; despieth for, pride, V-2-10; poured forth with plentifull dispence, II-12-42. Other constructions: past, spent, I-3-32; pure unspotted maid, I-6-16; pure unspotted life, I-10-3; puissant lords, spright, II-2-29; spyde, pace, II-12-68.

Substantiative and adj. st and t:

Stony towre, I-7-12; trickling streame, I-11-48; strong extremeties, II-2-38; twinckling starres, II-3-26; stedfast towre, II-8-35; up to a stately turret, II-9-11; stryfull termes, III-2-12; tragicke stage, III-12-3.

Verb with object or modifier:

Sturdie courage tame, I-6-26; termes established, I-9-41; from teares abstayne. II-1-56; with, teares did steepe, II-2-1; stablish terms betwixt. II-2-32; trembling still he stoode, II-8-46; trap his tomb-blacke steed II-8-16; strokes he told, II-8-11; tell, stay to tell, II-9-47; unto the, streame him to betake, II-10-16; restraining stealth and strong extortion, II-10-39; from, stocke was torne, II-10-36; towred still, II-12-30; turned in, stownd, III-1-21; trained up in, stowre, III-2-6; streightly straynd, and colled tenderly, III-2-34; tickle be the termes of, state, III-4-28; turne we our steeds: (also) retird their steeds, III-8-18; store of treasure, to tempt, III-10-29; trembling stood, III-11-40; establish in the troubled mynd, IV-3-13; tossed with his stormes which, still remaine, IV-11-38, tied were to stedfast chastity, V-7-9.

Other constructions:

Sterne and terrible, II-1-6; streames of tears, II-2-8, in time of storme II-12-24; tender feete upon the stony ground, III-4-34.

Such alliteration usually retains its individuality only when it forms the entire alliteration; when other words beginning with s, occupy emphatic positions in the verse, the first letters usually become alliterating; there are however a few instances where the position of the words separates them into groups, in which the second letter remains distinctly alliterative as: Now singing sweetly to suprize her sprights. III-10-8. But he then spotted with reproach, or secrete shame, VI-6-12.

The combination wr was in the transition period, so that as an alliterating term, it has a double function, rhyming, on the one hand, with w, on the other, with r. The former is the more frequent, which shows that the old pronunciation was still the prevailing one; examples for wr:

Substantiative and adj:

Wretched world, 1-10-21; wofull wretch, 11-1-17; wretched we, 11-1-32; wretched wight, 11-1-36; weary wretch, 11-1-17; wrathfull will, 111-1-11; unworthy wretch. 111-11-11; wretched weeds, 1V-8-12; wrathfull wight, 1V;-8-15; waters wroth, 1V-11-11; wretched wize, V-9-9; wretched woman, miserable wight, V-10-21; unworthy wretch.

Coordinate construction:

Wretched, and woefull, 11-10-62; weary wretched plight, 111-7-5; wretchednesse and wo, 111-12-11; wofull wretched (maid), 1V-7-14; in wretched thraldome, weake and wan, V-6-16; woe and wretchednesse, V-10-11; wretched wearie life, V1-5-5.

Verb with object or modifier:

(Weake wretch), I wrapt myselfe, in, weed, 11-1-52; awaite in, wretchednesse, 1-12-33; weene your wrong (to justify), 111-1-25; wexed, wroth, 1V-1-10; waste his wretched daies in wofull plight, 1V-7-39; weeping, wroth, IV-9-9; worke, wracke, 1V-9-25; war ye wrongfully have wielded, 1V-9-37; wrong the weaker, V1-2-23; (wight) should weet of me, nor worke me any wrong, V1-2-30, (vs. 5 & 6).

Other constructions:

Weary of that wretched life, 11-10-32; wretched man in, wofull cace, 111-10-14; wretched anguishe and incessant woe, 1V-9-39; wreckes of wrathfull winde, 1V-11-52; in wretched bondage, wofully, V-6-10; unweeting have you wronged, V-8-13.

The instances of wr and r do not afford sufficient variety to warrant a classification, the most important are the various combinations of right and wrong; these are so frequent that they alone would suffice to establish the class.

Right or wrong, 1-3-18; right and wrong, V-1-7; wrong and right, 11-4-42; right for, wrong, 111-1-3; of right, great wrong, V-2-31; wrong or right, V-2-15; wrongs, right, V-2-16; right in their wrongs rul'd by righteous lore, V-7-1; by, wrong, bereaved of right, 11-2-18; wrongfull outrage of unrighteous men, 111-11-10; care of right or ruth of wretches wrong, 1V-12-9.

Other examples: ransackt Greece, when they were wroth, 11-10-10, move to wrath, and indignation reare, 11-4-5; read who hath ye wrought; 11-1-18; royall gifts, wrought, V-7-21; wretched ruine, V-9-46; ruth of, wretched plight, V-9-50; wretched life bereave, V-5-37.

The initial h in such words as honor, hour, humble, still retained by Spenser its power of alliterating, as: And highly honourd in his haughtie eye, F. Q. I-7-16; Which hunt for honor, raised from below, ib. IV-1-19; And honourd him with all that her behoved ib. V-10-39; That made them grow so high t' all honorable hap. ib. VI-4-36; And heavnly honours yield, as to them twaine, M., VI-4; The which Rinaldo drunck in happie howre, F. Q. IV-3-45; Nor happy howre, beheld with gazeful eye, ib., IV-10-28; But ah! unhappy howre me thither brought, ib., IV-7-18; Presume so high to stretch mine humble quill? F. Q. III-1-3 (1); In lofty looks to hide an humble minde, ib., III-10-30; She did prostrate, and with right humble hart, ib., V-7-7.

Kn. and gn seem to be in the transition period. McClumpha gives for Chaucer the alliteration of knight, king. Such an alliteration does not occur in Spenser's poetry; king when alliterating, rhymes only with such words as crowne, kesar, conqueror. Knight alliterates frequently, but always with a word with initial kn or n; examples for the latter are: "A Stranger Knight," sayd he, "unknowne by name," F. Q. IV-6-6; Herein the noblesse of this Knight exceeds, ib., V-2-1; All were they nigh an hundred Knights of name, ib., V-8-50; When Calidore thus first, "Haile, noblest knight," ib., VI-1-4; The name of Knighthood he did disavow, ib., VI-5-37.

This manner of alliterating occurs by other words with initial kn: Some daily seene and knowen by their names, F. Q. II-9-50; To whom as he approcht, he knew anone, ib., V-11-37; Well knowne, and far renowned heretofore, ib., V-11-49. The frequent instances of such an alliteration show that it was the prevailing one; only in the word, knife does the initial k retain its original force, as is shown by the alliteration: A cruell knife that made a griesly wound. F. Q., II-1-39; Entrenched deep with knyfe accursed keene, ib., III-12-20; Through cruell knife that her deare heart did karve, ib., IV-1-4; With cursed knife cutting the twist in twain, ib., IV-2-48. The instances of the alliteration of gn are not sufficiently numerous to warrant definite conclusions, for from the few cases it is not possible to determine whether the alliteration is intentional, or whether in each case it is simply a matter of chance. It will be interesting to cite the examples noted for they in themselves show the double alliteration, gn ,g: And grimly gnash, threatning revenge in vaine, F. Q. II-4-15; But Radigund, full of . heart-gnawing griefe, ib., V-4-47; gn, n: Gnawing her nayles for felnesse and for yre, F. Q. IV-8-23; May by this gnatts complaint be easily knowen, V. G., 14 (ded.); Shall lighter seeme then this gnats idle name, ib., 1.

Formal alliteration which is common to the three poets:

Regel in his paper upon "the Alliteration in Layamon," Germanistche Studien, (Sup.), B. d., I., 171—, gave a classification for formal alliterations, which has been followed (with some slight variations in the different papers), by McClumpha, Petzold, Hoefer, Opitz, and Willert; also further, E. Kölbing in his edition of Byron's Siege of Corinth, Berlin, 1893, and J. Ellinger, "Zur Alliteration in der modernen englischen Proqsadichtung." The subject of this investigation lies in between the two periods, which have been handled in the above mentioned papers; for the older period we have Chaucer, discussed by McClumpha and Petzold, and Gower by Hoefer; for the later period, the alliteration of King James's Version of the Holy Bible, by Willert, Byron's Siege of Corinth by Kölbing, alliteration in Walter Scott's works, by Opitz. Zenner discusses alliteration in the works of Burns, Scott, Moore, and Byron, but does not follow the classification for formal alliteration. For the sake of comparison with the two periods, I have adopted the same method of classification, and to show the relation to Chaucer, have followed McClumpha, in his application of the classification. The other papers as before mentioned show some variations and hence would not be a means of so direct a comparison. The classification takes as a basis the three chief relations of alliterating combinations, etymological, ideal or associative, and grammatical. The following is a synopsis of the classification:

A.   Etymological: words of the same stem.

B.   Association.
    (1).   Concrete ideas.
    (2).   Abstract, or abstract and concrete.
    (3).   Emphasis.
    (4).   Contrast.

C.   Grammatical:
    (1).   Substantive and modifying adjective.
    (2).   Verb or adjective with modifying adverb or adverbial phrase.
    (3).   Substantive and verb, as subject and predicate.
    (4).   Verb and substantive as predicate and object.

In the following classification, Spenser is taken as the center and his combinations are the standard of comparison. The different classes are not distinctly separated, and often an alliterating combination falls under more than one class: in such instances it is given in but one class, for I have considered it best to avoid, as completely as possible, repetitions. This principal is also applied in citing the examples for the different poems: a combination is given only once for each poem, unless some variation warrants a repetition, with the exception of the Fairy Queen, where the books are grouped into two divisions according to the publication, and examples given for each group:

A. ETYMOLOGICAL.

Sp. angels and archangels, II. II. B. 11;—Dr. angels and archangels, Mn. Mn. 493.

Sp. armed, unarmed, F. Q. V-6-30; armd, unarmd, ib. III-1-63, arm'd, disarme, F. Q. III-4-27; armes, arming, F. Q. V-10-31; Dr. arm'd, arms. B. A. 76;—Dan. armes, armed. Mus. 882.

Sp. end, end, ending. B. I. II-8: ended, end;—Dan. end, ends, Cleo., 472.

Sp. band that bindeth, F. Q. IV-2-29; with bands, bynd, F. Q. I-12-30; bind, band, Epith. 396; bound, with, band H. H. L. 27; bound, with, bands, F. Q. IV-10-35; bond to binde, F. Q. II-8-56; bondage, unbind, F. Q. V-5-56; bound with, bond. F. Q. III-5-36;—C. 2;—Dr. bound with many a band, Leg. I. R. N. 11;—Dan. no band can binde, Pan. 22; bounds, bound, Mus. 105.

Sp. bidding, beades. F. Q. I-1-30; bidding of her bedes, F. Q. I-10-3;—C. 1 (2);—Dr. bidding, their beads, Pol. XXIV-1136; bidding of their beads, Pol. XIII-291; bidding of his beades, Leg. I. R. N. 120; beads, bid, II. E. III, J. M. 87.

Sp. blood, bleed F. Q. II-11-48; bleeding, bled, Ast. 143;—C. 1;—Dr. for, their bloods, bleed, M. M. 127; blood, bleed, M. M. 172.

Sp. bridegrooms, brides (g), F. Q. V-3-3;—bryde brydall, Epith. 17;—Dr. bride and bridegroom, Pol. XV-207; bridegroom bringing out his bride, N. F. 1011.

Sp. burning brond. F. Q. II-3-18; burning firebrand, F. Q. II-11-47; burning levin-brond, M. VI-30; burning brond-yrons, F. Q. III-12-21; C. 2;—Dr. brands, burn'd, M. B. M. II-185.

Sp. charged, surcharged. F. Q. IV-9-30;—Dan. discharge, your charge, Cleo. 1191.

Sp. charmes and, enchuntments. F. Q. I-8-14;—Dr. enchanted, by charms, M. M. 157; enchantress, charm'd, El. I. L. 64.

Sp. channgelings call, chaung'd, F. Q. I-10-65;—Dr. change, changeth, H. E. IV. M. J. 55; changing change, B. W. IV-31; chang'd, unchang'd, B. W. II-52;— Dan. changed, change, C. W. II-14.

Sp. choise, to choose, S. C. XII-62;—Dr. choice, to chuse, S. S. 112;

Sp. clad in cloth of gold; yclad in clothing, S. C. IX-188;—C. 1;—Dr. clad in, cloth, Pol. XI-17.

Sp. come, comely. F. Q. V-4-1; Dr. came, come, H. E. VII, E-A, 90; ib. XIX, M-C. B. 28.

Sp. comfort, comfortlesse, F. Q. III-5-27;--Dan. comfortlesse, comfort, Cleo. 969.

Sp. crowne with a coronall, Epith. 14;—Dr. crown'd with coronet, H. E. XX. C. B.-M. 126; crowned, crown B. W. V-23.

Sp. dawning day, F. Q. II-39; Ast. 6; R. R. 22; H. B. 35; day, dawning, F. Q. V-5-1;C. 6;—Dr. (dy'd), dawning day, Ode III. V. 4; day, from dawn, M. E. 1515.

Sp. death, dying, F. Q. I-8-38; death, die, F. Q. V-4-22; H. L. 35; death he dide, F. Q. I-5-48; deaths, to dye, F. Q. III-7-51; dead, death, F. Q. VI-11-34; death, deadly, S. C., VIII. 174; dead, dying, F. Q. I-9-30; dye, dying,F. Q. III-10-60; dyes, dying, B. I. VI-8; dying, dye, Daph. 62; dies, death, B. I. VI-8; die, dead, C. C. II. 205; die, deadly, F. Q. I-9-32; (daily), dyde, dyein, F. Q. II-7-58;--C. 5;—Dr. death that dies, H. E. IV. M. J. 79; deaths, die, Leg. I. R. N. 88; death, deadly M. C. 992; die, death H. E. XVIII, S. E. 77; die the death, M. B. M., III-252; dying, dies, Leg. I. R. N. 93; dying, dead, Pol. XXII, 939; dy'd, dies, B. W. VI-88;—Dan. death, die, C. W. VI-95; death and dying, Cleo. 492; death, dying, C. W. VI-77; death, die, Q. A. 1312; H. T. 1697; dead, die L. B. W. 24; die, death, C. R. 553, dyes, dying, C. W. IV-54.

Sp. doing, deedes, F. Q. I-10-3; VI-7-1; does deedes, (dims) F. Q. III-2-1; doo, deed, T. M. 77; did, in, deedes, F. Q. IV-11-37; done, deedes, F. Q. I-7-36; deedes, (day) donne F. Q. V-3-6;—C. 6 (9);—Dr. do the, deed, M. M. 35; deed to do, Leg. II. M. F-66; deeds were done, Pol. XII-344; by deeds, done, M. B. M. III-208;--Dan. do this deed, Q. A. 1838; doe the deed, C. R. 614; C. W. I-35; done the deeds, Mus. 491.

Sp. doing, doe, F. Q. IV-11-18; doe as did, S. C. V-171;--Dr. do, doth, M. C. 747; do as he had done, M. M. 80; did, do, El. VII. L. A. 92, done, do H. E. XVII, E. S., 139; Leg. III. P. G. 13;—Dan. do, by doing, dost, C. W. V-23; done, do Q. A. 2102; done, doth, C. W. IV-14, Cleo. 1169.

Sp. done, undoe, F. Q. IV-4-27; doen, undo, F. Q. I-12-19; did, un-donne, F. Q. III-2-51;—Dr. undo, done, Leg. I. R. N. 65;—Dan. doing, undone, Phil. 1723; doth, undone Phil. 766; did, undo; C. W. VI-80; undo, undone, Phil. 1657; undoo or be undone, U. S. 73; undoe, done, Q. A. 388; adoe, undone, Q. A. 790.

Sp. double, doubly, B. I. III-8;—Dr. doubled, redoubled, B. A. 219.

Sp. fayre, fairest, F. Q. I-12-21; Ast. 10, (l. 1); faire, fairest, faire, Ast. 10, (l. 2); fairer then fairest, F. Q. III-1-27; Am. 20; fayrest, fayre, Am. 11; fayrest, (of)faire), fairnesse, F. Q. IV-2-23; faire, fairenesse, Daph. 30;—Dr. fair, fairer, Pol. VI-169; fairest faire, H. E. XVII, E.-S. 2;—Dan. faire, fairely, T. D. 146; fairest, faire, (feedes), Cleo. 1511.

Sp. befell as, fals. F. Q. IV-7-24;—Dr. fell, fall, B. A. 207; fall, fell, H. E. XXIII, J. G.-G. D. 38;—Dan. fell, fall, Cleo. 1066.

Sp. fearfull, feare. B. I. II-6;—Dr. fearfull, fearfuller, B. A. 193, —Dan. fear'd, feares, Phil. 920.

Sp. floating through, fluds, M. VII-33; flow into, flood, F. Q. II-7-8, floating on, flood, Proth., 4; overflowing, of, flood, R. T. 83;—Dr. floods, set afloat, Pol. XXIX-131.

Sp. formed, formlesse. T. M. 85;—Dr. form in, deformity, H. E. IV. M.-J., 60; forms, deformities, Eclog. IV-20;—Dan. deformed forme, C. W. II-62.

Sp. freshest, fresher, B. I. III-5;—Dr. fresh a fresh.

Sp. gave goodly gifts. F. Q. I-9-18; gave, gifts, F. Q. V-4-51; given, goodly gifts of, grace, Am. 31;—C. 4 (6):—Dr. gave, gift, H. E. III, J.-M. 127; M. E. 2012; Leg. I, R. N. 135; gave, gifts, Eclog. VIII-7; give, gift, Pol. XV-107; give, gifts, Eclog. VIII-20; gift, gave, Pol. V-14;—Dan. give, gift, Phil., 1684.

Sp. gathered together, F. Q. VI-9-15; gather together, S. C. XII-145; —C. 1, 3.;—Dan. gathering, gathers, Mus. 714.

Sp. gold, golden, F. Q. II-8-14; gilden, golden, M. VII-33; gilded with gold;—Dr. gold, golden, Eclog. VII-12.

Sp. good, goodnesse, S. C. IX-85; V. W. V. 1; good, goodly, F. Q. IV-10-16;—Dan. good, good-like, C. W. V-22.

Sp. gotten, begotten, F. Q. VI-4-32;—Dr. begot, beget, H. E. XXIII, J. G. G. D. 35; begot, got, N. F. 31;—Dan. get, ungot, C. W. VII-46.

Sp. graced, to be, grace F. Q. VI-10-26; disgracing to grace, F. Q. IV-4-4; disgracing did, grace, M. H. T. 708; ungracious grace;—Dr. grac-ing, graced, M. E. 5080;—Dan. grace that graceth, Cleo. 1640; grac-ing, gract, Ep. IV, L. L. 27; grace with disgrace Cleo. 397; disgracing, grace, Cleo. 724.

Sp. great, greatest, F. Q. I-7-11; great, greater, F. Q. III-3-5; greatest of, great, Am. III, (2); greatest, greatly, Epith. 1; Dr. great, greatest, B. W. IV-63; great, greater, Leg. III, P. G., 88; H. E. VIII-A.-E. 31; Pol. XXVII-30?; great'st, greatness, Pol. XIII-31;—Dan. great, greater, C. W. VI-11; great, greatly, C. W. IV-28; greatest, greatness, C. W. VIII-61; greatnesse, great, O.-M. A. 13; greatnesse, greater, C. W. VI-24; Phil. 278.

Sp. hap, happened, (heare), F. Q. I-2-31; haples, hap., Ep. 10;—Dr. in, behalf, hap ill, or happen well, Pol. XXI-123.

Sp. hevenly, heaven, F. Q. I-10-59; VI-10-25; heaven, heavenly, M. VII, 2; heavens, heavenly, M. VI-11;—Dr. heav'nly; heaven, H. E., XXIII. J. G. G. D. 118;—Dan. heaven, and heavenly joys, C. W. II-45.

Sp. helpe, helplesse, F. Q. I-10-3;—Dr. help'd, helpeth, Pol. XXVII-179.

Sp. highest, hights, M. VI-36;—Dr. high, higher was, hap. Leg. IV. Crom. 59;—Dan. height, hie, Phil. 341.

Sp. judgment, unjust, F. Q. V-3 35; justice judgment, F. Q. I-9-38; just, unjust, H. H. L. 22;—Dr. judge, justly, H. E. VIII, A.-E., 114; just, unjust, H. E. H. H. R. 119;—Dan. injustice, justified, C. W. VII-65; unjustest, justest, C. W. I-73.

Sp. kings, kings, Ep. 7, (1);—C. 3.; Dr. king of, kings B. A. 168; king, kingdom H. E. IV, M.-J. 91; king, kingdoms B. W. III-55; king and kingdoms M. M. 47; Dan. kingdomes, and, kings C. W. III-90.

Sp. learne, learning F. Q. IV-12-13; learne, learned, S. C. XI-29; learnings lore, Epi. 2, (1); learned lore, T. M. 79; lore of learn'd (philosophy), F. Q. VI-1-35; C. 4; Dr. learn learn'd, (leave), M. C. 279; unlearned in learning H. E. XVII, E. S. 123.

Sp. leave (v), leave (s), F. Q. II-1-37; Dr. leave, leaving, (lack) M B. M., 1-243; leaving, left, Pol. XXIV-9-18; Dan. left, leave Q. A. 2215; leave, left, Mus. 74.

Sp. light, light (v), F. Q. I-8-19; light doth lighten, Am. 9; (lesser) lights in light F. Q. VI-10-26; lightning brond, light, F. Q. I-8-24; Dr. no light but lightning M. B. M. II-382; – Dan. light, lighter Q. A. 806.

Sp. life and livelihead F. Q. VI-7-20; Dan. life and livelihood C. W. V-15.

Sp. live, life F. Q. III-11-14; living, life F. Q. I-11-38; live, life Am. 19; live, in lives F. Q. II-1-36; live, living F. Q. III-6-43; Am. 44; lively, living F. Q. III-11-16; T. M. 43;—C. 4 (2); Dr. liv'd, a, life Pol. XI-240; a life that lives, H. E. IV; M.-J. 79; life, lives (pb) H. E. XXIV, G. D.-

J. G. 19; life, lively, Leg. III, P. G. 117; life, alive Pol. XXIV-159; lifeless, living Ids. 11;—Dan. live without life S. D. 20; live two lives Mus. 12; live a living (death) S. D. 9; life I loath to live S. D. 16; life and lives (unjust) depriving) C. R. 18; let him live, life C. W. VI-62; life, life, live too E. S. 12.

Sp. like, likest F. Q. V-9-28; lycke with his lycke M. H. T. 18;—Dr. like, unlike Pol. XXIV-1276; like, dislike H. E. VII, E.-A. 14; likeness, like M. M. 118; likewise, alike Pol. XXIV-695;—Dan. like, alike Pan. 68; lik't, alike C. W. V-105; alike to like (deserts) Pan. 37; (looking) alike on like (deserts) C. W. V-22; like, likewise Pan. 21.

Sp. longer, long S. C. XI-73;—Dr. long, at length Leg. III, P. G. 99; Dan. long have I long'd C. W. II-70.

Sp. lose, losing B. I. IV-6;—Dr. lose, lost, H. E. IX, L.-R., 143; lost, losse (less) M. M. 144;—Dan. lost, lose Q. A. 1936; C. W. VI-75.

Sp. love and lover F. Q. III-2-45; love, and lovers (life) F. Q. I-9-10; loving, lov'd F. Q. II-12-75; lov'd, and love F. Q. I-7-49; beloved love Epith. 2; love doth love, beloved, H. H. L. 117; of love, loveth F. Q. IV-1-4; (I); loving, love, C. C. H. 914;—C. 2;—Dr. love to lover, Pol. V-117; love, lovers (oaths) H. E. VII, E.-A. 160; loves, to see his love (possessed) H. E. XX O. B.-M. 34; loving, belov'd Eclog. IX-24; lov'd, lovingly Pol. XXVIII-217;—Dan. lovers with their loves Post. 66; lover, love C. R. 112; lover lov'd, Q. A. 2124; we love to be belov'd yet scorne the lover C. R. 539; love, lov'd Phil. 706; love, loves E. S. 1; loves, is loved C. R. 551; love, loving, (live) Q. A. 538.

Sp. lucke, lucklesse, lucky F. Q. I-6-19;—Dr. luckless, unlucky M. M. 252.

Sp. made by, Maker C. C. II. 561;—Dan. make, made C. W. IV-31; made, make Phil. 1009.

Sp. men, unmanly, F. Q. II-12-86; VI-6-25; for mans, sake, a man H. H. L. 117;—C. 1.;—Dr. man of men Pol. XVII-216; man, men, B. A. 73;—Dan. man of men Phil. 141.

Sp. mooving, unmoved M. VII-13; moove, mooved, B. I. IV-7;—Dr. remove, remov'd H. E. VII. E.-A. 58; motion, of, moving, El. I-49;—Dan. (according to) motion move, Mus. 527.

Sp. neighborhood, nere F. Q. IV-11-10; neighbours, neare Epith. 39;—Dr. nearest neighboring Pol. VI-222; near, neighborhood Pol. XX-282; neighboring, nigh B. A. 76; H. E. X. R.-L., 27; neighbouring near, M. B. M. I-221; nigh and neighborly Pol. VII-249; next, near, M. E. 1373;—Dan. neighbour neare Cleo. 656; next-neighbors H. T. 1602.

Sp. knew, unknowne, F. Q. III-5-17; Dr. knowing, knew B. W. III-69;—Dan. knew, known Q. A. 513; know, knew O.-M. A. 5.

Sp. knit the knot Am. 6; Dr. knit the knot M.-C. 741; knit, witch-knots H. E. XIII, E. C.-D. H. 110.

Sp. numbers, numberlesse F. Q. IV-12-1; Dr. in numbering, numbers B. W. V-21.

Sp. passeth in, passing day F. Q. II-12-75; passing, surpassing, F. Q. IV-10-10;—Dr. surpassing, pass Eclog. V-19.

Sp. praise disprais'd B. I. V-8; Dr. prais'd, praising H. E. VIII; A-B. P. 104.

Sp. pure, purest F. Q. II-2-9; purest, impure H. H. L. 98; -Dr. purest, pure Eclog. IV-21; pure, purer H. E. XXIII, J. G.-G. D. 88.

Sp. pyne, pyning S. C. 1-18; Dan. pine in pining S. D. 29.

Sp. rightfull, unrighteous F. Q. II-7-19; rightfull, rightly F. Q. IV-12-30; right (wrongs, rul'd), righteous F. Q. V-7-1; - Dan. right, rights C. W. I-1.

Sp. sacred, saints M. VII-7; saintlike as saint (Radegund) M. H. T. 497; Dan. sacred, design'd a saint S. D. 6; sanctuary, sacred Cleo. 266, sacred, sanctifies (sin) C. R. 304.

Sp. seeke, sought F. Q. V-7-24; unsought, seeking F. Q. VI-1-28; Dr. seek, sought (sack), H. F. VI. Mor. I. 88; sought, seeks H. E. III, J. M. 158; Dan. seeking sought S. D. 33; seeke, unsought O. M. A. 44.

Sp. see, seene, F. Q. II-1-15; M. VI-32; see, seeing, H. L. 19; seeing, (desired), see F. Q. III-9-24; seeing, saw B. I. III-1; saw, see Epith. 11, F. Q. II-4-3;- Dr. seen, seeing Pol. VII-60; saw, seeing B. W. III-42;—Dan. see, seeing C. R. 784; asham'd to see, seeing Phil. 149; to see er to be seene Q. A. 371; see, seene, see C. W. II-79; sees, see, C. W. II-75; saw, see H. T. 771.

Sp. see, sight F. Q. IV-9-9; V. P. 5; saw, sight, (smote) F. Q. III-8-31; sawe, sight, S. C. 1-52; Proth. 57; sights, saw, F. Q. IV-10-29; (sorie) sight, seene F. Q. V-1-14; sights, seene H. L. 371; sight, scene, F. Q. IV-5-13; F. Q. I-5-16; see, sight V. P. 5; scene, sight V. B. 4; -C. S (10); —Dr. see, sight, Mn. Mn. 28; sight, to see Eclog. IX (Sng. III), 4; sight, seen Leg. I. R. N. 133; sight, saw, Pol. XII 290; Dan. see so sad a sight Q. A. 2091; sight to see S. D. 36; in sight see Q. A. 1802.

Sp. serve observe B. I. V-3;- C. 3;—Dan. services will serve Phil. 124.

Sp. sinne and sinners H. B. 23;- Dan. sinn'd, sinne C. R. 364.

Sp. strike, stroke, S. C. XI-123; stroke, strike F. Q. IV-3-33; stroke, one stroke F. Q. VI-2-12; Dr. strike, (too great a) stroke Leg. II. Mat. F. 23; (one) stroke (have) strucken B. A. 196; strike, struck B. W. V-2; struck, strike II. E. VII, E. A. 22.

Sp. sung a song F. Q. I-12-38; sing, songs S. C. XI-77'8; song, sing Epith. 51;—C. 4 (5);—Dr. sing a song Pol. XIX-147; sing, song D. and G. 8; sang, song II. E. XX, C. B.-M. 122;—Dan. sing. song H. T. 1404; II. T. 1459.

Sp. swore, sweare M. II. T. 1057;—Dan. swore, sworne Cleo. 973.

Sp. tale, told F. Q. I-9-37; tale to tell, M. II. T. 36; tell, a tale of truth S. C. II-91; tell tales S. C. VI-87; tell, tale F. Q. II-1-9;—C. 29 (68);—Dr. tale to tell M. C. 163; tale is told M. E. 1700; tale as having told Pol. XVI-125; tell, tales M. E. 1676; tell her tale M.-C. 594; telling tales, B. W. VI-18; winter-tales, tell II. E. XXII, Ger.-II. II. 167;—Dan. tolde an idle tale Phil. 874; telling tales, Q. A. 1152; tell, old-tale, Q. A. 1714.

Sp. thinke, thought F. Q. IV-12-22; thought (v) and think I thought F. Q. I-7-49;—Dr. I think (it cannot be but) thought El. VI, L. P. C. 47; thought be, as I did think II. E. XX, C. B. M. 91;—Dan. thinke, thought Q. A. 1162; for a thought to thinke O.-M. A. 45; unthinke the thought Q. A. 2384.

Sp. time, untimely F. Q. V-5-29; tymely, tyme Epith. 20;—Dr. untimely, timeless M. B. M.;— Dan. time, untimely P. S. 33.

Sp. betrayd, betray F. Q. V-6-25; traytor, treason F. Q. VI-6-23; —C. 1;—Dr. treason, traytor's M. B. M. I-532; trait'rous, trait'rously, B. W. IV-9;—Dan. betrai'd, traitors Cleo. 989; traitor, treason Cleo. 849.

Sp. truth, trew F. Q. III-1-29; truth, trust, II. II. B. 157; in, truth, trusted, F. Q. V-8-30; true, untruely F. Q. V-7-38; true in trust, F. Q. IV-11-51;—C. 3;—Dr. true, truth II. E. I. R. II. 32;—Dan. truth, true C. W. II-51; truth with trust, Phil. 1603; truth, trust O.-M. A. 3; Q. A. 404; trust, untrue Q. A. 897.

Sp. twisting, twyne F. Q. V-5-22;—Dr. twisting, untwist II. E. XX. C. B.-M. 158; twist and twine Eclog. IV-13 (M.)

Sp. betwixt you twayn, F. Q. I-12-19; betwixt, (armes) twaine F. Q. VI-1-23; betwixt them two F. Q. III-6-4; betwixt us tway F. Q. IV-2-13; 'twixt them, twaine M. II. T. 1025;—C. 4 (8);—Dr. between them twain B. A. 212;—Dan. betwixt us twaine Q. A. 2017; betweene (them) two C. W. VIII-23; Q. A. 1637.

Sp. turnd, returnd. F. Q. III-8-18; III-10-49;—Dan. turnd, over-turned Mus. 711.

Sp. wake, waking F. Q. I-11-32; awake, awaking B. I. II-9; Dan. wake, awake Vs. Gd. 8; wak'd, awak'd, Q. A. 1759.

Sp. will, wilfull, F. Q. V-5-20; will, wilfully, Daph. 51; willing, will Am. wilfull, will F. Q. I-5-50;—Dr. wilfull, will Pol. XV-55.

Sp. winne, wonne F. Q. IV-3-36;—Dan. win, wonne, Q. A. 589; C. W. VI-76; winnes, won C. W. VII-21; wonne, win U. S. 70.

Sp. wittie, wise, F. Q. IV-2-35; unwise and witless S. C. XII-91; Dr. wisdom wise M. B. M. I-676;—Dan. wisedome, wise C. R. 130; unwise, witt, Cleo. 196.

Sp. worth, worthily (wonne) F. Q. VI-2-25; worthy, unworthy, F. Q. VI-7-29, (vs. 4 and 5); unworthy, worthy B. I. VI-10; worthy, worth, F. Q. II-1-33;—Dr. worthy, worthies, Ids. 18; worthiest, worthily Pol. VIII-392;—Dan. worth, worthy F. D. 390.

Sp. worse, worst, S. C. II-13;—Dan. worse than worst C. W. II-65.

THE MOST IMPORTANT ALLITERATING COMBINATIONS
PECULIAR TO SPENSER.

backs, backward, F. Q. V-1-2 (I); beg. beggers, M. H. T. 192; boldhe, boldest, M. H. T. 666; boldly, bold F. Q. IV-10-1; yborn of, berth, F. Q. I-3-28; (blowes), bore, forbore F. Q. V-5-7; daintie, daintier, B. I. I-6; darred, daring, M. VI-17; dearly deare F. Q. I-5-23; deare, dearest F. Q. I-4-45; dearest deare F. Q. VI-11-50; Am. 52; depth, deepe F. Q. V-9-6; dolefully, dole, S. C. VIII-193; adorne, adorn'd, F. Q. IV-11-31; doubtfull, redoubted F. Q. I-1-53; dreadfull (darknesse), dreadfully F. Q. VI-11-32; dread, dreadlesse F. Q. V-5-31; drive, drove F. Q. III-1-57; drover drive F. Q. III-8-22; redresse, redrest, F. Q. V-8-11; endu'd with dowre, F. Q. VI-8-20; chaste and unchaste F. Q. III-7-60; chased, chace F. Q. X-8-5; chearfull, cheard F. Q. III-2-17; cherish, cheare, F. Q. II-6-21; conne, conning, S. C. XI-52; conquer'd, conquerer, B. R. 11; conquer, conquerours, F. Q. IV-7-1; court nor courtesie, F. Q. III-9-3; cruell, crueller V. G. 59; fading, fade, F. Q. III-12-21; faith, faithlesse S. C. VI-110; find, fownd, F. Q. I-12-32; fit, unfit, F. Q. VI-10-37; with, food be fed F. Q. IV-12-4; force, forces, F. Q. IV-2-24; with, force, forced F. Q. IV-3-11, force, perforce F. Q. III-7-3; footing of feete F. Q. IV-2-34; fraud, fraudulently F. Q. IV-10-43; frayes, affrayd F. Q. I-1-52; freedome, free F. Q. V-5-32; of fullnesse fill H. H. B. 29; again -t, againe F. Q. V-8-9; gentle, gently B. I. V-8; gentle, ungently S. C. II-22;

ghosts. ghastly S. C. VI-24; God or Godlinesse M. H. T. 844; God, un-godly. V-8-49; God or godlike F. Q. IV-2-1; God, Godly, F. Q. I-11-7; guilt. guilty. F. Q. II-4-30; hard. harder, F. Q. IV-9-36; hardly hardi-ment. F. Q. II-2-37; joy. enjoy'd B. I. VI-3; enjoye'd, joy Ep. 8 (II); joy overjoyd. B. I. VI-3; joyes enjoyes S. C. XI-15; joying. enjoyd F. Q. III-6 48. joyous. joy. Am. 68; joy. joyes B. I. VI-8-; rejoyce. rejoyced F. Q. III-2-11; joyous, joyance F. Q. IV-10-23; forlorne, lorne, S. C. I-11; low. lowly. S. C. VI-9; man, inhumanitie, F. Q. VI-1-26; dismayd .dismayfull. V-11-26; mendes. amendes F. Q. II-1-20; dismem-ered. members. F. Q. I-5-38; messenger. message, F. Q. I-12-24; misse. missing. Daph. 24; mighty, mightier, F. Q. IV-3-48; immortall, mortall F. Q. III-8-38; T. M. 8; mortal, inmortall F. Q. IV-12-4; H. H. L. 17; mournd. mournful. F. Q. III-4-32; new, renewer, F. Q. III-4-57; new, anew. Am. 62; knight. knighthood F. Q. II-1-11; empaire, repaire F. Q. I-7-41; peace, pacifyde, F. Q. II-10-51; perle, perling, Epith. 9; point, appointed F. Q. V-1-1 (I); presence, present, F. Q. VI-2-37; prouder, proud F. Q. I-9-12; ragd. outragious, V. G. 63; outragiously, enraged, F. Q. II-12-22; arrayd (or rather) disarayd, F. Q. II-12-77; reach. raught F. Q. III-7-26; rest, rested F. Q. VI-9-3; (vs. 2 and 3); rule, rul'd, M. VII-56; saluting resaluted. F. Q. V-7-17; deceipt, self-deceiver F. Q. V-9-19; shamefast, shamefastnes, F. Q. II-9-43; sharpe. sharpest, F. Q. I-11-11; short. shortly. F. Q. IV-2-50; desire, desiring B. I. V-3. sweetest, sweet, F. Q. III-4-39; sweet, sweeter, F. Q. III-6-12; sweete. sweetly B. I. II-2; tidings, betide. F. Q. IV-8-18; tookest, take, F. Q. I-3-36; tooke. untooke F. Q. III-6-28; mistooke. tooke F. Q. III-9-23; wake, waking. F. Q. I-11-32; wept. weeping F. Q. I-4-30; winepresse, wine, F. Q. II-12-56; wishing. wish F. Q. III-1-16; wonder. wondred. F. Q. I-11-35; unwonted. wonted. F. Q. I-1-19 (vs. 1 and 2); world. world-ings. F. Q. II-7-8.

To Drayton:

beat. beaten, Pol. XVII-118; blue. bluer. Mn. Mn. 168; built, builded Pol. XXIX-340; curls. curled Pol. VI-176; fowls, fowler, Pol. XIX-56; begun. begin. H. E. XXIII, J. G. G. D. 36; behold, beheld, Pol. XXVII-404; honour. honoured. Pol. XXIV-1330; hope. never-hoping Ids. 26; ugly. kind. Pol. XVI-36; larger. largely Pol. XXV-326; commends and commends Ids. 42; merry, merrier, Pol. XXVI-359; nations, na-ture. B. W. V-15; nations, naturally, Pol. V-251; unnatural, natural B. W. I-9; pities. pitied, B. W. II-19; expos'd, opposed, B. W. IV-31; reading. read El. VI. L. P. C. 121; rough and rougher Pol. XXVI-368;

ruin'd, ruines, Pol. XVI-133; season, unseason'd II. E. X. R. I. 52; sieging or, besieged, Pol. XVIII-510; beseig'd, siege II. F. VII. E. A. 155; besieged, besiegers B. A. 106; entertain, attained, Pol. XXVII-168; external nor internal B. W. IV-49; interring, inter'd, Pol. VIII-330; valley, vale Pol. X-179; varying, variously Pol. XXVI-134; Virginia, virgin Pol. XVII-348; west, westerne. Pol. XVI-156; whet-stones, whet, Pol. XXVI-392; wound, wounded, Ids. 36.

To Daniel:

Ayld, ayle, II. T. 88; ever, every, Phil. 2014, errd, error. Cleo. 1521; order, disordered Phil. 764; offers, offering, C. W. III-71; owner, owne, C. W. IV-52; breath'st the breath, C. R. 338; breaths, breath, C. R. 666; cleere, cleer'd Phil. 2209; deface, face Mus. 107; offence, offender, Phil. 2240; offender, offence Phil. 1817; offince, offend, O. M. A. 27; confound, confusion. Q. A. 1465-6; confusd, (affect), confound, C. R. 795; unbelieve, belief, (Q. A. 2389; believe, unbelieve, Mus. 640; mercie, mercilesse E. S. 23; apart ,part, B. W. II-87; impart a part, B. W. V-72; appearing, disappears, Des. B. 4; powre, powers, C. W. V-9; oppression to oppresse, C. W. VI-1; oppression is opprest, Phil. 750; oppressor, opprest, Phil. 1899, arrivd, arrive B. W. VIII-82; shewes, shew, II. T. 1072; spinning wheel, spun P. C. 18, staid, stay, II. T. 594; staying, staid II. T. 597; stood, standest, Cleo. 611; strong, strength C. W. V-15; taste, distastes, Mus. 69; contend, content, C. W. IV-93; contention, Discontent, C. W. VI-37; farewell, well II. T. 1320.

B. ASSOCIATION.

1 CONCRETE IDEAS.

The names of objects and ideas which are associated in every-day life are frequently connected by alliteration. We have to consider under this class the names of concrete ideas, of concrete and abstract, and of abstract.   1. Concrete:

Sp. archer, arrow, F. Q. III-2-26;—Dr. archer, arrows, B. W. II-21; archer, arrow-head, B. A. 149.

Sp. (the) earth, the ayre, H. L. 12; earthly, ayre, R. R. 20; aire, earth, Muiop. 27;—Dr. earth, air, Pol. XX-152; M. C. 967; earth and air, Pol. II-135;—Dan. earth, and, air and all C. W. I-116.

Sp. eyes, eares, B. I. II-4; T. M. 30; eare or eye F. Q. VI-1-1 (I); eares and eyes, F. Q. II-9-51;—Dr. eyes and ears, M. E. 1188; B. W. VI-93;

eye or ear, Mn. Mn. 252; ears and eyes, M. B. M. II-214;—Dan. eyes, ears, H. T. 192; Phil. 612; care, eye, Q. A. 2389.

Sp. banck nor bush, F. Q. III-10-55; banck and bush F. Q. III-1-17; Dr. banks, bushes Pol. XVIII-5.

Sp. beasts and burds, F. Q. IV-2-35; C. C. II. 297; beasts, birds F. Q. III-6-35; bird and beast, F. Q. III-10-16;—C. 8;—Dr. beasts and birds, N. F. 153; the birds, the beasts, N. F. 763; birds and beasts, D. and G. 756.

Sp. bed and bord, F. Q. III-10-51;—Dr. both at board and bed O. 1033; bird and beast Eclog. I-4; X-12, (blood of) birds, (of) beasts, H. F. II. II. R. 91.

Sp. belles, and babes, S. C. V-240;—Dr. belles and babies, M. C. 768.

Sp. bird on bough, F. Q. II-6-25; birds, in, boughs embowring V. G. 29; Dr. birds, boughs, M. C. 1249; Owl. 1157; boughs, birds Owl. 1172.

Sp. birds in bushes, S. C. III-66; bramble bush, byrdes, S. C. VI-7; braunch, bird F. Q. II-6-13;—Dr. birds from, bush and brier, M. E. 1565.

Sp. blades, with, blond, F. Q. IV-9-29;—Dr. blades, with blood, M. M. 136.

Sp. blosomes, buds, S. C. I-34; bud and blosome F. Q. III-6-30; bud, blossome, F. Q. II-6-15; Am. 61, (similar) blossome or, blade, F. Q.V-2-10;—Dr. blossom'd, bloom (v), M. E. 78.

Sp. bodie, nor blond F. Q. VI-4-5;—Dr. body, blood, Ids. 49.

Sp. brakes and briers, F. Q. VI-5-17; (similar) holy-bush, nor brere, S. C. VI-3;—Dr. brakes and briers, Pol. II-204; through brake, through brier Nym. 39; (bring into), brake of brier, M. C. 1116; (similar), broom and brakes, Pol. XIII-28.

Sp. brakes and brambles, S. C. XII-102; Dr. (compare) briers and Brambles, Nym. 57.

Sp. branch with blossomes, F. Q. IV-10-22; braunch, blossomes, Daph. 35; branch, bud S. C. XI-91; budding braunch S. C. II-58; boughs with blossomes, S. C. XII-103;—C. 3;—Dr. blooming branches, B. W. VI-38; buds every branch and blossoms every spray, Owl. 4.

Sp. braunches broad, and body F. Q. II-7-53; braunch of, body, S. C. V-196; bodie, braunches (broke), S. C. II-170;—Dr. branch and bo. Pol. XIV-58.

Sp. briers and bushes, F. Q. IV-7-8;—Dr. (see above) birds from brier.

Sp. chests, and coffers, F. Q. II-7-30;—Dr. chest or coffer N. F. 141.

Sp. kings, crowne. F. Q. II-7-11; -Dr. king. crowne B. A. 11;—Dan. king, crowne, C. W. VIII-9.

Sp. cockle for corn, S. C. XII-12 i:—Dr. cockle in the corn, M. E. 921.

Sp. crowne, countrey, F. Q. V-7-23;—Dr. (similar). court and country II. E. IV. M. J. 131; Pol. XXIV-157:— Dan. country, crowne Cleo. 55.

Sp. crownes, kingdomes, M. VI-32; crowne and kingdom F. Q. II-1-2; crownes and kingdomes, F. Q. II-7-11; kingdomes crowne F. Q. V-10-26; Dan. kingdom, crownes, C. W. VIII-3.

Sp. curds and clouted cream. S.C. XI-99; (compare) cakes and crack-nells and, country cheere, S. C. XI-95;—Dr. curds and clouted cream Eclog. IX-12; curds and clouted-cream and country (dainties), Pol. XIV-271.

Sp. face and feature, Proth. 10; H. B. 6; face. and front V. B. 9; feature of, face Am. 21;—Dr. feature of my face, II. E. V. I-Mor. 65.

Sp. fields, floods. F. Q. I-9-12; field, forrest (farre) M. II. T. 578; field and forest. Ast.. 11; (feeds) in forest or in field, C. C. II. 821; -Dr. floods, field, Pol. XXIX-180; forest, flood, or field Pol. VII-117; forests, floods, Pol. IV-55; (flesh) of forest and of flood. M. B. M. III-102; forest, fields. X. F. 419.

Sp. fields, flowers, (freshly) F. Q. II-6-24; flowrs, fields F. Q. II-6-15; flowers, field Proth. 5; flower in field, F. Q. IV-10-22; flowers in fieldes. V. G. 17; flowring field F. Q. II-6-16; fields with faded flowers, C. C. II. 25;—Dr. fields, in flowers, Q. C. 1; fields, flowers. D. and G. 331; fields of flow'ry (Picardy) II. E. XIX, M-C. B. 12, fields, flow'ry meads, Pol. VII-215; flow'ry fields, M. B. M. I-605; fields with flowers, Eclog. VII-2:—Dan. field of flowers, Ode XIII.

Sp. fields, and flockes, R. T. 17; my fields my food, my flocke F. Q. VI-9-20; flocks and fields, C. C. II. 620; (feede) flocke in fields, S. C. VI-76; —Dr. in, fields, flocks, Eclog. IX-2; fields, (fathers) flock, D. and G. 193; fields, folded flock, M. E. 1703; flocks, fair fields Owl. 11;—Dan. flockes into the fields, II. T. 210.

Sp. fish nor fowle F. Q. II-12-8; fowle, fish F. Q. I-2-10;—Dr. fish and fowl, Pol. XXV-195; fowl and fish, Pol. XX-275; fowl, fish, Ode XX, V. V. 5; (fruit) fowl and fish Pol. XVIII-661.

Sp. flame, unto, fire. F. Q. II-5-8; flames, fire F. Q. II-7-17; flame with fire F. Q. IV-8-16;—C. 3 (1):—Dr. fire, flame B. W. VI-10;—Dan. flame, fire, Mus. 551; fire, flame. O. M. A. 41; fire, in flame C. W. VIII-12 fire, flames Q. A. 823.

Sp. flocks, in, fold, F. Q. VI-9-17; fell upon, flock in folde, M. II. T. 535; Dr. flocks, and folds Eclog. VIII-23.

Sp. fowle, flight F. Q. II-8-9; fowles, fluttering F. Q. II-12-35;—C. 1; Dr. fowl, flight, N. F. 363.

Sp. hart and hand, F. Q. I-12-40; my hart, my handes F. Q. II-4-28; hand, nor hart (so hard) F. Q. V-5-13;—Dr. heart, hand, Pol. IX-289; hearts, (in need) of hands B. W. II-1; hand, heart, B. A. 60; hands, hearts B. A. 249; hand and, heart, Leg. II Mat. F. 65;—Dan. hearts and hands, Phil. 1712; hearts, hands C. W. V-87; Pan. 73; hands, harts C. W. II-64; have thy hand against thy hart C. W. VII-90.

Sp. harpe in hand, F. Q. IV-2-1; in hand, harp, Am. 44:—Dr. harp in hand, D. and G. 279.

Sp. head and helmet, F. Q. V-5-11; V-7-34;—Dr. head, helmet, B. A. 152; helmet on her head, B. W. II-11; helmet from his head, D. and G. 398; helmets from, heads, Nym. 38; helm, upon, head, Pol. IV-455; helm, head, Pol. XXX-197.

Sp. heads, harts, F. Q. II-11-10;—Dr. head, heart, Pol. II-469; heart, head, B. W. III-11.

Sp. hunters horn, (hanging had), F. Q. VI-2-5; hounds, hunters (hew)), M. VI-15;—C. 2 (3);—Dr. hounds and huntsmen, Pol. XIII-111; horn, hunter, Pol. XIII-127; hound to hunt, hawk, Pol. III-135; hunt, hart, Pol. XVIII-65, hart, hunter's, (game), Pol. XIII-94.

Sp. lampe, light, F. Q. I-2-6; light, and, lampe F. Q. I-3-27; lamp of, light, C. C. II. 873; lampe of light, F. Q. V-1-7 (1); lampes of light F. Q. V-9-50; lampe of light, II. H. L. 7; light, lampe, II. L. 19;—Dr. lamp, lights (be lost) II. E. XX-166;—Dan. lampe of light, Des. B. I.

Sp. life and light, F. Q. III-5-7; Lord of life and light, F. Q. I-1-37; Lord of life, F. Q. II-7-62; (lyfe) Am. 68; Lord of, living (wight) II. H. L. 17;—C. 1;—Dr. light and life, lord Pol. XVII-131.

Sp. lords and ladies, F. Q. I-4-7; V-3-2; lord and lady, F. Q. I-12-2; ladies and lordes. F. Q. III-6-13; ladies, lord. F. Q. I-5-3;—C. 4;—Dr. lords and ladies Eclog. VI-10; VII-7.

Sp. lord of, land F. Q. I-12-3; VI-4-30;—Dr. Lord Protector of the land, H. E. XIII, E. C. D. II. 66;—Dan. Lord, land, C. W. I-85.

Sp. (my) Lord, my Liege F. Q. II-3-35;—Dr. liege, lords, B. A. 128.

Sp. lump of lead, F. Q. II-1-15; lomp of lead, F. Q. II-8-30;—Dr. lump of lead, II. F. XIII, C. E. D. II. 112.

Sp. man or monster, F. Q. V-12-15; more like a monster than a man, F. Q. I-4-22; Dr. men, sea-monster, Eclog. IV-23; monster art of men, D. and G. 746;—Dan. monster man II. T. 1674.

Sp. mind of, man, F. Q. II-12-87; mindes of men F. Q. V-7-11; V. G.
12; T. M. 32: (minds) II. B. 86; man, minde F. Q. V-8-1:—Dr. minds
of men, Pol. X-270: men whose minds. Pol. XXI-27; man whose,
mind, Pol. XXIII-330: B. W. V-51: man, whose minde, Pol. VI-284;
sundry men, sundry minds, Ids. 42;—Dan. mindes of men, II. T. 38
(prol.); mind of man Cleo. 103: men of might and mindes, C. W. I-22;
man, mind, Phil. 2173.

Sp. moores and marshes, F. Q. V-10-18: moorish fennes, and marshes
R. T. 20: Dr. (similar) in meadows and in marshes, Nym. 9.

Sp. name and nation, F. Q. I-9-2: names and nations, F. Q. IV-12-3:
—Dr. name, native country Kent. M. M. 52.

Sp. name, nature, F. Q. I-8-31: names and natures, F. Q. III-12-26;
Dr. names, nature M. E. 1458; name, nature Pol. XVII-60; name and
nature Owl. 963: nature, name Pol. XVIII-156.

Sp. (what) pen, what pencill Am. 17;—Dr. pen, pencils B. W. VI-57.

Sp. princes pallace, S. C. X-81: princes pallaces,, M. H. T. 1175;—
Dr. princes, palaces, M. E. 1607.

Sp. prince, peare, F. Q. V-10-15: nor prince, nor peare, R. R. 23;
(pere) F. Q. III-2-37; princes, peares M. H. T. 901: Dan. princes,
peeres, C. W. II-117; peeres and princes, Phil. 384.

Sp. realmes, and rulers, F. Q. II-7-13:—Dr. (compare) as kings rules
realms. God rules the hearts of kings Owl. 231.

Sp. sheepe and shepheards base attire, F. Q. VI-9-24: sheepe, shep-
heard S. C. VII-53, sheepe, shepheards swaine, F. Q. II-9-14; shepheards kept sheep, Ast. 35;—C. 1;—Dr. sheep nor shepherd, Eclog. IV-
101; shepherd sheep Eclog. VIII-17; shepherds, sheep, Pol. III-131;
(shepherd) M. B. M. I-688.

Sp. shield, and sword, F. Q. I-7-36; shield, sword F. Q. I-3-11; sword
and shield, F. Q. II-8-54; IV-6-11; sword or shield F. Q. II-3-16: sword
on, shield F. Q. II-6-31:—Dr. sword and shield, Pol. XII-451.

Sp. sight, sense F. Q. V-8-38;—Dr. sight and senses, Pol. XXVIII-
358:—Dan. sense, sight C. W. IV-15.

Sp. sire, nor sonnes, F. Q. V-6-35; sonnes, syre, T. M. 11:—Dr. from
son to sire from sire again to son, Leg. II., Mat. F. 83;—Dan. sire,
sonne Q. A. 2561; sonne, such a sire, C. W. VI-86.

Sp. smel and sight, B. I. II-5;—Dr. sight and smell, M. E. 1114.

Sp. smoke and sulphure, F. Q. III-2-32;—Dr. sulphurous smoke Pol.
XXIX-264.

Sp. tilt and tournament. F. Q. V-8-7: taught to tilt and tournament,
F. Q. III-1-14; tilt or tourney, F. Q. III-2-9;—Dr. tilts and turneys,

M. M. 20: (tourneys) Leg. III, P. G. 63; (compare) tilts and triumphs, H. E. XVII, E.-S. 158; Dan. tilts and tournaments, C. W. III-34.

Sp. (your) tongue, your talk, F. Q. VI-6-7;—Dr. tongues, talking Leg. I. R. N. 16; (compare) tongue, tale Leg. IV, Crom. 66; tale of, tongue, Leg. III, P. G. 96.

Sp. towres and terras F. Q. V-9-21;—C. 3 (toun and tour);—Dr. (compare) towers, towns, Pol. XVIII, 238; town, and tow'r M. M. 57.

Sp. waves, winde, R. R. 16;—Dr. waves, winds Leg. I, R. N. 3.

Sp. weapon, (wont), warre, F. Q. V-4-44; warre, and weapons, F. Q. II-6-31;- Dr. weapons, war, B. W. I-40.

Sp. weapons, wounds V. G. 63;—Dr. weak with wounds, weapons, B. A. 232.

Sp. wynd and weather F. Q. I-12-1; winde, F. Q. V-12-4; wind or wether, F. Q. V-2-31; wether, and wind, F. Q. II-12-87;—C. 1;—Dr. with wind, with weather, H. E. XXI, H. H. Ger. 37.

Sp. wynd, and, waters, F. Q. VI-6-42; (instruments) windes, waters F. Q. II-12-70;—C. 1;—Dr. winds and waters, N. F. 140.

Sp. (with) word, work, Am. 23; with his word, his work, S. C. IX-175; witty words, and, works, M. H. T. 416;—C. 5;—Dr. words, works, N. T. 210.

Sp. woods, and waters C. C. II. 635; Epith. 1;—C. 1:—Dr. waters, woods, Pol. II-112.

Sp. world, waters wide F. Q. I-1-39:—Dr. world of water, N. F. 213.

Sp. worlde's wealth, F. Q. I-9-31;—Dr. wealth of, world, Eclog. V-17; world's huge wealth, Pol. XVII-15.

ALLITERATION COMMON TO SPENSER AND CHAUCER.

life and limbes F. Q. III-1-6;—C. 1;—Sp. gemmes of, gold H. H. L. 29:--C. 1:-sp. head, hood, F. Q. VI-2-5: headlesse, hood, S. C. II-86;—C. 1:- Sp. mery moneth of May, S. C. V-1;—C. 2;—Sp. ystabled his steeds, S. C.:— C. 1 (steedes in stalle);—Sp. water of this well, F. Q. II-2-40;— C. 4.

ALLITERATION COMMON TO DRAYTON AND CHAUCER.

Dr. corn and cattle, Pol. XXVII-269;—C. 1 (calf, corn):—Dr. head, -. B. W. V-33; D. and G. 711;—C. 2.:—Dr. (high-palmed) harts, nds, Pol. XXVI-113;—C. 1.;—Dr. hart with, hind, N. F. 281;—C. Dr. horse and hound, Pol. XXV-230;—C. 1.

ALLITERATION COMMON TO DANIEL AND CHAUCER.

Dan. kings, court, C. W. 1-28;—C. I.

TO DRAYTON AND DANIEL.

Dr. fuel to, fire II. E. I. II.-R. 44; fuel to that fire, Leg. III. P. G. 25;
fuel, fire Ids. 40; M. B. M. 1-54;—Dan. fuel to this fire, C. W. I-81;
(similar) fuel, flames, C. R. 483;—Dr. prince, people, Pol. XVII-171;
(similar) the peasant and the peer, B. A. 197;—Dan. prince and people
Ep. I. T. E. 194; nor peeres nor people. C. W. 1-39.

ALLITERATING TERMS PECULIAR TO SPENSER.

backe and, bodie, F. Q. IV-1-13; bed, nor bowre, S. C. VIII-167; bowres,
and beds, F. Q. I-1-55; bever, brow, F. Q. IV-3-11; bow and bolts, S. C.
III-65, bowes and braunches, F. Q. II-12-53; brest, bauldrick brave F.
Q. 1-7-29; brest, and bosome, F. Q. VI-12-19; card and compas, F. Q.
II-7-1; kid, cosset S. C. XI-46; kiddes and cracknelles, S. C. I-58; con-
quours and captaines, F. Q. III-11-52; flint, and fethers, F. Q. II-11-21;
floods and fountaines, F. Q. IV-11-52; groome or guide, F. Q. III-10-
36; haberjeon, helmet, F. Q. III-11-7; helmets, hawberks, F. Q. IV-9-27;
leman and, lady, F. Q. III-8-40; liegmen to, ladie, F. Q. III-1-44; lungs
and lites F. Q. VI-3-26; mariners and merchants F. Q. II-12-19; men,
master, M. H. T. 467; pathes and perils past, F. Q. VI-9-2; powers and,
potentates H. H. B. 13; realme and race, F. Q. II-10-4; rhymes and
roundelayes, S. C. VI-7; royalties and realmes, F. Q. III-5-53; scribe,
scale M. VI-35; shield and shining helmet, F. Q. I-6-41; shoulder, shield,
F. Q. V-5-3; silke and silver F. Q. II-12-77; storme, stowre, T. M. 42;
stockes and stubs, F. Q. I-9-34; sun and starres, V. G. 73; swords and
speares, H. L. 33; teeth and tayle, V. W. 10; thorns and thickets, F. Q.
IV-7-21; time, tide, F. Q. II-6-26; wine and water, F. Q. I-10-13; woods
and wastnes wide, F. Q. I-3-3.

Spenser as seen from the above examples, not unfrequently employs
alliteration for terms applying to weapons and war, but in such a use
Drayton far exceeds him. Examples of such alliteration by Drayton are:

Arms, and arches, B. A. 56; archers in ambush, B. A. 184; arms and
ensigns, B. A. 79; battle-axes, bills, B. A. 191; bills, bows, B. A. 211;
bills and blades, B. A. 149; brown-bills with their well-strung bows,
M.M. 94; blade, battle Leg. I. R. X. 88; bows, bills and battle-axes, Pol.

XXII-678; bows and, blades, B. A. 1; bow and quiver on, back, Eclog.
VII-18; sword, from side, D. and G. 799.

Terms applying to the body, alliterate occasionally by Spenser; (see
examples above); such alliteration is more frequent by Drayton, and especially in Poly-olbion, where it is applied to the bodies of the animals
which haunt the regions and rivers described, as: beards, bosoms, M.
B. M. III-327; back, belly, Pol. VI-71; breast and buttock, M.-C. 524;
head, heels, Pol. XII-337; heels, head M.-C. 727; herds, horn and hair,
Pol. XXVI-199; hoof and hair, M. E. 6072; horns and hoofs, Pol. XXII-
715; root, rind, Owl. 6; shape and skin, M. C. 1094.

Drayton frequently connects the names of the objects of a land-
scape by alliteration, a method employed very seldom by Spenser, not-
withstanding the fact that he uses alliteration so extensively in describ-
ing natural objects. Examples of such alliteration by Drayton: nor
dale nor ditch nor bank nor bushes M. C. 1318; heathes, and high-cleev'd
hills, Pol. XXIII-214; frith and, fell, Pol. XVII-388; hills and, holts,
Pol. XXVI-112, holts and hills, Pol. XV-289; moss and mere, Pol.
XXVII-2; rush and reed, Pol. XXV-95.

A few miscellaneous examples will serve in completing this class of
alliteration by Drayton: bells and bonfires, B. W. IV-23; coat and
cap, M.-C. 21; corn and cakes, D. and G. 411; drink and dice, M.-C. 312;
fire and flood, H. E. XIII, E. C.-H. 136; fodder, fold, Eclog. X-1; gob-
lin, ghost, H. E. XIII, E. C. H.,138; garter, glove, B. A. 61; hart, nor
hare, M. E. 291; lute and lyre; M. E. 1059; noon and night, Pol. XIII-
162; pen and paper, B. W. VI-98; poop and prow, B. A. 79; post, with,
packets, Leg. III, P. G. 81; sheaf and sickle, B. A. 78; sheaf with scythe
or sickle, Pol. XIV-101; woof and warp, Pol. XXIII-271.

--

2 ABSTRACT, OR ABSTRACT AND CONCRETE.

Words which represent abstract ideas, or an abstract and concrete idea
which are naturally associated, often alliterate. Abstract, or abstract
and concrete:

Sp. beauties blame, H. B. 155:—Dr. beauty's blame H. E. XII. O.
T.-C. 155.

Sp. bosome of, blis. T. M. 52; H. L. 20;—Dr. bosom full of blisses,
Ode H. N. Y. 10.

Sp. borne and bred, F. Q. I-10-51; bore and bred, Muiop. 33; bred,
or borne, F. Q. V-10-1; beene ybredd and, borne F. Q. III-4-38;—Dr.

(in Britain) born and bred, Pol. XXIV-153: born nor bred, Pol. XXIV. 1166: born and bred, Pol. XV-282:—Dan. borne and bred, C. W. IV-9: borne, but bred, C. W. VII-38.

Sp. care and count, F. Q. V-10-16:—C. 1 (cost and care): —Dr. (compare) cost and care. Pol. XXIX-325; cost, yet, care, B. W. II 67;—Dan. care and cost, O. M. A. 31.

Sp. dread of death and dolor doe, F. Q. II-8-7: dread of death, and dangerous dismay, Am. 63: dread and death M. H. T. 966: death, and dreaded sisters deadly spight, S. C. XI-163:—C. 5;—Dan. (compare) dead, darknesse. Cleo. 331.

Sp. death and dolor, F. Q. II-7-23: death, dolour. F. Q. III-4-6; deadly, dolorous Daph.. 65: in dolorous and, deadly feares, F. Q. V-10-6; dolorous (dismay) and deadly plight, F. Q. VI-3-27;—Dr. doleful, dead, B. W. V-5.

Sp. Redemer's death, F. Q. II-1-27:—Dr. dear Redeemer's death, Pol. VIII, 326.

Sp. doome of death, F. Q. I-10-53: doome, death. F. Q. VI-8-8:—Dr. death by, doom, Pol. XXIV-82;—Dan. (compare) doome to die Phil. 2027.

Sp. dred or dout, Daph. 23; dread and doubt, F. Q. IV-1-8; doubt or dreed, F. Q. VI-5-10; doubt and dreed, F. Q. III-1-48;—Dr. (compare) death and doubt, Pol. IT-293.

Sp. fortune and, fate, F. Q. III-10-3; fortune of fate, F. Q. II-7-60: fortune, fate F. Q. III-3-19; fate, and fortune, F. Q. VI-4-26; fate, fortune, F. Q. III-3-24; by fate or fortune, Ast. 25; fate or, fortune (faultless) Muiop. 53;—Dan. fate and fortune, C. W. I-84.

Sp. fortune, and, force, F. Q. V-4-47;—Dr. force and fortune, Pol. XII-83;—Dan. his fortune and his force, C. W. VI-11; fortune, force C. W. VI-78.

Sp. fortune, favour (gives) M. H. T. 594;—Dan. fortune, favour, C. W. III-19; fortunes, favours, F. D. 148; C. W. VII-96..

Sp. glorie, greater then, gayne, S. C. X-20; glory of, gaine, Epith. 14: —Dan. glory and not gaine, Ep. I, T. E. 188: gaine of glory, Mus. 959.

Sp. God of, grace, F. Q. V-7-2; of God, of grace, F. Q. I-10-19: Goddesse grace, C. C. II. 359; grace of God, F. Q. VI-8-38;—C. 1:—Dr. grace, great God, Pol. XXIV, 625: grace, in, godlike (hearts) Leg. III, P. G. 53.

Sp. grace, nor goodnes, F. Q. II-10-7: by grace, and goodnesse, M. VI-34; goodnesse, and grace, C. C. II. 588; Ast. 3; goodnesse, grace, F. Q.

III-11-9; good, grace, F. Q. III-11-10; all good, all grace, (growes), C. C. II. 324; grace and goodnesse, M. VI-34;—Dan. grace or goodnesse, Pan. 70; to good, to grace, Pan. 54: (congratulate) the good and the grace, Q. A. W. D. 8.

Sp. grace and glorie, Daph. 71; grace, glory, F. Q. VI-6-4;—Dan. grace and glory, C. W. VI-15; (compare) glory greatnesse, Pan. 64.

Sp. guifte of, grace, F. Q. II-2-6; gifts nor graces, F. Q. IV-11-2, grace, and gifts (of great availe), F. Q. V-5-49;—Dan. gifts and grace, Phil. 24.

Sp. gifts, gold, F. Q. I-12-12; ib. V-7-24;—Dr. gift, bought with gold, Owl. 688.

Sp. happinesse that heart, (desires), M. H. T. 609;—Dr. heart so happily, Leg. II. Mat. F. 49.

Sp. hart and hope, F. Q. II-8-39; hart, with hope, F. Q. V-6-8; hope, hart (hope,v), Am. 51;—C. 4 (6);—Dr. hope, heart, M. M. 46.

Sp. heaven, happines, R. T. 86; heavens, happie (hower), Proth. 6;—Dr. heaven, happy, Leg. III. P. G. 53.

Sp. hevens hight, F. Q. I-10-20; heavens height, II. L. 27; II. B. 16; II. H. L. 4; S. C. XI-177, heavens in height, R. T. 773;—Dr. height of heaven Eclog. VII. (Sng. II) 20.

Sp. hell with horrour, F. Q. V-11-12; horor of, hell, II. II. L. 130;—Dan. hell of horrour. II. G. 1513- 14.

Sp. helpe of, hand F. Q. II-11-30:—Dr. helpe of, hand, M. B. M. 111-57: Leg. IV. Crom. 20.

Sp. hope, and hate, C. C. H. 192;—Dr. hate of, hope, B. W. IV-15.

Sp. hope and help, F. Q. II-3-5; hope of helpe, F. Q. V-10-22: M. H. T. 327;—C. 1: Dr. hopeless as helpless, Leg. IV. Crom. 11;—Dan. hopes and helpes, C. W. V-26.

Sp. length of, launce, F. Q. III-4-16:—Dr. launce's length, Pol. XXII-1514.

Sp. libertie and life, S. C. XII-36; libertie, love and life, F. Q. IV-8-60; life and liberty, F. Q. II-5-13;—Dr. life and liberty, II. E. XXIII, J. G. D. G. 40; in life, liberty, II. E. V. I. Mor. 12.

Sp. life and love, F. Q. VI-1-15; Am. 7; love or life, F. Q. IV-12-16; love before, life II. L. 20; living, and loving, F. Q. IV-9-39; lives, loves, F. Q. IV-8-63; live, and love, F. Q. III-11-37, lovers, life II. L. 38; love ungri g life, F. Q. I-9-29; Dr. love, life, II. E. XXIV, G. D. J. G. ... Dr. love, of life, C. W. II-107, my love and life S. D. 27; love, ... 154; (Ode) Past. 94; liv'd and lov'd. S. D. 55, live because I S. D. 46; loving her that lives, S. D. 22.

Sp. losse of love, (losse), F. Q. II-1-31; ib. IV-9-13; losse, love as lyfe, wayd, S. C. VI-17; Dan. losse of love, II. T. 658.

Sp. love of lady, F. Q. II-6-33; love of ladies, F. Q. IV-9-37; loves, ladies, M. H. T. 757; ladies love, F. Q. IV-1-16; ib. I-6-21; lover, T. M. 56; ladie's, loves, F. Q. III-7-16; ladies, loved F. Q. I-1-21; lady or, love, F. Q. III-1-27;—C. 3;—Dr. (upon), lady, love, M. M. 201; love, ladies, II. E. XIV, II. E. C. 48.

Sp. loves delight, F. Q. V-9-31; R. T. 81; Ast. 9; Epith. 22; II. B. 35, Proth. 179; loves delight, II. L. 39; love, and, delight II. B. 3;—C. 1;—Dr. ôn love, delight, Eclog. VII-16; my dear delight my love, M. E. 150; love, delight, M. C. 267;—Dan. love, Delight, Cleo. 722; love, delight, Q. A. 1279; O. M. A. 22; in love, delight, Pas. F. 12.

Sp. love or liking, F. Q. V-5-16; love, liking F. Q. IV-2-8; liking to, love, F. Q. VI-3-7; liking, love, F. Q. III-12-13;—Dr. lik'd or, belov'd, M. B. M. 1-48.

Sp. love is lord, C. C. II. 883; love is lord, (loialtie), II. L. 26; love and lordship, M. H. T. 1027; loving Lord, II. H. L. 30; Lord of love, II. H. L. 19; lord of love, (law), Am. 10; liege Lord, love F. Q. I-1-51; lordly love, S. C. X-98; lord, love F. Q. IV-1-52, lovers of lordship, S. C. V.-123;—C. 3;—Dr. lord, love, Leg. II-Mat. F. 37; II. E. XIV, II. E. C. 40;—Dan. love, lord, C. W. IV-72; love, the lord of kings, C. W. VIII-50, love knew never lord, Q. A. 189; Lord and love, Cleo. 1106.

Sp. love and loialty, F. Q. I-12-31; (loialtie), C. C. II. 575; love, loialtie, F. Q. V-6-2, love, disloyalty, F. Q. III-5-46;—Dan. loyalty and love, Phil. 443.

Sp. loves and lustyhed, F. Q. I-2-3; love and lustihead, S. C. X-51; of love, of lusty-hed, F. Q. III-11-29;—Dr. love and lusty-head, Eclog. VII-9.

Sp. lordship with, land, F. Q. IV-9-13; land and lordship, (life), F. Q. IV-9-15;—C. 1;—Dr. Lordships in my lands, Pol. XIII-408.

Sp. man of mickle might, F. Q. II-1-7; ib. IV-1-32; manhood and, might, F. Q. IV-1-35, manhood, nor, might, F. Q. V-11-1; mickle might and manhood, F. Q. VI-3-10; (vs. 2 and 3); might in man, F. Q. VI-8-18; —C. 1(2); Dr. man, of (wondrous) might, Pol. XII-133; man of might, M. B. M. 1-257; men of, might Pol. XVIII-283; B. W. 1-50; men. mighty, M. M. 10; might in mortal man, D. and G. 365; Dan. man of might, C. W. V-83; (men) men of, might, C. W. IV-16; men of (worth) and might, T. F. 119.

Sp. mercy, and, might, II. H. B. 16;—Dr. mercy and, might, M. B. M. II-115; mercy, mightiness, X. F. 930.

S. ...ght of magick, spell, F. Q. I-7-36; in. magick, might, F. Q. I-
... Dr. magick ..., might, Pol. IV-330.

S. ..igh and main, F. Q. I-11-13; ib. IV-8-45; R. T. 9; S. C. III-
...; V. G. 66; maine and might, F. Q. VI-12-23: amaine with, might,
F. Q. VI-6-27; C. 2: Dr. might and main, M. M. 97; Nym. 78; Leg.
IV., Crom. 19.

S. ..radi.. of pleasure, Am. 76; pleasure, paradice, Am. 77;
..es..e..t, paradise, Muiop. 24;—Dr. paradise for pleasures, M. B. M.
...92.

Sp. peace and pleasures, F. Q. II-6-37; pleasure, ib. IV-4-7;—Dan.
.eace with pleasure, Cleo. 535.

Sp. plenty and, pleasure, F. Q. III-6-41; pleasaunce, and plentifull
.stor), F. Q. II-6-11;—Dr. pleasure in, plenteous (cup), Leg. III. P.
G. 59; pleasures, plentifully, Leg. I. R. N. 3;—Dan. pleasure, plenty,
Vr. Gd. 186; (supply) pleasures with plenteousnesse, II. T. 480.

Sp. pledge of peace, F. Q. V-9-30;—Dan. pledge of peace, S. D. 46.

Sp. powre to, princes, F. Q. V-1-10. (I);—Dr. power in, princess hand,
M. B. M. I-363; prince of pow'r, M. M. 226; prince, power, Leg. II, Mat.
C. 2.; Dan. power of princes, Q. A. W. W. 28; powers of princes Mus.
.16; powers of princes mindes, C. W. VI-70: pow'r and princes (jealous-
nes) Phil. 1140; prince, power, C. W. I-44, prince, power (dispence),
Cleo. 388.

Sp. prayre and, praise, F. Q. I-5-11;—Dr. praise nor prayers, M. E.
905.

Sp. (peerlesse) price, praise, C. C. H. 549;—Dan. price, prayse, Des.
B. 4.

Sp. rule and reason, F. Q. V-5-25; reasons rule, F. Q. I-4-41; V-7-
.t: Dr. rules (v). no reason, Eclog. VII-25.

S.. rule of right, F. Q. II-2-36; to rule them right, T. M. 93;—Dan.
...t that rules, Cleo. 271.

S. shame and sorrow, F. Q. III-1-7, T. M. 88: (compare) shame and,
.orne, F. Q. V-11-52;—C. 2;—Dan. sorrow, shame and scorne, C. W. II-
51: sorrow, shame, sin O. M. A. 38, shame a sinne, C. R. 143; sinne and
.... C. W. V-6: Q. A. 1525.

S.. sign of silence, F. Q. III-12-4;—Dr. sign of silence, Pol. IX-69.

S.. tenor of my tale, C. C. II. 98;—Dr. tenor of my tragick tale,
L.. III. P. G. 117.

S.. ..ct of time, F. Q. V-4-8; S. C. V-117;—Dr. tract of time, Pol.

Sp. travell and, toile, F. Q. VI-1-25; (compare), troubles and, toyle V. G. 19; toyle nor traveill, F. Q. II-12-19; - Dan. toyle and travell, Ep. III, L. M. C. 107; toyle, and, travelling, Mus. 111.

Sp. want of words, F. Q. III-1-2 (I):—Dr. want of words, H. E. VIII, A. E. 20;—Dan. wanteth words, (v) C. R. 805.

Sp. words, wits, M. H. T. 71;— C. 1;—Dr. in, words, no wit, Eclog. VII-22.

Sp. worth and wealth, F. Q. V-10-7; Dr. (compare) worth and wit, B. A. 264.

Sp. wonder of, world, F. Q. III-9-45; Dan. world's wonder, C. R. 486;

Spencer and Chaucer:

Sp. beauty, bounty; F. Q. I-10-30; ib. IV-3-39; C. 2.

Sp. fancies were foolries, S. C. II-211;— C. 1 (fool of fantasie).

Sp. perill and, paine, F. Q. II-3-11; perils and, paynes, H. L. 35; perill, paine, F. Q. V-11-55; paines ne perill, F. Q. VI-10-32; C. 1.

Sp. right withouten reason, S. C. V-146;—C. 1.

Sp. (sad) sighes and sorrowes, F. Q. III-2-28; C. 2.

This method of alliterating is extensively employed by Spencer, and with a great variety of combinations. The following examples will show something of the extent to' which it is used:

Causes nor, courses, F. Q. V-2-12; change, and, chaunce, F. Q. V-2-36; chaunce, choyce, F. Q. VI-8-16; crime with cruelty, F. Q. VI-8-7; countenance and, cheare, M. VI-12; danger and, dreed, F. Q. II-1-52; daunger with dread, F. Q. IV-10-58; death, daunger, F. Q. IV-12-28; death, destinie, F. Q. IV-6-18; (deepe) disdaine and, indignity, F. Q. IV-7-36; the doubts, the daungers, H. L. 38; his faith, his fortune, H. L. 32; for favour or for feare, M. VI-12; folly unto fate, F. Q. V-1-28; force, ne fraud, (found), F. Q. V-1-9, (I); force and furie, F. Q. V-12-17; friendship and afffection, F. Q. IV-3-50; gard and government, F. Q. V-1-3; glorie or, guerdeon, F. Q. IV-7-1; god and goodnes, F. Q. I-10-16; grace and gaine, F. Q. IV-7-11; grief, and, gall, F. Q. IV-3-43; griefe or gall, F. Q. V-10-4; griefe, grace, F. Q. IV-7-38; leasure, and liberty, F. Q. III-10-16; lewd loves and lust, F. Q. IV-9-16; love and lewdnesse disolute, F. Q. III-8-14; love, lucke, F. Q. VI-8-32; luck and loves, lore, S. C. XII-63; love, and, lustfulnesse, F. Q. IV-1-7; mind and meaning, F. Q. VI-1-46; note and name, F. Q. V-11-19; pains, and, praise, F. Q. I-5-43; paines or punishments, F. Q. III-12-26; penurie and pyne, F. Q. V-5-22; pleasure and repast, F. Q. V-3-40; pleasure nor.

play, Ast. V; powre and peerlesse majestie, H. H. B. 27; powre and, oppression, F. Q. V 10-9; praise or pitty, F. Q. I-12-17; prayse, pride, V. W. V. 10, pride, praise, portlinesse, Am. 5; pryde and proud submission, F. Q. I-3-6; pride and puissaunce, F. Q. VI-2-8; reproach, ruine, F. Q. III-6-22; reproch, repentance, F. Q. III-12-24; prowesse and, prize, F. Q. VI-6-35; reason, remedy, F. Q. III-2-36; sacrilege, sinnes, F. Q. II-8-16; sorrow and consuming smart, H. B. 4; strength and stifnesse, F. Q. IV-1-19; sternesse, strength, V. W. V. 10; want, woe, F. Q. V-7-15; woe and wretchednesse, F. Q. V-10-11; worth and wealth, F. Q. V-10-7; wretchednesse and woe, Daph. 62.

Such alliteration is frequently employed in phrasal construction, as the following examples show:

Care of cold, F. Q. II-10-7; care of credite, F. Q. III-10-11; cause in combat F. Q. I-4-13, chaunge of chear, F. Q. I-2-27; cloke of cowardice, F. Q. V-3-15; course of kinde, F. Q. III-6-38; Am. 30; II. B. 21; craft in, countenance, S. C. IX-168; crop of, care, F. Q. I-4-47; S. C. XII-122, doubt of daunger, F. Q. III-5-12; dore of death, F. Q. I-5-41, dore of death and deadlie dreed, V. G. 15; face of falsehood, F. Q. I-8-19; fansie, from former follies, S. C. VI-37; feare of, fates, F. Q. I-12-37; feare of, foes, F. Q. I-10-5; fear of fraude, S. C. V-224; force of flame, H. L. 2; foe of folly, F. Q. II-6-37; fortunes freakes, F. Q. I-3-1; to fortune, foeman, S. C. II-21; flowre of faith, F. Q. I-3-23; garland or, glorie, H. B. 26; glorie of his guile, F. Q. I-1-42; governannce, to guyde, F. Q. II-1-7; grace, be guerdon of, griefe, C. C. II. 943; guerdon of his guile F. Q. I-3-10; heat of hardiment F. Q. I-9-12; houre in, happines, M. H. T. 983; lacke of love, B. T. IV-4; lampe of love, Epith. 288; lay of loves delight, F. Q. III-12-5; of lassie love C. C. II. 766; league of love. F. Q. III-1-1; delights of life, light, M. H. T. 762; in, life, delight Daph. 2; lightnesse, in love, F. Q. I-4-4; love of, lasse, F. Q. III-12-43; lore of love, F. Q. III-6-51; losse of, lives, F. Q. II-9-5; love of letters, M. H. T. 829; love of lillyes, Epith. 43; unto, lust, a law, F. Q. IV-8-30; makers majestie, T. M. 87; makers of might, F. Q. II-9-46; matter of myrth, S. C. XI-56; matter by, might, H. B. 18; maystery of might, F. Q. VI-1-36; measure of, mynd, C. C. II. 363; might in medicine, F. Q. I-5-43; mother of, might, F. Q. I-8-3; mone with many a mocke, S. C. VIII-120; muses might, S. C. X-30; musickes mirth, S. C. XII-40; muses merrie, S. C. XI-34; paines of purgatorie H. L. 40; partmer of plight, F. Q. partner of, payne, F. Q. III-9-40; part of, paine, M. H. T. of plight F. Q. I-10-24; compassion, of, plaints F. Q. III-

7-10; compassion of plight. F. Q. VI-4-3; perill of, pride. F. Q. V-4-38;
perill of, place, F. Q. I-1-13; perill of, paineful plight. F. Q. I-5-52;
place of paine. F. Q. III-5-23; place of punishment, F. Q. V-10-36;
plumes of pride. F. Q. I-10-39; pierlesse pleasures, in, places, S. C. VI-
32; picture of. punishment. F. Q. VI-7-24; pitty of, payne. F. Q. I-10-
28; pitty of the pray, F. Q. IV-7-8; pitie of. plight Daph. 25; poets praise,
S. C. XI-23; report of perlous, paine, F. Q. II-9-17; powre of patience,
F. Q. III-11-11; praise of pollicies, F. Q. II-9-18; prayses of, prince, F.
Q. V-9-21; praise of prowesse F. Q. II-2-30; pricke of, prayse. F. Q. II-
12-1; pride of, praise, Ast. 2; prince, with pacience, F. Q. II-8-17; prince
of peace F. Q. IV-1-1 (I); princes pleasures. F. Q. III-2-31; proofe. of,
powre, F. Q. III-3-3; puissance of. push, F. Q. I-3-35; wrecks of.
wretches. F. Q. III-4-22; rod of righteousnesse H. II. B. 23; roote of,
wrath F. Q. II-4-10; safties sake, F. Q. II-10-16; sea of sorrow, F. Q. III-
4-8; signes of sorrow, F. Q. III-11-37; sights of semblants, F. Q. III-4-54;
signe of shame. F. Q. VI-3-17; slaughters sake. F. Q. V-12-8; sorrows
sourse. F. Q. IV-7-20; sternesse of. stile, M. VI-37; strokes of. steele,
F. Q. II-2-22; terrour of. tortures. F. Q. II-7-63; weaknesse of, widowhed
or woe, F. Q. I-12-28; witnesse of woe, S. C. VIII-151; workmans witt
F. Q. I-4-5; worke of, witt, F. Q. II-12-11; womens witt, F. Q. I-6-31.

Some other forms by Drayton:

brow, beauty, Leg. II. Mat. F. 10; Mn. Mn.. 131; burthen from, back,
B. A. 35; on, back, burthen, II. E. XIV, II. E. C. 154; heart. hatred,
Pol. XXII-1175; kings, conquests, Pol. XI-27; liberties and laws. B. W.
IV-30; means and might, Pol. XXIX-15; penitence and prayer, Pol.
XXIV-1005; pomp, power. Pol. XXIV-212; poverty and prayer. Pol.
XXIV-911; providence and power, M. B. M. II-653.

By Daniel:

counsels, customes, Phil. 1169; feare and flattery, Pan. 73; force and
feare, C. W. IV-39; grace and greatnesse, Phil. 436; majestie and might,
C. W. II-19; mischief, malice, C. W. VIII-23; repentance and com-
II-19; mischief, malice, C. W. VIII-23; repentance and compassion, Q. A. 1910; applause and pleasure, S. D. 198; his powre his
paines, C. W. VII-10; pride, oppression, C. W. V-19; imprisonment and
poyson, Ep. VI, II. W; waste and warre, C. W. I-2; wealth and wits. V.
Gd. 122; their wit, their wealth, C. W. IV-109; wit and worth, C. W. IV-
63; wounds and wearinesse, C. W. VIII-21.

Words expressing the same general idea, or ideas which are closely
allied, are often joined by alliteration, thus rendering the effect more

emphatic, not only by repetition of thought but also **by repetition of sound.**

₃ EMPHASIS BY REPETITION.

Sp. bare and barrein, S. C. XII-105;—Dr. (similar) barren, bleak, Pol. V-341.

Sp. beastly brutish (rage), F. Q. II-4-6; brutish, beastly, F. Q. III-7-15; brutishnesse and beastlie (filth), T. M. 15;—Dr. (compare), barbarous brute, Pol. XIX-339.

Sp. beastly and blont, S. C. IX-109;—Dr. (compare), beastly base M. E. 1133; baseness and thy beastly will, B. W. III-78.

Sp. blew in black, S. C. XI-107;—C. 2;—Dr. black and blue, Nym. 9.

Sp. cryes and clamours, F. Q. VI-11-32;—Dr. cries and clamours, B. A. 246.

Sp. darke and dampish, H. H. B. 24;—Dr. (compare) dark and deep, Pol. XXVIII-292; dark and (wondrous) deep, Pol. II-321.

Sp. deare and dainty, F. Q. VI-11-1; dainty deare, F. Q. I-11-48;—Dr. deare and dainty (nymph), Pol. XXIII-309.

Sp. faire and free, F. Q. I-10-6; fayre, free Epith. 405;—C. 2 (5);—Dr. fair and free, Eclog. IV, (motto) 9; so fair so free, H. E. III, J. M. 157.

Sp. false and fayned, F. Q. VI-6-42;—Dan. (compare) false and faithlesse, Phil. 1782.

Sp. false, and fraught with ficklenesse, F. Q. I-4-25;—Dr. fickle, falsely, Eclog. X-10.

Sp. fawne and flatter, F. Q. VI-6-42; fawning of, flatterer, F. Q. III-8-38; Dan. flatterie, fawnd, C. W. II-18.

Sp. inflame, set on fire, H. H. L. 39; flaming, fiery, F. Q. I-7-31; flames and flashing (light) M. VII-23;—Dr. inflam'd with, fires, Leg. I. R. N. 1; Dan. fire inflam'd, C. W. VIII-51; firie, flaming, C. W. VI-77.

Sp. flourishbing fresh leaves, F. Q. II-3-30;—Dan. fresh and flourishing, Des. B. 9; so flourishing and so faire, C. R. 675.

Sp. forme and, fashion, F. Q. III-6-38; C. C. H. 615;—Dr. forme fashion H. E. IV, M. Juo. 75;—Dan. forme and fashion, Mus. 992.

Sp. fowle ill-favor'd (sight) F. Q. II-7-3;—Dr. foul ill-favour'd, H. E. XVI, M. W. 64.

Sp. fresh, and full, F. Q. III-12-18; VI-7-5; Dr. so full s fresh
Pol. XVII-75; (similar) most full, most faire, Pol. XXVI 165; (t o)
fair and full-brim'd floods, Pol. XXIX-110; Dan. (compare) faire ard
full of modestie, Q. A. 614.

Sp. fret and fome, F. Q. VI-12-31; fret and frowne, F. Q. V-8-11;—
Dr. (similar), fret and fume, Pol. XXIX-318; fumes, frets Nym. 57.

Sp. full and free, H. H. L. 38;—Dr. fully take what freely I poss-
est, Leg. III, P. G. 60; and his free bounty fully, found, M. B. M. III-97.

Sp. goodly, godly, F. Q. I-10-1;—Dr. godly (man), good (a king), Pol.
XVII-263; godly, good (instruction) gave, Pol. XXIV-663.

Sp. goodly, glorious, F. Q. IV-8-33; Am. 70;—Dr. (compare) godlike, glorious, Pol. V-5.

Sp. goodly, and gay, F. Q. III-6-11; so goodly and so gay M. H. T.
590; goodly, gay, Am. 27;—Dr. (compare) gild and make, gay, H. F.
XX1, H. H. L. Ger. 124.

Sp. goodly golden (chayne), F. Q. I-9-1; goodly golden (fruit), F. Q.
II-7-55; goodly gilden, F. Q. VI-2-33; golden (words) and goodly (countenance) F. Q. IV-2-9; golden, goodly, F. Q. IV-10-8;—Dr. (compare)
goodly glitt'ring (east gilds) Pol. XIII-18.

Sp. glorious, glistereth, F. Q. I-10-50; H. H. B. 17; glorious, and
glistering, Muiop. 12; glorious glitterand (light), F. Q. I-1-16; glorious
golden, Am. 82; glistering glorious, H. H. L. 8; - Dr. glistering wings,
gloriously, B. A. 155.

Sp. greatest glorious (Queen) F. Q. I-1-3; greatest and most glorious,
F. Q. II-11-30; great, glorious, F. Q. II-2-40; Proth. 157; glorious,
great, F. Q. I-5-1;—Dr. great and glorious, B. W. 1-17; greatest, gloriously, Pol. XVIII-400; (similar) great and godlike, B. W. I-19; (compare also) great and goodly (woods) M. E. 7015; goodly, and greatest,
Pol. XVI-228.

Sp. long, late, Epith. 273;—C. 1;—Dr. long, late, M. C. 1295; (similar) latest, last, H. E. IV, M. J. 192.

Sp. pearle and pretious stone, F. Q. IV-1-15; perles and pretious
stones F. Q. III-4-18;—Dr. precious orient pearl, Pol. XXX-116.

Sp. plaine and pleasaunt, F. Q. I-10-6;—Dr. (compare) plaine and
poor, Pol. XXIII-59.

Sp. plaints and piteous (griefe), F. Q. III-1-53;—Dr. (compare)
plaints and pleas, H. E. XI. C. O. T. 150.

Sp. plaints, prayers, Am. 14;—Dr. complaint or prayer, Ids. 52.

Sp. plant or prune, F. Q. III-6-34;—Dr. prune and plant, Pol. III-353.

Sp. prate and play, F. Q. V-9-13;—Dr. (compare) prate, preach, Owl. 909.

Sp. rare and rich;— Dr. rich (attire be), rare, Pol. XVIII-49.

Sp. rule and raigne, M. VII-58; M. H. T. 980; reign and rulen, S. C. VII-155; Dr. rul'd, raign'd, Pol. XVII-352.

Sp. sad and sorrowfull, F. Q. IV-8-19; sorrowfull and sad, F. Q. VI-5-3; sad and sorie (for, sight), F. Q. IV-3-14;—C. 1;—Dr. (compare) sad forsaken (night) M. E. 1331.

Sp. sett or sow, F. Q. III-6-31;— Dr. set and sow, Pol. III-353.

Sp. shrill and shrieke, F. Q. VI-8-46; shrill (outcryes) and shrieks, F. Q. I-6-7;—Dr. with, shrill scream, shrieking, M. B. M. III-539; (similar) shieks and shouts Pol. XXII-1143; shouts, and shrieks, B. A. 96.

Sp. sicke, sore, F. Q. VI-5-40;—C. 1;—Dr. sore and sick, H. E. III, J. M. 115;—Sp. sign'd and seald, F. Q. I-10-13;—Dr. sign'd and sealed, H. E. VII, E. A. 6.

Sp. smooth, and soft, B. I. III-9; smoothest softnes, B. I. III-9; (similar) so smirke, so smoothe, S. C. II-72;—C. 2 (swote, smothe, softe; —Dr. smooth and soft, Pol. XXIII-30.

Sp. solemne sad, F. Q. II-6-37; sad and solemne, F. Q. II-10-36;—Dr. (compare) solemn, sullen, H. E. VII. E. A. 66.

Sp. sternely, strong, F. Q. VI-5-25;—C. 2 (stern and stoute);—Dr. stern, strong, M. M.

Sp. so stiffe, so state, S. C. IX-45; (similar) so stiffe so stanck, S. C. IX-47; Dr. (compare) stiff and strong, Nym. 62; strongly stiff'ned, N. F. 649.

Sp. stout and, strong, F. Q. I-5-7; strong and stout, F. Q. V-11-47; Dr. stout and strong, Pol. XXII-1118; strongly, stoutly, Pol. IV-276; (similar) strong and stubborn, D. and G. 617.

Sp. stout and sturdy, F. Q. I-3-17;—Dr. (compare), stout and sted-fast, Pol. XIX-403; (similar) stedfast, strongest, Pol. II-148.

Sp. strove and struggled, F. Q. V-2-11;— Dan. striv'd and struggled, C. R. 388.

Sp. sullein, sad, F. Q. III-12-18;—Dr. sad and sullen, M. E. 1133.

Sp. sure and strong, F. Q. V-12-11;—Dan. (compare) sure and sen, Cleo. 119.

Sp. tossing and turning, F. Q. II-9-58; tost and turned with continuall change, M. VII-21: - Dr. (compare) turns and twinings, Pol. XXII-23;-- Dan.turne and tosse, C. W. VII-11.

Sp. watch and ward, F. Q. I-3-9; S. C. IX-234; (was) watch, and, ward, F. Q. III-11-31; watch and, ward, F. Q. IV-10-17;—Dr. watch and ward, II. E. VII. E. A. 115. Washes, to watch and ward Pol. XX-279; watch, ward, Eclog. VII-26;—Dan. watch and ward, II. T. 1206.

Sp. watch and, waite, S. C. IX-237; (wait) F. Q. I-11-50;—Dr. wait, watch, II. E. XX, C. B., M. 7.

Sp. weake and wearie, F. Q. I-9-20;—Dr. (compare) weak and worthless. M. B. M. II-237;—Dan. weary and weak, O. M. A. 31.

Sp. weeping, and wailing, S. C. II-50; (in way), weepe and waile, F. Q. I-3-24; weepe, and waile, ib. IV-9-7; Am. 18; wept, and wayld, F. Q. I-3-22; ib. IV-8-2; wail and weepe, F. Q. I-2-8;—C. 5 (7);—Dan. a weeping eye a wailing face, Cleo. 728.

Sp. wildnesse and wastefull (desert), F. Q. I-3-3;—Dan. wastes and wildes. Ep. III, L. M. C. 11.

Sp. wise and wary (was), F. Q. I-8-7; unwise, and warelesse, F. Q. IV-2-3;- C. 2 (4) (war and wys);—Dr. (similar) watchful and too wary (foes), B. W. V-46.

Sp. wounded and weake, F. Q. V-4-15;—weak with wounds, B. A. 232.

SPENSER AND CHAUCER.

Sp. courteous kind, F. Q. V-5-35; courteous and kynde, F. Q. III-5-55; kind and courteous (use) F. Q. III-7-15;—C. 1;—Sp. cald, and cryde, F. Q. VI-12-8; cry and call, C. C. II. 879;—C. 1;—Sp. covert, close, F. Q. II-12-76;—C. 1;—faire and fresh, as freshest flowre, F. Q. I-12-22: faire and fresh, T. M. 7; freshest faire (attire), M. VII-11; —C. 4 (faire, fresh, fre);—Sp. (in forrest) fresh and free, M. H. T. 630;—C. 3;—Sp. feeble, and faint, F. Q. I-10-2; faint and feeble, ib. I-7-5; ib. VI-5-40; faint and feeble (in folde), S. C. I-1;—C. 1;—Sp. fiers and fell. F. Q. I-6-26; (similar) to fearelesse and so fell, F. Q. I-6-25; --C. 1;—Sp.firmely, faithfull, F. Q. III-3-27;—C. 1;—Sp. gladsome, glee, F. Q. IV-9-13; glee, gladsome chere, F. Q. IV-3-51; glee, goodly (feast) F. Q. VI-6-41;—C. (good, glade) 1; goodly glad, 1;—Sp. griev'd, and groning, F. Q. V-4-22; (compare), groveling and groning, F. Q. VI-5-5;—C. 1 (grone and grete):—Sp. to ride to ronne, M. H. T. 905;—

(l (renne, ryde): Sp. say or sing Epith. 20; sing, and, say El. 16;—C. 1: Sp. sighes and sobs, F. Q. III-1-53;—sigh and sob, ib. III-11-8; sighing and sobbing sore, F. Q. IV-7-10; sighed, sobd, swound, III-10-7; (similar) sighed and sorrow'd, F. Q. VI-3-6;—C. 2:—Sp. slug, or sleepe in slothfull shade, F. Q. III-7-12;—C. 1 (slomber, sleep, slouth);—Sp. swincke and sweate, S. C. XI-151; M. H. T. 163; swinck and sweat, F. Q. II-7-8; sweat and swinke, F. Q. VI-1-32; forswonck and forswatt, S. C. IV-99;—C. 2. (swelt and swete);—Sp. sugrie sweete, M. H. T. 819;—C. 1, (sucre, or soot);—Sp. wake, and, weepe F. Q. V-6-25;—C. 1 (forweped and forwaked);—Sp. wett, and weary, F. Q. III-9-19;—C. 2:—Sp. wylie witted, F. Q. II-3-9; —C. 1: (wily and wis.).

Drayton and Chaucer:—Dr. sit and sing, Ids. 53; C. 1 (sate and songe).

The above classification represents very fully this method of alliterating, as employed by Drayton and Daniel, with the exception of a few phrases used by the former, which are distinctly characteristic for the class and peculiar to him; such are:

curl'd and crisped, Ids. 8; crisp and curled, Eclog. IV-64 (motto); helpless, harmless, Owl, 343; unheard, unhelp'd, II. E. II, II. R. 62; nigh and haughtily, Owl. 1198; integrity and truth, B. W. I-62; trampled, and trod, B. W.; loose and large, Owl. 505; loud and long, Pol. XXX-163.

But for Spenser, however, the above classification represents only a small portion of such alliteration. This is a favorite method of the poet, and is applied in a great variety of combinations and constructions. It is strongly characteristic and is of special importance for two reasons; first, it reveals everywhere a conscious use of alliteration on the part of the poet, and secondly, it shows clearly that the purpose of such a use is to procure an emphatic effect. In order that the importance of this class may be clearly set forth, it will be necessary to give here the phrases and combinations, which are most distinctly characteristic and which do not appear in the above classification. A coordinate construction of nouns, adjectives and verbs, is very frequently employed. The following are examples for the noun:

blame and, blemishment. F. Q. IV-2-36; buffets and, blowes, F. Q. III-1-9; constancy and care, F. Q. II-12-38; discomfort and disquiet, F. Q. IV-8-8; dust and drosse, H. H. L. 10; fowlnesse and deformity, F. Q. V-11-25; powre and puissaunce, F. Q. I-10-20; plague and pestilence, M. H. T. 8; pompe, and pride, R. T. 75; wrong and robbery, F. Q. II-7-20;

shade and semblant, F. Q. III-2-38; simple show, and semblant, F. Q. II-1-21; sighes and singulfs, F. Q. V-6-13; stock and ston, Ast. 1; restraint or stay, Epith. 11; taunts and termes, F. Q. V-4-23; by treatie, and by traynes, F. Q. I-6-3; woods and wanton wildernesse, F. Q. III-6-22.

A variation of the same construction is made by alliterating a modifying adjective instead of the Substantive which it qualifies, as:

debate or bitter strife, F. Q. VI-9-18; cares nor cumbrous thought, F. Q. VI-9-22; death or deadly paines, F. Q. I-12-36; dread and dolefull teene, F. Q. I-9-31; dreams, nor dreadfull sights, Epith. 19; filth and foule incontinence, F. Q. II-12-87; filth and foule iniquitie, F. Q. V-1-5; (dreadfull) force and furious intent, F. Q. IV-3-6; geares and goodly ray, F. Q. V-2-50; gold and gorgeous ornament; F. Q. I-9-19; grace and goodly carriage, F. Q. II-2-38; grace and goodly modesty, F. Q. III-5-55; joy and jolly merriment, T. M. 35; pomp, and princely majestie, F. Q. I-5-5; puissaunce and impetuous maine, F. Q. II-9-14; rage and rancorous yre, F. Q. I-11-14; of troubles and of toylesome paine, F. Q. VI-9-31.

Adjectives:

bestial and blinde, F. Q. III-12-24; so blessed, and so blythe, C. C. D. 21; blinde and brute, F. Q. VI-10-38; carelesse, and unkind, F. Q. III-12-24; coy and curious nice, F. Q. IV-10-22; cruell and unkind, Am. 56; dimme and darke, S. C. XI-67; dim and dulled, II. B. 3; faire and fensible, F. Q. II-9-24; faire and fruitfull, F. Q. II-12-12; false and fayned, F. Q. VI-6-42; false and fraudulent, F. Q. IV-12-23; fearfull, and, faint, F. Q. IV-1-5; fearlesse and free, Daph. 16; fierce and fervent, Daph. 28; fierce and furious, V. G. 65; francke and free, F. Q. II-7-9; free and fortunate, F. Q. VI-9-19; fresh and fragrant, F. Q. IV-1-31; furious and fell, F. Q. I-6-43; (fell and furious, I-2-15); grim and ghastly, F. Q. V-11-12; grim and griesly, M. VII-16; loose and loathsomely, F. Q. V-12-29; meeke, and merciable, S. C. IX-174; meeke and myld, F. Q. III-7-15; dispised and dispraized, F. Q. VI-8-26; rough and rude, F. Q. III-10-48; sage and sober, F. Q. I-12-5; safe and sound, F. Q. II-12-82; slow and sluggish, F. Q. II-6-46; smooth, and subtile, F. Q. V-9-5; sober, and sage, F. Q. IV-3-43; unsuccour'd and unsought, F. Q. IV-8-51; sure and sound, F. Q. V-11-38; strong and streight, F. Q. V-5-33; so wanton and so wood, S. C. III-55; so wimble and so wight, S. C. III-91.

This method of alliterating is frequently varied, by omitting the connective; with such an arrangement, the slow and measured tone of the expression gives way to a hurried, more vividly emphatic one, as the following examples show:

bitter balefull stound; F. Q. I-7-25; bitter byting wordes, F. Q. I-12-
29; comely courteous glee, F. Q. I-10-6; constant carefull mind, F. Q.
I-5-28; crafty cunning traine, F. Q. I-7-1; cruell, cursed enemy, F. Q.
I-7-11; cursed cruell sarazin, F. Q. V-2-1; doughty dreaded knight, F.
Q. III-1-21; fowle deformed wight, F. Q. I-8-49; ghastly griefful eies,
F. Q. VI-8-40; griesly grim aspect, F. Q. V-9-48; hatefull hellish snake,
F. Q. III-11-1; heavy hapless curse, M. VI-55.

Verbs alliterating in coordinate phrases:

barke and ball, S. C. IX-190; barking and biting, F. Q. VI-12-40;
barke and bay, F. Q. V-12-41; bay and barke, V. G. 44; bet and bounst
F. Q. V-2-21; beate and bruse, F. Q. VI-7-40; burne, and boyled, F. Q.
IV-1-17; brusht and battered, F. Q. V-12-7; checkt and changed, M.
VII-51; creep, nor crouch, M. H. T. 727; cry, and curse, F. Q. I-3-25;
decke or adorne, F. Q. VI-10-23; fade and fall II. B. 14; give or graunt,
M. H. T. 1143; glaunce and glide, F. Q. II-5-2; gibe, and geare, F. Q.
II-6-21; jest and gibe. F. Q. V-3-39; lament and mourne, M. H. T.
580; mourne, and, mone, T. M. 28; mumming and, masking, M. H. T.
802; hackt and hew'd, F. Q. V-7-29; rag'd and ror'd, F. Q. IV-11-3; rored
and raged, F. Q. III-7-33; rage and rayle, F. Q. II-8-37; raile and rend,
F. Q. I-3-35; rashing and ryring, F. Q. V-3-8; wrest and wring, F. Q.
VI-1-7; yrid'd, and, yrent, F. Q. IV-6-15; rob and ransacke, F.
Q. II-7-32; robbe and rend, F. Q. III-10-40; serve and sew, F.
Q. II-7-9; shake and shiver, V. G. 43; shiver, and shake, M.
VII-23; srike and squall, F. Q. VI-4-18; stagger, and stare, F.
Q. V-1-11; stop or stay, F. Q. II-6-42; stopped nor withstood, F. Q.
V-10-8; stouping (low), or stealing, F. Q. IV-10-18; talke and tellen,
S. C. IX-53; tosse, and teare, F. Q. IV-9-23; trast and traverst, F. Q.
V-8-37; tride, and tempted, F. Q. V-5-48; tug and teare, F. Q. VI-11-17;
waste and wear away, Am. 25; wast and woxen old, S. C. I-28; watch, and
weare, (weary night), F. Q. V-6-26.

Alliteration is often employed for the sake of emphasis in antithesis:

(4) EMPHASIS BY CONTRAST.

No blisse, to balefulnesse, F. Q. II-12-83; blisse, halefull, F. Q. V-10-
6; blisse into bale, Daph. 16;—C. 1 (blis, bitternesse);—Dr. (similar)
baneful poison spiced with, bliss, Leg. IV, Mat. F. 26;—Dan. blisse
bale, C. R. 137.

drowsie night, F. Q. I-3-15; (similar) darksome night, to

day, F. Q. III-3-12;- Dr. (compare) blacke and darksome nights, the bright and gladsome days, Pol. XIII-174;—Dan. daylight sets and all is dark and dull, H. T. 1311, 12.

Sp. of, fayrest, made, fowlest, F. Q. II-12-83; faire grew foule, and foule grew faire, F. Q. IV-8-32; fowle, faire, ib. I-7-3; fowle or faire, M. VII-22;—C. 6 (7):—Dr. so faire a rising had so foul a set, ids. 60; fair, foul, M. B. M. II-195; foule or faire, Pol. XXX-28; foul, fair, Eclog. IV-20;—Dan. faire, foule, C. W. V-12; fairest, fowle, P. S. 55; faire, foully, C. W. VII-109; fowlest, finest, Mus. 513.

Sp. fayrest, fiercest, F. Q. V-10-9;—Dan. my fierce Faire, Ode. 17.

Sp. fayrer, false, Am. 59; false, (seemde as) faire, F. Q. I-2-37; false Lady faire, F. Q. I-4-37;—Dan. (compare) faithfull, false, Cleo. 851; falshood, faith, O. M. A. 23; false, faith, Cleo. 857.

Sp. flourish, vade, F. Q. V-2-40;—Dan. flourish now, and fade, C. R. 252; fade that made the fairest florish, S. D. 50.

Sp. friend or foe, F. Q. IV-7-16; friend nor foe, ib. I-12-28; friends profest, to foemen fell, F. Q. IV-4-1; fayned friends, foes, H. L. 38; friendes and feeble foes, S. C. VII-194; friend, feare of foe, Muiop. 48; 'foe and frend, H. B. 39; foe, friend, F. Q. I-3-39; foes, to faithfull friends, F. Q. IV-4-1; former foes, friends, C. C. H. 851; foe, frend, Ast. 24; foes, friendly, F. Q. IV-3-49;—C. 3 (6):—Dr. friend and foe, Pol. XII-161; H. E. VII, E. A. 78; friends, foes, M. M. 103; such friends became such foes, M. M. 94; friend, foes, Leg. 11-82; foe, friend, Leg. I, R. N. 32; foes, friends, B. W. IV-33;—Dan. friend, foe, C. W. 1-64; friends, foes, C. W. VII-1.

Sp. glistring beames, gloomy ayre, F. Q. I-5-2; (similar) into, glooming world, gladsome ray, Am. 62;—Dr. (compare) from glitt'ring arms in palmer's, gray, Leg. I. R. N. 121; glittering crown, (made, hair,) gray, B. W. V-20.

Sp. heaven and hell, F. Q. V-2-31; H. L. 34; (hap from) heaven or hell, F. Q. VI-11-29; hell and heaven, F. Q. I-5-31;—Dr. heaven or hell, M. C. 100; heaven, hell, Mn. Mn. 478; Ids. 39; shewest us heav'n and yet in hell doth leave us, H. E. XXII, J. G. G. D. 44; hell is heaven and heaven is turned to hell, B. W. III; Dan. hell, a heaven, Phil. 656.

Sp. ilefe or loth, F. Q. III-9-13; VI-1-44; (similar) dislikes, loved meanes, H. L. 13; - Dan. lov'd, loath, C. W. III-9; C. W. 1-64; love, and loath, C. W. VIII-21; dislike, love, C. W. II-78.

Sp. lowly, lofty, F. Q. II-2-32; low, lofty, F. Q. III-7-12; ib. (loftie) V-10-22; lowlinesse, lofty, Am. 13; loftie, low, F. Q. III-1-53; loftie, lowly, S. C. X-96; aloft, layd, alow, F. Q. VI-8-13; lowly, loftie, C. C. II. 938; Dr. lofty, lower, M. E. 7033.

Sp. (the) lyon with the lamb, F. Q. IV-8-31; S. C. V-169;—Dr. lamb was closed in lion's den, Leg. II Mat. F. 58; a lion is become a k. b. B. A. 113.

Sp. make, mard, F. Q. IV-1-29; make, marre, F. Q. III-2-3;—Dr. made, mar, B. W. VI-6; mar, or make, Pol. XXII-916; (mar, makes) Eclog. VIII-7; (mar, or make) Leg. II,P. G. 89; marrs nor makes, Ode, N. D. C. 1;—Dan. mend, marre, C. W. V-94.

Sp. mirth to mourning, F. Q. III-8-46; nor merth, nor mone, Am. 54; Dr. mirth is turn'd to moan, S. S. 350.

Sp. (things) amisse to mend, F. Q. IV-11-47; amisse, mend, F. Q. III-10-38; amend what was amisse, F. Q. VI-5-10;—Dr. where I miss amend me, M. E. 1358.

Sp. painefull pleasure, to pleasing pain, F. Q. III-10-60; pleasure, payne, Am. 47; pleasure, paine, F. Q. II-6-1; R. T. 4; Displeasure and Pleasaunce, F. Q. III-12-18; pleasing payne, F. Q. VI-9-10; pleasing, in, paine, Am. 42;—C. 1 (2):—Dr. please, for, pain, Ode. XIV, Cr. 9;— Dan. pleasing paine, C. W. V-10.

Sp. plenty made him pore, F. Q. I-4-29; plenty makes, poore, Am. 35; plenty and pennurie, H. L. 8:—Dr. plenty makes us poor, Leg. II. Mat. F. 29; plenty, penury, Ids. 62;—Dan. plenty doth make us poore, Phil. 1582.

Sp. right or wrong, F. Q. I-3-18; right and wrong, F. Q. V-1-7; right, wrong, Daph. 35; right, wrong, F. Q. V-2-34; wrong and right, F. Q. II-1-42; by wrong, by right, T. M. 53; right my wronged fire, B. I. IV-7; wrong or right, F. Q. III-2-46:—Dr. right and wrong, II. E. XI, C. O. T. 149; right and wrong, Pol. XVII-240; right, the cloak of wrong, B. W. IV-56; wrong, right, B. W. V-55; right our wrongs, M. M. 217; rightful, wrongful, Pol. XII-363; right or wrong, Ids. 12:—Dan. wrong right, C. W. VIII-36; wrongs to right C. W. VI-3; wrong your right, Ep. II. II. II. 126; righting wrong, Cleo. 759.. rights them, doo them wrong, C. W. VIII-108.

Sp. shady, sunny, S. C. VI-54;—Dan. shades, sunny, S. D. 6.

Sp. spare, (shortly) spent, F. Q. IV-3-6; spend, spare, T. M. 80;—Dr. spent, spar'd, Pol. XV-24; spend, spar'd, Pol. VIII-288.

Sp. sweete, sowre, F. Q. I-3-30; sweet without sowre, Ast. 5; sweet, with sowre, Am. 26; sowre, sweet, F. Q. I-7-3; sowres, with, sweet, F. Q. VI-11-1;— sweet, yet soure enough, Am. 26;—C. 1;—Dr. sweets with

sours, M. B. M. I-111; sweet and sowr, Leg. I-R. N. 15; sweet. sour, M.
B. M. II-166; set my sweets unto my sours Ids. 3;—Dan. sweetest, soure,
S. D. 26; sweet sowre bread, Cleo. 1009.

Sp. swift, slow, F. Q. II-6-10;— Dr. or swift or slow, Eclog. II-8,
swiftest wind were slow, Pol. XXIII-312; swift, slowly. El. I,
L. L. 18; the swift-wing'd swallow and the slow-wing'd owl, N. F. 697.

Sp. thicke and thin, F. Q. III-1-17; F. Q. VI-2-10;—Dr. thro' thick
and thin M. M. 141; M. E. 708; (through) Nym. 39; (thro') M.
C. 1317; (through) Pol. XXIII-256.

Sp. vertue, vice, F. Q. IV-11-51; C. C. II. 323; M. H. T. 812;
C. 1;—Dr. vices, vertues, Ids. 35;—Dan. virtue, vice. C. W. V-12.

Sp. wele or woe, F. Q. I-8-43; ib. (wo) V-6-23;—C. 7 (12);—Dr. weal
and woe, Elg. VII, L. A. 96; of our weal or of our woe, Nym. 85; come
weal, come woe, M. M. 200; weal, woes, Ids. 60 (vs. 1 and 2);—Dr. weale
or woe, Cleo. 777.

SPENSER AND CHAUCER.

Sp. baile nor borow, S. C. V-131;—C. 5 (bote ne bale);—(now) bright,
now brown, M. VII-50;—C. 1 (2);—Privie or pert, S. C. IX-162;—C.
4 (5);—high, humble, F. Q. III-1-3 (1); humble, hie, C. C. II. 784;—C.
(1) (humble and hye);—rode, ne. rest, F. Q. V-11-35; (compare C. reste,
ryse);—rotted ere, ripe;—C. (2) (roten, rype);—save or spill, F. Q. I-3-
43; C. C. II. 815;—C. (4);—salves, to. sore, F. Q. IV-11-6; salve for
my sore, S. C. VIII-103;—C. (2).

DRAYTON, DANIEL AND CHAUCER.

Dr. downs, dales, Pol. XVII-119;—C. 1:—Dr. helps and hurts, B.
W. IV-26;—C. 1 (helpe, hyndre);—Dan. never till now, Q. A. 2107;—
C. 2.;—Dr. prince and peasant, H. E. XVII, Ed. S. 120; page to prince,
Leg. III-P. G. 10 prince and peasant, M. B. M. II-189; princes and peas-
ants, B. A. 16; prince, page, B. A. 116; (similar) the peasant and the
pier, B. A. 197;—C. 1;— Dr. wane or wax, Mn. Mn. 312; wanes or wax-
eth, M. E. 6027; waxing still do wane, Pol. I-138;—Dan. waxe, wining,
S. D. 11;—C. 3.

DRAYTON AND DANIEL.

Dr. publick, private Pol. XVII-107; private hate, popular applause,
B. W. IV-30;—Dan. privately made and publikely undone, Mus. 886;

private profit, publique good, C. W. V-79; private pulike, Phil. 777;—
Dr. cowl, crowne, Pol. XVII-260;—Dan. (compare) cloyster, crowne
C. W. V-53.

Some other contrasting terms and expressions by Spenser not included
in the above classification:

budde fayre, burnt and blasted, S. C. XII-99; cheerefull, cheerelesse
S. C. VIII-182; chearefull day to chearelesse night, F. Q. I-3-27; chearefull, chill, F. Q. I-7-6; drawes, drives away, Am. 21; gentle, grevious,
F. Q. VI-5-39; good, guilty, II. B. 24; mighty man demeane, F. Q. VI-7-
39; wretch, rich, F. Q. VI-9-30; semblaunt, substance, F. Q. II-9-2;
spinnes, but spils F. Q. V-12-36.

By Drayton: curing, killing, Ids. 50; costliest silks and coursest rags,
M. B. M. II-190; fledds't thy foes but followedest misery, B. W. IV-34;
frown'd and flatter'd, Leg. III, P. G. 94; largest, lesser, Pol. IV-17; last,
yet not, least, Pol. XVIII-199; a prison and a paradise, II. E. III, J. M.
170; right, awry, II. E. VIII, A. E. 26; uncertaine, sure B. W. VI-63;
sorrowes, smiles, M. B. M. I-140.

By Daniel: best, badnes, Cleo. 743; grief was glad, C. W. V-103; majestic and miserie, Cleo. 313; scarlet sinne as snow, C. R. 298; scorne
what now is so desired, C. R. 250; sorrow for, sweetnesse, Cleo. 562;
sweetest grace, saddest cheere, Cleo. 736.

C. GRAMMATICAL.

The grammatical relations form a ready means for alliteration, with
all the various combinations which the structural relations will permit;
but only the most important word-relations in the sentence, such as substantive and qualifying adjective, verb and adverbial modifier, subject and
predicate, and predicate and object, are emphatic enough to cause a
repetition and a constancy in the application of alliteration, sufficient
to form a distinct class so formal that it may be taken as a basis for
comparison, for the works of the different poets.

1. SUBSTANTIVE AND MODIFYING ADJECTIVE.

Sp. balefull bowre, F. Q. III-3-8; S. C. X-29; R. T. 19; baleful bowres,
F. Q. I-5-14; —Dr. baleful bower, M. C. 112.

Sp. banners broad, F. Q. IV-3-5;—Dr. banner, broad, B. A. 72.

Sp. battell brave, F. Q. I-1-3;—Dr. brave battles are to bring, B. A.

Sp. beames bright, F. Q. III-1-4 (I); M. VII-44; H. B. 35; beames more bright, Epith. 93, 4; beame so bright; S. C. VIII-81; beames, bright, II. B. 23; bright, beames, C. C. II. 518;—C. 5. (6);—Dr. bright beams, B. W. I-47; Mu. Mn. 397;—Dan. brighter beames, H. T. 1171,

Sp. beautifullest bride, Epith. 6;—Dr. beauteous bride, M. M. 18.

Sp. bended bow, F. Q. II-11-21;—Dr. bended bow, Pol. XXV-296.

Sp. blessed byrd, S. C. VIII-184;— Dr. blessed birds Owl. 1246.

Sp. blessed bowre, F. Q. II-9-47;— Dr. (compare) bless, bower (o), M. E. 1272; blessed bowers, M. E. 105.

Sp. blessed brooke, S. C. IV-37; Dr. blessed brook, Pol. XXX-72; Ids. 53.

Sp. bloody batteiles, F. Q. I-10-65; bloody batteill, F. Q. III-4-24; ib. VI-12-3;—Dr. bloodier battle, M. M. 131; bloody battle Pol. XI-383.

Sp. bloody buthren both, F. Q. II-10-33;—Dr. bloody brothers, M. M. 256; brother's blood, Pol. XXII-525;—Dan. (compare) brothers blood-shed, C. W. IV-79.

Sp. bodie bigge, S. C. II-106; V. B. 9;—Dr. big-grown bodies, N. F. 57.

Sp. bared bosome, F. Q. II-12-74;—Dr. bosoms bare, M. C. 79 (bosom) Leg. II, Mat. F. 31.

Sp. bragging brere, S. C. II-115;—Dr. bragging bryer, Eclog. II-15.

Sp. brave a band, F. Q. V-8-18;—Dan. brave army with, these ready bands, C. W. IV-61.

Sp. brydall bed, F. Q. I-10-42; (similar) bridale bowers, Epith. 3;— Dr. bridal bed, II. E. VIII; A. E. 80; bride-bed, M. E. 3046.

Sp. broken bowes, F. Q. III-11-46;—Dr. bow, broken, Eclog. II (El.) 1; bow broken, Ode. VI, C. 5; M. E. 2012.

Sp. brute beasts, T. M. 90; brutish beast, F. Q. I-4-21;—Dr. brute beast, Leg. IV; Crom. 5.

Sp. beautie bright, F. Q. I-6-9; VI-7-29; beautie as brightest sky, F. Q. I-6-4; F. Q. IV-2-4; B. I. III-2; beauties bright, Proth. 3. (st.);— Dr. brighs't beauty, M. M. 6; bright star of beauty, Ids. 4.

Sp. borrowed beauti, F. Q. IV-1-31;—Dan. (compare) no borrowed blush which bank-rot beauties seeke, C. R. 112.

Sp. carrion crowes, S. C. III-110;— Dr. carrion crow, N. F. 101.

Sp. cleare as christall, F. Q. I-7-6; V. B. 12; S. C. VIII-80; clearer than cristall, Am. 15; more cleare then cristall glasse, S. C. VII-159;— C. 2;—Dr. clear and crystall (limbs), Pol. VI-128.

Sp. conscience cleare, F. Q. I-12-30;— Dr. conscience clear, H. E. XXXIII, J. G., G. D. 52.

Sp. costly cloth, R. T. 84; costly clothes, F. Q. III-1-31;—Dr. costly oth, Pol. XII-275.

Sp. crowned as king, S. C. V-30; —Dr. crowned king, Pol. XXII-883; crowning of kings, Pol. XXIII-92;— Dan. crownd a king, C. W. I-84.

Sp. craggy cliff, F. Q. I-9-33; craggy cliffes, F. Q. V-9-15;—Dr. craggy cliffs, B. W. VI-52.

Sp. cruell clawes, F. Q. I-3-19; ib. VI-12-29;—Dr. (compare) the cruel kite because his claws were keen, Owl. 201.

Sp. daungers dread, F. Q. IV-3-20; daunger drad, F. Q. VI-1-10; daunger, dreaded, F. Q. IV-10-17; dreaded daunger, F. Q. VI-2-29;—Dr. dreadful danger, B. W. VI-87;—Dan. dreadful danger, C. R. 353.

Sp. daughter dear, F. Q. I-3-22; Daph. 67;—C. 4 (5);—Dr. daughters dear, Pol. XXIV-1109; dear daughter, Pol. XXIV-1116; darling daughter, Pol. XXVIII-54;—Dan. deare daughter, Q. A. 2432.

Sp. deadly dart, F. Q. III-12-21; deadly darte, S. C. IV-22; deadly darts, F. Q. I-9-29;— Dr. deadliest dart, B. W. V-24.

So. deadly dint, F. Q. I-11-35; deadly, dint, Ast. 21;—Dr. deadly dint, Pol. IV-284.

Sp. dearest darling, M. VII-50;—Dr. dear, darling, Leg. II, Mat. F. 10.

Sp. dismall day, F. Q. IV-7-12; ib. II-6-43;—Dr. dismal day, B. W. II-18; Eclog. VI-4; Pol. VIII-95; dismal days, H. E. XXIII, J. G., G. D. 165.

Sp. dreddest day, F. Q. IV-3-3;—Dr. dreadful day, B. W. II-24; B. A. 170; Pol. IX-236.

Sp. face, filthy fowle, F. Q. I-5-30; face, fowle, filthy, F. Q. IV-1-27; Dr. filthy, face, Ids. 31.

Sp. face deform'd, F. Q. V-3-38;—Dan. deformed face, Q. A. 2293.

Sp. faith so firme F. Q. V-12-1; firme, faith, F. Q. II-8-53;—Dr. faith as firm, H. E. XXII, G. H. II. 7; faith as firmly, H. E. XXIII, J. G. G. D. 125.

Sp. faithfull friends, F. Q. IV-2-28; faithfull friend, F. Q. VI-3-15; faithfull friendship, F. Q. IV-6-16;—Dr. faithful friend, M. M. 115; Leg. I. R. N. 68; faithfull friends, M. M. 252; Pol. XXII-877;—Dan. faithfull friend, F. D. 389.

Sp. fairer faces, F. Q. I-1-24; fair face, Am. 13; F. Q. III-9-27; M. H. T. 1267; Muiop. 44; faire, in, face, Ast. 3; face, fayre, H. H. L. 16;

face, more faire, Epith. 232; face, the fairest face, Ast. 27; C. 1;
Dr. fairer face, B. W. VI-57; Leg. III, P. G. 30; faire faces, Pol. XXIV-
1195; fairest face, Ode. XI, D. C. 6:— Dan. so faire a face, Q. A. 559; sn-
faire within her face, C. R. 815.

Sp. fayre fieldes, S. C. XI-188;—Dr. fair fields, H. E. XV, W. M.
131; fair and fertile fields, Pol. XXV-220.

Sp. fayre flocke, S. C. VIII-118;—Dr. fair flocks, Eclog. IX-9; M. B.
M. I-635; fair, flock, Pol. XIV-265.

Sp. fairer flood, M. VI-10;—Dr. fair flood, Ids. 32.

Sp. fayrest flowre, F. Q. II-3-10; ib. IV-2-11; S. C. XI-75; fairest
flowre, Daph. 71; fayre, (lyke) flowres, fade, Am. 79; fayrer flowre, F. Q.
VI-1-4 (1):—C. 3 (5):—Dr. fair flower, Eclog. IX (Sng.) 5;—Dan. fairest flower, S. D. 40.

Sp. fairer form H. L. 28; fair formes, H. H. B. 3;—Dan. fairest
forme, S. D. 13.

Sp. fairer fortune, S. C. IX-257; fortunes faire, F. Q. IV-10-17;
fayrest fortune, F. Q. III-1-17;—Dan. fortunes fairest (side), Cleo. 11.

Sp. falser friend, F. Q. II-4-21;—Dr. false friends, Ids. 10.

Sp. fearfull fowle, F. Q. II-3-36;—Dr. fearful fowl, B. W. VI-65;
Pol. XX-238; H. E. XXIII, J. G., G. D. 80.

Sp. feeble feet, F. Q. I-10-9; ib. IV-7-17;—Dan. feeble feet, Ep. H.
L. M. C. 17; Q. A. 460; feeble footing Cleo. 520.

Sp. fervent flames, F. Q. IV-9-21; (similar) fervent fyre, F. Q. II-7-37;
—Dan. fervent is the flame, S. D. 11.

Sp. infernall Furies, F. Q. I-3-36; ib. IV-1-26;—Dan. infernall Furie,
C. R. 501.

Sp. professed fone, F. Q. IV-2-28;—Dr. professed foe, H. E. XIII,
E. C., D. H. 185.

Sp. fewe such friendes, S. C. IX-259;—Dr. few friends, M. C. 272;
B. W. IV-58.

Sp. fields, fresh, S. C. XI-189; fresh flowring fields, F. Q. I-1-37;—Dr.
fields, fresh and fragrant, M. B. M. I-6-26; fresh fields D. and G. 318.
Sp. fingering fine Muiop. 16; fine fingers, full featously, Proth. 27,
finest finger's (touch), F. Q. III-1-61:—Dr. fingers neat and fine, Pol.
XV.-140.

Sp. flesh is frayle and full of ficklenesse, F. Q. VI-1-11; fleshes frailty.
T. M. 83; fraile flesh, Daphn. 13; fraile fleshly wight, Muiop. 29:—Dr.
fraile flesh's (embicility) H. E. XXIII, J. G., G. D. 110:—Dan. fraile
flesh, C. R. 359; the state of flesh and what our frailties are, C. R. 203.

Sp. former feare, F. Q. IV-7-34;—Dan. former feare, C. W. V-78.

Sp. fortune false, F. Q. I-2-22; but ah false fortune, S. C. V. 198;—C. 2 (3); Dr. false fortune, Leg. III, P. G. 62.

Sp. fowle offence, F. Q. V-5-33;—Dr. foule offence, H. E., I. R. II. 15; Dan. foule offence, C. W. II-45.

Sp. fowle confusion, F. Q. III-7-18;—Dan. fowle confusion, O. M. A. 19.

Sp. fragrant flowers, S. C. XII-109; Epith. 3; Am. 64;—Dr. fragrant flow'rs, M. C. 1284.

Sp. franticke fit, F. Q. V-8-49;—Dr. frantick fits, M. E. 1847.

Sp. gay girlands goodly, Epith, 3; girlands gay, F. Q. IV-10-37;—Dr. garlands, gay, M. E. 1113; garlands fresh and gay, Pol. XXVIII-265.

Sp. (girt in) gawdy greene, S. C. V-4;—C. 2;—Dr. gaudy green, Pol. XVIII-26; gawdy, green, Eclog. VII-2.

Sp. goodly grace, F. Q. I-10-30; ib. IV-8-6; H. H. B. 30; good grace, F. Q. IV-1-13; -Dr. goodly graces, M. E. 4013; good graces, Owl. 635; gales of your good graces, Owl. 463.

Sp. goodly garments, F. Q. II-1-39;—Dan. goodly garment, Ep. V. L. A. C. 29.

Sp. goodly government, F. Q. IV-2-36;—Dan. good government, C. W. IV-93.

Sp. goodly girlands, F. Q. III-5-53;—Dr. goodly garlands, M. E. 649.

Sp. glory great, F. Q. III-9-16; glorie, C. C. H. 301; great glorie, V. B. 10; greater glory, F. Q. II-6-35; Am. 49; greatest glory, F. Q. V-2-1; Dr. great glory, Mn. Mn. 39; greater glory, Leg. III, P. G. 3; Pol. XXIV-187; greatest glory, Pol. XXVII-91;—Dan. glories greater, C. W. I-20; greater glory, Pan. 18; C. W. VI-62; greatest glory, Pan. 21.

Sp. great, griefe, F. Q. IV-8-9; S. C. XI-113; great grief, Ast. 35; griefe, great, F. Q. I-7-10;—Dr. greater grief, Leg. III, P. G. 7, greatest grief, H. E. IV. M. J. 82.

Sp. grassie ground, F. Q. I-7-7; S. C. VI-6; grassie, ground, F. Q. VI-7-48; (similar) grassy greene, F. Q. II-12-12; S. C. IV-55; ib. XI-189; Ast. 35; V. G. 23; Dan. (compare) ground, whose grasse, Mus. 627.

Sp. greater grace, F. Q. I-9-26; greatest grace, F. Q. VI-1-3; grace, great, C. C. H. 187; great in grace, M. H. T. 1200; grace, great, C. C. H. 187; C. 1:—Dr. greater grace, Pol. XXVIII-210; greatest grace, H. E. XII. O. T., C. 61;—Dan. greatest grace, Ep. I. T. E. 124; so great a grace, Phil. 299; great grace, Phil. 517; grace made greater, Phil. 1582; graces not so great, Phil. 621.

Sp. greatest God, F. Q. II-7-8; V. P. 1; greatest of the Gods, C. C. H. 767;—C. 5;—Dr. great and fearful God, M. B. M. I-701; great God, Eclog. I-5; N. F. 16; B. A. 152.

Sp. great disgrace, F. Q. IV-7-30;—Dr. great disgrace, Pol. XXVIII-141;—Dan. great disgrace, C. W. II-54.

Sp. great regard, M. H. T. 885;—Dan. great regard, C. W. VII-52.

Sp. happie houre, F. Q. IV-3-15; unhappy houre, F. Q. IV-7-18; F. Q. I-2-22; happy howre, F. Q. II-10-57:—Dr. happy hour, B. W. III-80; Bal. A. 2; Eclog. I-1; M. B. M. III-210; unhappy hour, M. M. 211; (happy) Pol. XV-202; Ode. III, V. 2.

Sp. hardie hand, F. Q. VI-11-15; M. H. T. 974:—Dr. (compare) hard, hand, H. E. IV, M. J. 9;—hand, did so hardly deal, B. W. VI-90.

Sp. hard mishap, F. Q. I-3-39; ib. IV-7-39; Daph. 11; hard, hap, F. Q. II-4-43:—Dr. hap so hard, H. E. XIII-223, E. C., D. II.:—Dan. hard mishap, C. R. 652; hard hap. Q. A. 1705.

Sp. hardest hart, F. Q. III-8-1; hard hart, Am. 18; hard, hart F. Q. VI-8-19; Am. 31; hart so hard, Daph. 36:—Dr. hard, heart, H. E. XIX, M. C. B. 120; hard heart, E. S. 14;—Dan. hardest hart, S. D. 11: Q. A. 1886; hard hart, S. D. 19; Q. A. 1964; hard is her hart, S. D. 13.

Sp. hardned hearts, F. Q. V-8-1;—Dr. harden'd hearts, Pol. XXIV-547; harden'd heart, M. B. M. II-106.

Sp. heavie hand, F. Q. I-5-13; F. Q. VI-7-18; heavy hands, F. Q. VI-8-11;—Dan. heavy hand, S. D. 28.

Sp. heavie hap, F. Q. I-3-20;—Dan. heavy hap, C. R. 395.

Sp. heavie, harts, F. Q. I-8-14; Am. 52; heavy hart, F. Q. III-4-57; M. H. T. 1222; F. Q. V-4-22;—Dr. Heavy hearts, M. M. 174; heavy heart, H. E. XIX, M. C. B. 43; B. W. V-24; Eclog. III-11, heavy hearts (relief), H. E. X, R. I., 33; M. B. M. II-618; hearts so heavy, B. A. 255;—Dan. heavy heart, S. D. 28; heavy carefull hart, C. W. III-62

Sp. heavenly hymne, H. L. 44; H. H. L. 1:—Dr. heavenly hymns, Pol. XV-271; M. E. 7084.

Sp. helping hand, F. Q. II-10-65; ib. VI-9-15;—Dr. helping hand, H. E. XXIV, G. D., J. G. 83; hand that help'd, M. B. M. III-663.

Sp. highest head, M. VI-36; head more high to reare, F. Q. V-12-19; —Dr. head so high, Pol. XII-520; (hills) which high'st heads, Pol. V-116.

Sp. highest heaven, F. Q. I-4-9; high heaven, Epith. 21 (so; high hevens, Am. 16; highest heaven, R. T. 55; high in heaven, **Muiop.** 7; heaven hie, R. R. 8; C. C. II. 483;—C. 3;—Dr. highest heaven, Eclog. V-3; highest heav'ns. Ids. 51; high heav'n M. M. 156; (heaven) Pol. XXVII-137; Dan. (compare) heaven, hie, C. W. II-111; heaven, highest, C. R. 151.

Sp. high on, hill. V. W. V. 3; high hills top, V. B. 2; hill so hie, S. C. VIII-57; C. 1;—Dr. higher hills, Pol. III-415; highest hills, Pol. XXVII-103; high'st hills, N. F. 596; high-topt hills, Pol. IX-64; high-embattled hills, Pol. X-51;—Dan. (hopes) **on hills of high desire. S. D. 36.**

Sp. hideous hedd, F. Q. 1-7-31; hideous, **huge her bed, F. Q. VI-6-10;** Dan. hideous heads, Q. A. 1920.

Sp. hoarie head, F. Q. 1-3-38; head, hoary, F. Q. IV-11-25; (similar) hoarie haires S. C. VI-10; **R. R. 28;**—C. 4;—Dr. hoary heads, Pol. **XXX-126.**

Sp. hoarie hill, F. Q. II-12-30;—Dr. hills whose hoary heads, Pol. X-85.

Sp. holy hermit, F. Q. IV-7-42;—Dr. holy hermit, Leg. 1, R. N. 97; Pol. XVIII-127; holy hermits, Pol. XXIV-806; holy hermitage Pol. XXIV-897.

Sp. holy hilles S. C. VII-38;—Dan. holy hill, C. W. III-22.

Sp. humble hart, F. Q. V-7-7; humble harts, Am. 10; (hearts) C. C. II. 784;—C. 3;— Dr. humble heart, **M. M. 24;** humble hearted, Pol. XXIV-624;—Dan. humble heart, **H. T. 3 (Ded.).**

Sp. labors long, F. Q. 1-10-17; ib. VI-1-6; labor long F. Q. 1-9-2; longer labours, F. Q. 1-1-26;—Dr. long labour, **N. F. 835.**

Sp. labours lost, F. Q. IV-2-34; labour lost, F. Q. I-3-24;—Dr. labour lost, N. F. 819; M. E. 474.

Sp. learned ladies. F. Q. 1-10-51;—Dan. learned lady, Ep. IV, L. L. 333.

Sp. longer life, F. Q. 1-9-13; life, long, Am. 36;—Dr. long life N. F. 183;—Dan. so long as I had life, Q. A. 1952.

Sp. lesser lights. F. Q. 1-7-30;—Dr. lesser lights, H. E. XX, C. B. M. 133; B. W. III-18; lesser light, Pol. 1-257.

Sp. liege lord, S. C. II-150;—C. 2;—Dr. liege lord, Owl. 1147; liege sovereign lord, B. A. 12.

Sp. little leasure, F. Q. III-8-13;—Dan. little leasure, Cleo. 189.

Sp. little loves, F. Q. IV-10-12;—Dr. (compare) little god of love, Eclog. VII-17; Dan. little leaning love, Q. A. 305.

Sp. loathsome lazars (lay), F. Q. I-4-3; Dr. (similar) lothsome leprosy, Pol. XXII-66.

Sp. locks all loose, F. Q. V-8-4; locks, loast, V. B. 9; looser golden lockes F. Q. II-1-11; long loose locks, Epith. IX; looser locks V. G. 15; —Dr. looser locks, Pol. XX-142.

Sp. lookes, loftie, M. H. T. 678;—Dr. lofty looks, Pol. XXVIII-130.

Sp. lordly love, S. C. X-98; Dr. lordly love, Eclog. VI-2.

Sp. lord alone, M. H. T. 1026; like a lord, alone, S. C. II-222:—Dr. lords alone, Pol. XX-223;—Dan. lord, alone, C. W. II-87.

Sp. loving lord, F. Q. III-5-26; loved lord, VI-12-22;- Dr. (compare) unlike to my lov'd lord, H. E. IX, I. R. 27.

Sp. loyall love, F. Q. IV-8-30;- Dan. loyall love, S. D. 18.

Sp. lythe as lasse, S. C. II-74;- Dr. lythe as lass, Eclog. IV-27, (motto).

Sp. many miles, F. Q. IV-9-19; many a mile, F. Q. VI-2-40;- Dr. many miles, Pol. XX-256; many a mile Pol. XVI-103; B. A. 105.

Sp. many miseryes, F. Q. I-6-19;- Dr. many, miseries, B. W. I-9; M. B. M. II-410.

Sp. many mischieves, F. Q. I-4-31:—Dr. many mischiefs, Leg. I, R. N. 60; from this mischief many more, B. W. I-56; mischiefs more, Owl. 1223; much mischief, M. M. 103.

Sp. many moneths, (mourne), F. Q. V-3-4;—Dr. many a month, Eclog. 8-1:—Dan. many monthes, many yeares, L. B. W. 36.

Sp. manie, moe, M. H. T. 13:—Dr. many more, Pol. XXIV-1248.

Sp. man so mercifull, F. Q. IV-4-30; (similar) of no man mercified, F. Q. VI-7-32:—Dr. merciful'st of men, Pol. XXIV-60.

Sp. mad, man, F. Q. III-9-6:—Dr. madder men, M. E. 705;—Dan. men, mad, Q. A. 1161.

Sp. manly mind, F. Q. V-4-32:—Dr. manlike mind, Pol. II-428.

Sp. matchlesse man, Ep. 4 (II):- Dr. matchless man, Pol. VIII-167.

Sp. matchlesse might, F. Q. II-7-40; ib. IV-11-16; Dr. matchless for, might, Pol. XVIII-119.

Sp. maistring might, F. Q. II-5-13:—Dr. (compare) o'er master'd in his might, M. M. 100.

Sp. meanest man of many moe, F. Q. IV-10-19; men of meane degree Am. 61;—Dr. meanest men, H. E. IV, M. J. 125; meaner men, H. E. XVIII, S. E. 155;—Dan. meaner men, C. W. III-69; men of meaner skill, Phil. 1165.

S. men dismayde F. Q. VI-3-24; Dr. man, dismay'd, Pol. XXII-542

Sp. mighty mayne, F. Q. II-11-44;—Dan. mighty maine, Mus. 277.

Sp. mightie men, F. Q. IV-2-38; mightie man, F. Q. IV-8-38; I-5-50, (men), Muiop. 2; C. 1:—Dr. mighty men, M. M. 33; mighty were, men, Pol. I-485; These mighty men the mighty vanward led, B. A. 164; men so mighty, Nym. 71; men were mighty, M. M. 10; mightiest men, Pol. XI-14; Dan. mighty men, Cleo. 567; C. R. 197; mighty man, F. D. 143; mightie men, C. W. III-11.

Sp. almightie Maker, F. Q. IV-10-35;—Dr. mighty Maker, N. F. 7.

Sp. mightie monarch, F. Q. I-5-48;—Dr. mightiest monarchs, Eclog. V-3; mightie monarchess, Leg. I, R. N. 74;—Dan. mightie monarch, F. D. 453; C. W. II-1; mightiest monarchs (warres) Ep. III, L. M. C. 20; monarchs might, C. W. I-113.

Sp. mortall men, F. Q. I-8-44; ib. V-7-1; S. C. XI-154; V. P. 7; M. H. T. 150; T. M. 78; Daph. 55; V. G. 26;—C. 1;—Dr. mortal men, Pol. I-139; mortal man, N. F. 871; Owl. 23; Eclog. X-4, Pol. IX-121; immortal men, Pol. X-216;—Dan. mortall men, F. D. 119; Cleo. 1406.

Sp. mournfull muse, F. Q. IV-8-5; mournfulst muse, S. C. XI-53; Muiop. 2;—Dr. (compare) mournfull'st maiden, Leg. III, P. G. 3, (referring to the muse); mournful maidens El. IV, L. S. 2; melancholy maid, M. E. 1023.

Sp. passage plaine, F. Q. II-3-41;—Dan. passage plaine, Pan. 12.

Sp. perfect part, F. Q. III-1-1 (I);—Dr. perfect each, part, M. B. M. I-453.

Sp. perfect plight, F. Q. III-1-1;—Dr. perfect plight, B. A. 5; pinious in, perfect plight, Owl. 716.

Sp. perlous passage, F. Q. II-12-17;—Dr. passage perrillous, B. W. II-51.

Sp. purple pall, F. Q. I-4-16; ib. V-9-50;—Dr. purple pall, Eclog. III. (sing.) 1.

Sp. perke as peacocke, S. C. II-8: (similar) peacocks, pride, F. Q. I-4-17; Dr. peacock, proud, Owl. 917.

Sp. pitteous plight, F. Q. II-8-24; ib. V-8-22; S. C. IX-245; S. C. VIII-92; Dr. piteous plight, B. W. IV-61; M. M. 36; S. S. 325; Owl. 316.

Sp. appointed place, F. Q. II-4-28; ib. V-8-27; C. C. II. 128;—Dr. 'nted place, Pol. XII-221; M. B. M. III-613; M. M. 35.

Sp. imperiall powre, F. Q. II-9-3; powre imperiall M. H. T. 972,

II. II. B. 28: Muiop. 39;—Dr. imperial power, B. W. II-13; (pow'r) Leg. IV, Crom. 31; imperial powers. B. W. 1-58.

Sp. powre imperious, F. Q. III-12-22;—Dr. (similar) proud power of his imperious hand, M. B. M. 1-586; imperious power, Leg. II, Mat. F. 23.

Sp. present perill. F. Q. 1-4-49;—Dr. present peril, B. A. 215; Leg. III, P. G. 108; Owl. 1120; M. B. M. 1-476; present perils, Pol. XVIII-339; peril present, B. W. 1-57.

Sp. present pray, F. Q. VI-10-43;—Dr. present pray, M. C. 1106.

Sp. purchast pray. F. Q. V-8-26;—Dr. lately purchas'd prey, Leg. I, R. N. 121.

Sp. raskall routes, 1-7-35; raskall route, F. Q. II-9-15; raskall rent, F. Q. V-2-54; (similar) raskall rablement, F. Q. III-11-16;—Dr. rascal, rout, B. A. 297; rout of, rascals, B. A. 124.

Sp. rayling rhymes, F. Q. V-9-25; (compare) rufull rime, S. C. XI-55; ragged rimes, rude, F. Q. 1-12-23; T. M. 92; rimes, rugged, S. C. XI-51; rhymes, rough and rudely (drest) S. C. VI-77;—Dan. rayling rimes, C. W. II-99; rural rhyme, Eclog. V-7.

Sp. rich array, F. Q. 1-4-6; (array), ib. V-3-3;—Dr. rich array, Pol. IV-53; in rich and brave array, Pol. XVII-8;—Dan. rich aray, Cleo. 1474.

Sp. roses red, F. Q. II-5-29; red as, rose, F. Q. II-8-39; red, roses, Ast. 28; red roses, Epith. 13; redde rose, S. C. IV-68;—C. 5 (9);—Dr. roses red, Eclog. III, (sng.) 6; ib. IV-92 (motto); roses white and red, M. E. 1363; the white rose, and the red, Pol. XXVIII, 96.

Sp. roiall robes, F. Q. V-11-60; II. II. B. 185; richely in robes of royaltye F. Q. II-7-44;—Dr. regal robe, Pol. XXIV-126; (compare) more rich than robe, II. E. XVII, E. S. 70.

Sp. rude, rablement, F. Q. 1-6-8; rude, rout, F. Q. III-12-25;—Dr. (compare) rude, rout. Pol. XXII-1387.

Sp. rural routes, S. C. X-26; (compare) mustick rout, F. Q. VI-9-45; —Dr. rural rout, Eclog. VIII-16; (routs) Pol. X1-136.

Sp. sacred seate, F. Q. II-10-76;—Dr. sacred seat, Pol. XXIV-597.

Sp. sacred sisters, Daph. 2;—Dr. sacred sisters, M. E. 1005.

Sp. secret shade, F. Q. 1-5-15; M. II. T. 952; secret shadow, F. Q. 1-3-4; S. C. XII-4;—Dr. secret shades, Q. C. 36; secret shade, Pol. XXII-51.

Sp. secret skill, F. Q. IV-5-15;—Dr. secrets of his skill, Eclog. VIII-12.

Sp. setting sunne. F. Q. III-1-3;—Dr. setting sun, Pol. II-455;—Dan. setting sunne. Q. A. 112.

Sp. sharpe showre. F. Q. V-1-38; shape, showres, S. C. V-157;—C. 1;—Dr. sharp, show'rs, B. W. VI-19.

Sp. shouting shrill, Epith. 8;—Dr. shouts, shrill, Pol. IX-57; so shrill a shout, Pol. XXVIII-490; shrill, shouts, Pol. I-63;—Dan. shouting shrill, C. W. IV-15.

Sp. shrieckes shrill, F. Q. VI-1-18; sharp shrilling shriekes F. Q. I-5-33; shrilling shriekes F. Q. III-8-29;—Dr. (similar) sharp shriek B. W. VI-65.

Sp. silver scales, F. Q. II-12-23:—Dr. (compare) silver-scaled shoals, M. E. 1639.

Sp. silken skin, F. Q. III-1-65:—Dr. skin as soft as, silk M. E. 384; skin, soft, Eclog. IV-28, (motto).

Sp. silver song, S. C. IV-46;—Dr. (compare) silvan songs, M. E. 1598.

Sp. simple sheepe, S. C. VIII-117; simple as simple sheepe, S. C. VII-130;—Dr. (compare), silly sheep, B. A. 291; D and G. 246.

Sp. simple song. F. Q. I-10-55; H. L. 44;—Dr. (compare) of simple shepherds sing, Pol. XX-206; (also) that simple age as simple sung of love, Eclog. IV-16.

Sp. sinfull soule, F. Q. III-5-23; ib. IV-7-32; sores of sinfull soules unsound, H. H. L. 24;—C. 1;—Dr. with such a sin upon my soul, H. E. VIII, A. E. 70; soul, sinful body, Pol. XXIV-194.

Sp. solemne silence, F. Q. I-8-29:—Dr. (similar) sober silence, Pol. XXII-93.

Sp. sommers shade, H. B. 10; sommer shade, S. C. XI-12;—Dr. (compare) summers heat, sweet shades, H. E. XXI; H. H. Ger. 210; summers shade, M. E. 87; shadow of summer bowers, Eclog. IX-13.

Sp. soundest sleepe, F. Q. IV-5-43; sounder sleepe, F. Q. V-6-14; S. C. VIII-189:—Dan. soundest sleepe, Phil. 1220.

Sp. soveraigne seat, M. VI-12; soverayne see, F. Q. III-6-2;—C. 1;—Dr. sovereign seat, Pol. XV-126.

Sp. snowy swan, F. Q. III-11-32; (snowie) R. T. 81;—Dr. swans were white than snow, M. E. 553; white as swan or snow, M. E. 1880.

Sp. sudden shower, F. Q. IV-4-17;—Dr. sudden show'r, B. W. VI-29; M. M. 100; M. E. 7034; on the suddain coming like a shower, B. A. 254.

Sp. sun-brode shield, F. Q. III-7-40; Dr. (compare) sun-bright sword, Pol. XVII-245.

Sp. sundrie shapes, F. Q. 1-1-15; ib. IV-10-15:—Dr. sundry shapes, Leg. III, P. G. 38; Pol. VIII-251.

Sp. sondry shayres, F. Q. II-10-37;—Dr. sundry shires, M. M. **185**.

Sp. sundry sort, F. Q. II-2-13; sundry sorts, Ep. 3 (II):—Dr. sundry sorts, M. C. 1281; sundry sorts of soil, Pol. III-345.

Sp. sunned sheepe, S. C. [-77;—Dr. sunned sheep, Eclog. VI-30.

Sp. sumptuous shew, F. Q. 1-4-7;—Dr. sumptuous shows, M. M. 24; Dan. sumptuous showes, C. W. II-62.

Sp. surging seas, F. Q. IV-11-50;—Dr. unsurging seas, Leg. II. Mat. F. 49.

Sp. swift than swallow shores, the sky, F. Q. II-6-6; swallow swift, S. C. XII-20;—C. 1;—Dr. the swift-wing'd swallow, X. F. 391.

Sp. sweet sleepe, soft in swound, F. Q. VI-7-18; sweet sleepe, V. G. 18; —Dr. sweet sleep M. C. 553.

Sp. scattered sheepe, F. Q. V-6-30;—Dr. scatter'd like sheep, M. M. 143.

Sp. steadfast starre, F. Q. II-7-1:—Dr. unstedfast star, Leg. I, R. X. **53.**

Sp. stormi stowre, F. Q. IV-5-32; stormy stowres, S. C. [-27; ib. V-**156**; —Dr. stormy stowrs, Eclog. IV-26.

Sp. tedious toyle, F. Q. IV-7-3; Am. 33:—Dan. tedious toyle, Phil. 81

Sp. tedious travell, F. Q. VI-5-34; Dr. tedious travels, Ids. 1.

Sp. tender tears, F. Q. 1-5-18; (teares) ib. IV-7-9:—Dr. (compare) tears, tender breast, Pol. VIII-115.

Sp. thousand thankes, F. Q. I-12-12; ten thousand thankes, F. Q. IV-1-15;—Dan. thousand thankes, Q. A. 1312.

Sp. thousand thoughts, F. Q. III-4-5; ib. V-7-17;—Dr. thousand thoughts, II. E. I, R. II. 108; a thousand strange thoughts, M. B. M. I-154.

Sp. thousand times, F. Q. VI-12-20:—Dr. thousand-thousand times, II. E. VII, E. A. 190;—Dan. a thousand times, S. D. 25.

Sp. tokens trew, F. Q.II-8-55; token true, F. Q. V-5-34; Dr. 'tis a true token, II. E. X, R. I. 46; true tokens, M. B. M. I-380.

Sp. toylsome trade, Daph. 70;– Dr. (compare) toiling tradesman, II. E. XVII, E. S. 117.

Sp. trickling teares, F. Q. III-7-9;—Dr. from top, tears, trickling, Pol. 1-95.

Sp. trusty trew intent F. Q. III-7-55; true intent, H. B. 32;—Dr. true intent, B. W. IV-1.

Sp. turtle truer, F. Q. VI-8-33; turtle true, C. C. II. 308; **truest turtle** dove, Epith. 2;—Dr. turtle, (that's) so true, II. E. III, J. M. 147.

Sp. warlike weapons, F. Q. II-2-18; wonted warlike weapons, F. Q. IV-7-39;—Dr. warlike weapons, Pol. XIX-134.

Sp. warlike wize, F. Q. I-12-18; warlike wise, ib. IV-1-11;—Dr. warlike wise, Pol. XVIII-210.

Sp. weake, woman, F. Q. II-4-45;—Dr. weaker woman, M. C. 181; women, weak, Eclog. VIII-11; woman-like a weakness, II. E. IV, M. J. 72; woman's weakness II. E. VIII, A. E. 3.

Sp. unwearied wings, Muiop. 5;—Dr. unwearied wing, N. F. 851; Pol. XI-1; wearied wings, Pol. III-128.

Sp. western winde, F. Q. II-11-9; (westerne) S. C. IX-49;—Dr. west wind, M. E. 681; western winds, El. VII. L. A. 57.

Sp. wicked wayes, F. Q. I-10-21;—Dr. wicked wayes, N. F. 221.

Sp. wicked woman, F. Q. I-8-28;—Dr. wicked woman, II. E. I. R. N. 46.

Sp. wicked world, F. Q. VI-1-8;—Dr. wicked world farewell, B. W. V-10; wicked world, Pol. XXIV-910; N. F. 618.

Sp. wight, weake, F. Q. VI-5-30;—Dan. weak, wight, C. W. V-50.

Sp. wisest, wight, F. Q. IV-2-10; R. T. 64;—Dr. wise and **warlike** wights, Pol. XXII-879.

Sp. wylie witted, F. Q. II-3-9; wily wit, F. Q. V-9-5;—Dan. **wary** wit, C. W. IV-20; in womens wiles unwitty, Cleo. 167.

Sp. wide wildernesse, C. C. II. 198;—Dr. (compare) wildernesses wild D. and G. 61.

Sp. woefull widow, F. Q. V-10-11;—Dr. woful widow, II. E. II, H. R. 55;—Dan. wofull widow, C. W. VIII-52; wofull widowes, C. W. III-51.

Sp. wofull word, S. C. XI-93;—Dr. woful words, B. W. VI-70; words so woful, II. E. X, R. I. 11.

Sp. woman worthy, F. Q. II-10-42; woman of, worth, F. Q. II-3-21; Dr. worthy women to the world, Ids. 18.

Sp. wondrous work, F. Q.; wondrous workmanship, F. Q. I-10-42;—Dr. wond'rous works, N. F. 19.

Sp. worthie wight, S. C. VI-100; worthie wights, F. Q. IV-5-17; **wight** unworthie, F. Q. IV-5-28; worthy wight V. B. 3;- C. 1; Dr. worthy wight, Leg. I. R. N. 10.

Sp. woundes wide, F. Q. I-5-15; S. C. II-176; wound, wyde, F. Q. I-11-20; wownd so wide and wondrous, F. Q. II-11-38; wide wounds, V. G. 52; woundes soon wexen wider S. C. VIII-96; wyder, wound, F. Q. V-5-28; wide wounds, H. L. 12;—C. 1;—Dr. wider wounds, Leg. I. R. N. 62; width of, wound, B. A. 142; wounds, gaping wide, B. W. II-39; wounds gap'd wide, Pol. XVIII-304; made their wounds so wide. M. M. 254; wide listred wounds, P. S. 21; wide, wound Pol. XII-113; Dan. set wide for wounds, C. W. VIII-8.

ALLITERATION COMMON TO SPENSER AND CHAUCER.

Sp. blessed body, F. Q. I-2-24; (bodie) H. H. L. 22;—C. 1;—Sp. bent lowring browes, F. Q. II-2-35; bending her browes, M. 6-12; brows, bent, M. VII-32;—C. 1 (2);—Sp. big embodied braunches, F. Q. III-3-22;—C. 3 (braunches brode);—Sp. broken bands, F. Q. IV-1-24;—C. 1 (brosten bands);—Sp. coverts close, F. Q. II-9-40;—C. (court close);—Sp. falsed fayth, F. Q. II-12-14;—C. 1 (fals faith);—Sp. false fox, S. C. V-236; M. H. T., 304;—C. 1;—Sp. (the) faire feature, F. Q. III-9-21;—C. 1;—Sp. feend more fowle, F. Q. II-7-26; foule feend, ib. VI-4-31;—C. 1;—Sp. freshest flowre, F. Q. I-9-9; ib. VI-12-3; fresh flowre, H. B. 42; freshest flowres, Proth. 5; fresh as flowre, C. C. H. 106; flowres of freshest youth, F. Q. I-8-12;—C. 9 (11);— Sp. frothy fome, F. Q. I-7-37;—C. 1 (frothen as fome);—Sp. firie face, S. C. IV-78;—C. 1;—Sp. great degree, F. Q. II-4-19; great in gree, S. C. VII-215;—C; greene gras, F. Q. II-1-49; greene grasse, V. G. 10; grassy greene, V. G. 23; grassie greene, Ast. 35; S. C. IV-55; grasse, greene, S. C. XI-189;—C. 2 (3);—Sp. long, locks Epith. 9; long locks, F. Q. II-1-15;—C. 1;—Sp. labour lost, F. Q;—C. 1;—Sp. lovelie lady, F. Q. I-1-4; (lovely) ib. VI-12-34;—C. 1 (2);—Sp. lovely lookes, F. Q. V-5-34;—C. 2;—Sp. loves longing, S. C. V-134;—C. 2 (4);—Sp. hardy hart, F. Q. IV-7-5;—C. 1;—Sp. mister men, F. Q. VI-11-39;—C. 1 (2);—Sp. mylder mood, F. Q. V-6-15; mood, mildly, F. Q. V-5-17;— C. 1;—Sp. mickel might, F. Q. II-4-7; ib. V-9-22;—C. 2 (3);—Sp. as, rubine, red, F. Q. II-12-54;—C. (rubies red);—Sp. sommer season, S. C. XII-56; summers (day), season, Muiop. 7;—C. 2;—Sp. sorie sight, F. Q. VI-2-11;—C. 1 (sorrowful sight);—Sp. sorrow sad, F.

Q. II-12-28; C. 2 (1) (sorrues sore):– Sp. starris seaven, T. M. 78;–
C. 2 (3); Sp. starrie sky, V. G. 5; starre in sky, F. Q. IV-3-13;
Sp. starrie (skie), S. C. X-91; star in skyes, Ast. 32:—C. 1;—Sp. steede,
strong, F. Q. VI 5-7; stoute as steede, S. C. VII-156;—C. 2;—Sp.
smelling sweete, F. Q. II-6-12; smell, sweet, Daph. 60;—C. 7 (8);—Sp.
sharpe speares, Muiop. 11; sharp bore-speare, F. Q. II-3-29;—C. 4
(6); Sp. sweetest season, Proth. 4;—C. 3:—Sp. tale, of truth, S. C.
II-91; C. 1; Sp. wedded wife, F. Q. IV-9-15;—C. 2;—Sp. whist-
ling wind, F. Q. II-3-20; V. G. 30;—C. 1:—Sp. wicked wight, F. Q.
I-1-31; Muiop. 31; wicked wights, F. Q. I-2-1;—C. 2;—Sp. wicked
will, F. Q. IV-10-36;— C. 1; wicked working, F. Q. IV-5-23; wicked
worke, Muiop. 32;—C. 1:—Sp. wilde, woods V. G. 80; wild woods,
F. Q. IV-7-23; wilde woods, S. C. VIII-166; wilde, wood, F. Q. II-
5-43;— C. 2:—Sp. wretched world, T. M. 21;—C. 1;—Sp. world so wide,
V. G. 17; worlde so wide, F. Q. III-5-11; wide, world, M. H. T. 90; wide
world, T. M. 84;—C. 6 (7).

Drayton and Chaucer:

Dr. broad buttocks, B. A. 187:—C. 1;—Dr. false flatteries, Leg.
III. P. G. 26;—C. 5;—Dr. merry man, Pol. XXVIII-71; merry men,
Pol. XXVI-343:— C. 2:—Dr. seven great sins, Leg. IV, Crom. 99;—
C. 1:—Dr. sharp, sword, Pol. XVIII-485;—C. 2 (3);—Dr. worthy
wife, Pol. VIII-333; Pol. XXIV-1259;—C. 1.

Daniel and Chaucer:

Dan. greater good, Phil. 1577; greatest good, Phil. 128;—C. 1:—
Dan. wofull woman, Cleo, 341;—C. 1.

(2) VERB OR ADJ. WITH A MODIFYING ADVERB or Adver-
BIAL PHRASE:

Sp. (on) backe, bare, F. Q. I-8-16; on backe, beare, V. W. V. VIII;
at, back, or F. Q. V-9-11; bearing, at, back, S. C. V. 239; backes,
to beare, F. Q. I-6-24; behind his backe, bore, F. Q. II-1-38:—C. 2;—
Dr. (on) his back, bear, Leg. III. P. G. 25; on, back, bear, H. E. VI.
Mor. I 60; on back, bears, Pol. VII-120.

So. backe, rebownd, F. Q. II-11-12; backe rebownding, F. Q. II-1-
..; a backe rebowndes, F. Q. IV-4-12; back rebownded, Am. 19;—Dan.
r ownding backe, Cleo. 966.

S backward bent, F. Q. IV-10-12;—Dr. backward bend, Eclog.
II. Sne...

Sp. backe, to be borne, V. G. 58; F. Q. V-11-29;—Dr. back, born,
B. A. 233; back, bear, B. A. 203; M. M. 139; backward bear, N. F. 915,
bear them backward, Pol. XX-120; bear, back, M. E. 1674;—Dan.
backward he bears, C. W. III-77; bears back, C. W. V-44.

Sp. basely, borne, F. Q. VI-6-36; M. H. T. 808; borne to base hu-
mility, F. Q. V-5-25;—Dr. basely borne, Pol. XXIX-334.

Sp. bathed in, bliss, F. Q. I-1-47; bathes, in, blis, F. Q. II-3-40;
bathe in blisse, Am. 72;—Dr. bath'd in bliss, Leg. III, P. G. 16.

Sp. bathe in bloud, F. Q. I-5-15; to bath, in blood, F. Q. IV-6-17;
bath'd in bloud, F. Q. V-5-12; bloody bath, Am. 31;—Dr. bathing, in
blood, M. M. 95.

Sp. rebeaten back, F. Q. VI-8-40; bet abacke, F. Q. VI-12-29; backe
did beat, F. Q. V-7-15;—Dr. beaten back, H. E. XI, C-0, T. 92; B.
A. 212; Pol. XXIX-324; beat, back, Pol. VIII-197; H. E. V, I-M. 131.

Sp. beaten, from, battilement, F. Q. V-2-20;—Dr. (compare) upon
bulwarkt, beat, Pol. II-412.

Sp. (unto) bed, bring, F. Q. I-1-48; to his bed was brought, F. Q.
IV-12-26; brought a bedde, S. C. X-68;—C. 3;—Dr. brought to bed,
Pol. I-139; M.-C. 64;—Dan. bring, to bed, W. C. VI-11.

Sp. bearing, abrode, F. Q. VI-12-7;—Dr. abroad, bear, B-W. I-5;
bearing, abroad, B. W. IV-18.

Sp. boldly bad, F. Q. III-5-18; boldly, forbad, ib. VI-3-38; boldly
she bid, M. VI-11;—Dr. boldly bid, B. W. I-32.

Sp. bought with, blood, F. Q. I-7-26; with bloodshed, bought, R.
T. 17;—C. 1 (2);—Dr. with, blood be bought, B. A. 261; Leg. I, R. N.
23; with blood was bought, M. M. 16; with blood, buy, B. W. I-24;—
Dan. buy with blood, C. W. II-13.

Sp. Bravely beare, F. Q. IV-9-30; (similar) boldly beares, F. Q. II-
2-25;—Dr. barvely bears, Pol. VIII-103; bravely borne, Elg. V. L. I.
S. 21; M. E. 752; beare, more bravely, Leg. I. R. N. 115.

Sp. (on) breast, beare, F. Q. IV-8-22; in breast, (blessed image)
beare, H. H. L. 37; in breast, beares, H. L. 32; bore before her breast,
F. Q. V-6-39.—Dr. in, breast, bear, M. M. 206; in, breasts, bear, H. E.
XIV, H. E. C. 139; with, breasts, bear, N. F. 237; in bosom bears D
and G. 376; bare in, breast, M. C. 620.

Sp. (against) brest, bent, F. Q. II-1-11; at, breast, bend, F. Q. IV-
2-14;—Dr. upon breast, bent, H. E. XIV, H.-E. C. 109.

Sp. breathed, with blast of bitter wind, F. Q. IV-8-26; with breathed
sighs, blowne and blasted, S. C. I-7;—Dr. blasted with, northern breath,
Eclog. VI-22; blasteth, with, breath, M. B. M. II-166.

Sp. breath'd into, breast, C. C. II. 824;--Dr. (similar) into, bosom breathe, H. E. XXIII, J. G. G. D. 123; in her bosom breathe, Pol. II-002.

Sp. embrew in blood, F. Q. V-7-40. (vs. 4 and 5); embrewd in blood, F. Q. I-7-47; embrew, with, blood, V. B. 6; in, bloud, embrew, F. Q. V-1-16, Dr. in blood, embru'd, B. W. IV-43; Leg. I, R. N. 75; (imbrew'd) Pol. XVII-293; in, blood, imbru'dst, Pol. XIII-332.

Sp. bring in bondage of, brutishness, F. Q. V-11-44; in bondage, brought, F. Q. V-6-3; Dr. from, bondage, bring, M. B. M. I-726.

Sp. brings, to blis, F. Q. I-10-52;--C. 3:--Dr. (compare) bliss could bring (o), Leg. III, P. G. 59.

Sp. brought her backe, F. Q. V-8-46; backe, brought, F. Q. II-765;--Dr. back, bring, M. M. 218; Pol. VI-313; back unto, banks, brought, Pol. L-189:--Dan. brought it backe, Q. A. 1732; brings us backe, Pan. 55; bring backe, O. M. A. 45; bring backe, C. W. I-69.

Sp. brought, in bands, F. Q. III-7-47; brought into, band, F. Q. VI-42-39 (vs. 3 and 4); brought, bound, Daph. 17;--Dr. bound, basely did, bring, Leg. I, R. N. 86.

Sp. bubble blowne up with breath, S. C. II-87;--Dr. a bubble, blown up by deceitful breath, Leg. I, R. N. 20.

Sp. burnen, bright, F. Q. I-12-37; bright doe burne, Epith. 23 (vs. 2 and 3):- C. 3:--Dr. with, beams more brightly made, burne, H. E. XXI-II, H. L. Ger. 76; burning bright, H. E. XXII, L. Ger. II. II. 37; M. B. M. I-703.

Sp. busie, about, F. Q. III-7-7;--Dr. busied, about M. M. 105.

Sp. call to count, F. Q. IV-1-3 (L.) ib. V-2-42; called to accounpt, I. O. VI-8-22;--Dr. to account, call, Leg. III. P. G. 59; Leg. IV Crom 57.

Sp. over-came with care, S. C. I-46;--Dr. overcome with care, Eclog. VI-20.

Sp. keepes in coverts close, F. Q. II-9-40:--Dr. keep I close, M. C. 310:--Dan. keep it close, Phil. 214.

Sp. kept on, course, F. Q. V-12-21; kept on her, course, F. Q. III-1-5;--Dr. keeping on her course, Pol. XXVIII-86;--Dan. kept in course, by kinde, Pan. 40.

Sp. clad in colours, F. Q. IV-11-47; cloath, in colours, V. G. 86; colours meete to clothe, S. C. II-132:--Dr. in, colours clad, M. C. 729;--Dan. in, colours clad, Cleo. 1586; clad in colours, V. G. 91; cloathe in colours, Q. A. 1984,5.

Sp. keepen carefully, F. Q. I-8-29; keepe with carefulnesse. F. Q. III-11-53, carefull keeping, F. Q. VI-5-21; carefully he kept, A-t. 1; Dr. carefully, kept, B. W. II-1; with, care, keep, Pol. XXIX-367; care had it kept, Leg. II. Mat. F.-77.

Sp. (from) cold to keepe, F. Q. III-5-33;—Dr. from cold, to keep Pol. VII-211; kept from cold, Pol. XV-11; keep, from, cold, Eclog. IX. (sng.) 8.

Sp. comes by course, F. Q. VI-6-17; come into, course, F. Q. VI-12-2;—Dr. coming in, course to cross, Pol. XVI-269; on, course, came, Pol. XVII-127.

Sp. to, court, came, F. Q. III-6-52; come to corte, M. H. T. 107; from, court, came, M. H. T. 607;—C. 2; Dr. come to the court, H. E. III, J. M. 187; camst, into, court, B. W. III-56; into the court, came, Leg. III, P. G. 10; unto, court, come, Pol. IX-335; com'n, to, court, M. M. 211.

Sp. coverd with charmed cloud, F. Q. I-5-29; covered with cloudie storme, F. Q. IV-5-32; with, cloud, covering, F. Q. V-11-11; Dr. cov er'd, with clouds, Pol. VII-104; coverd, with cloudy kels, Owl. 766; clouds that cover, Leg. I, R. N. 17.

Sp. creeping close, F. Q. III-10-53; S. C. V. 251; C. C. II. 698. (closely) V. W. V. 6; closely, crept, F. Q. III-10-22;—Dr. of, close coverts creeps, Pol. XIII-85; closely creeps, Owl. 1091.

Sp. cruelly to kill, F. Q. VI-3-49;—Dr. cruelly did kill M. B. M. II-585.

Sp. crowing cranck, S. C. IX-16;- Dr. crowed crank, Eclog. IV-11 (str).

Sp. (in) darknes dwels, F. Q. III-4-13; ib. VI-10-13; in darknesse and dread horror dwell, H. H. L. 13; dwell in darknesse M. H. T. 1187; Daph. 69; T. M. 82;—Dr. in darkness, dwell, Leg. III, P. G. 1; M. B. M. II-485; dwellt in darksome groves Pol. I-36.

Sp. dayly doth, F. Q. VI-4-31; daily doe, F. Q. VI-9-28; dayly doest, F. Q. IV-10-17; daylie doth, Daph. 22; does each day, F. Q. V-8-19; Dr. daily, as I do, Mn. Mn. 327; daily did, Owl. 108; did each day, M. M. 104;—Dan. daily doe, Q. A. 2221.

Sp. daily dying, F. Q. IV-12-9; daylie die, Daph. 63; dying dayly, F. Q. II-6-15;—Dan. the day thou dyest, H. T. 1210.

Sp. (with) dainty daysies dight, S. C. VI-6; Dr. (compare) with daffodilies dight, Q. C. XIX.

Sp. daunce deftly, S. C. IV-III;- Dr. deftly dancing, Pol. XXII-29.

So. death, ordayned oy destinie, F. Q. I-9-12; ordayn'd, to die, F. Q. IV-12-31; (compare) damne to death, M. H. T. 1244;—C. 2 (damned to death, Dr. destined, to die, B. W. II-59.

Sp. (to) death, drive F. Q. I-9-38; ib. V-9-41;—C. 2:—Dr. (similar) drawing to my death,. Eclog. VI-5; drawn to death, B. W. IV-59.

Sp. deemed deare, S. C. V-277;—Dr. too dear, deem, Leg. III, P. G. 70.

So. bedecked daintly, F. Q. I-7-32; deckt, daintily, F. Q. II-9-46; deckt, with dainties, M. VII-34; decke, with, dainties (store), H. B. 49; Dan. (compare) dresse daintily, Q. A. 2022.

Sp. dew'd with drops, F. Q. IV-8-33; with, drops, dew, F. Q. IV-8-20; with, dew bedight, F. Q. III-6-13;—Dr. bedew'd with drops, Pol. XXI-211.

Sp. does each day, F. Q. V-8-49;—Dr. in that day, done, Pol. XXII-351; —Dan. to doo that day, C. W. IV-49; done this day, C. W. VI-87; done to-day, Q. A. 1787; this day is done, C. W. II-65.

Sp. doen to dye, F. Q. I-8-36; doe him die, F. Q. III-7-32; doest not unto death, F. Q. II-3-7; doen to death, F. Q. II-5-26; doe me not to dy, Am. 12; do I die, Am. 7; did to die, M. H. T. 10; doing him die, H. H. L. 23; Dr. did to die, Pol. XXII-1135; to death, had done, Pol. II-261; to death, done, Pol. XXIV-98;—Dan. death, done, Q. A. 2149.

So. (in) doome ordained, Muiop. 29 (vs. 1 and 2);—Dr. dooming heaven ordain'd, Leg. IV, Crom. 8.

Sp. drawne into danger, V. G. 67;—Dr. out of this danger to withdraw, M. M. 143; danger that they drew, M. M. 27.

Sp. driven downe, M. H. T. 1237; downe, drive, F. Q. VI-9-22;—Dan. (similar) drawne, down, Cleo. 131.

So. dropped downe, F. Q. II-12-65;—Dr. dropt, down, Pol. XII-307; drops down, M. B. M. III-604; drooping down, M. E. 187; down would drop, Pol. XXVI-434;—Dan. down like, drops, Q. A. 2164.

Sp. duly everie day, M. H. T. 119; duly her attended day and night, M. VI-94; Dan. every day, duly, H. T. 1167.

So. falling them beforne, F. Q. II-2-27; before him fall, F. Q. IV-11-30; fall, before, H. H. B. 22;—Dr. falls before, H. E. I. H. E. R. 146; before it fell, M. C. 814;—Dan. before those altars fall, H. T. 1242.

Sp. falling flat, F. Q. I-12-25;—Dr. falling, flat, Pol. XIX-9; fall B. W. II-3.

So. far away wasted, F. Q. I-2-7; fled farre off, M. H. T. 576; full fast, flies, and farre afore, F. Q. IV-7-21;—Dr. far doth fly, Pol. XXV-308;far have fled, B. A. 257.

Sp. fare on foot, F. Q. V-3-35; far'd on foot F. Q. III-11-10 (vs. 3 and 4); fairely fare on foot, F. Q. II-2-12; fare on foote, R. R. 24;   Dr. on foot, set forth, Pol. XXII-881.

Sp. fed in field, S. C. XII-11;—Dr. in fields found feeding, Mu. Mu. 78.

Sp. fell before her feet, F. Q. IV-8-9; at her feet did fall, F. Q. V-12-24; at her feet downe fell, F. Q. IV-8-13; fall lowly at, feet, Am. 2; at feet, feld, F. Q. II-6-32;—C. 3;—Dr. falling at my feet, Elg. VI. L. P. C. 31;—Dan. at, feet, fall, H. T. 779; C. W. V-1; fall at her feet, H. T. 295.

Sp. fell, in fight, F. Q. II-10-35;—Dr. to the fight, fall, B. A. 267; falling to the field, in, fight, Pol. XII-121.

Sp. feeds on, flesh, (feede), F. Q. III-7-22; fed on, flesh, F. Q. III-9-19; fed, with flesh; F. Q. V-8-28 (vs. 6 and 7); feed on fleshly gore, F. Q. IV-7-5; upon their fleshes, fed, M. H. T. 319;—Dr. on flesh, feed (fish), N. F. 199.

Sp. fetch from far, F. Q. I-12-38; Muiop. 26;—Dr. fetcht from far, B. A. 19; far doth fetch, B. A. 165; M. E. 963; D. and G. 338; falcon like from far doth fetch, Pol. II-128.

Sp. (from the) fielde, fly, F. Q. I-10-4; through fields, before him flie, F. Q. V-4-14; into fields, fled, F. Q. VI-9-1;—Dr. from the field, flies, B. A. 213; flying o'er the field, Pol. XXII-1486;— Dr. the field doth fly, B. A. 218; fled the field, Pol. XXII-266; from the field, fled, Pol. XXII-1330.

Sp. fiercely, flies F. Q. I-2-17; fiercely flie, F. Q. IV-9-33; fiercely flying forth, F. Q. V-6-10; fierce, flye, F. Q. II-8-47; fiercely flew, upon foend, F. Q. III-7-32; fiercely, flew, F. Q. VI-1-20; with force he fiercely flew, M. H. T. 1371;—Dr. fiercely, flew, B. A. 215; Pol. II-365; (similar) furiously doth fly, B. A. 224.

Sp. fiercely fall, F. Q. I-11-40; (compare) falls so forciblye F. Q. II-11-13;—Dr. (compare) furiously not falls, B. A. 94; furiously doth fall, Leg. 1, R. N. 31; fearfully, fall, B. W. II-11.

Sp. first falleth, F. Q. VI-8-31; first, fell, ib. VI-8-31;— Dr. first here fell, M. M. 171;—Dan. first to fall, Cleo. 128.

Sp. finely, foote, S. C. IV-109;—Dr. foot it finely, M. E. 398.

Sp. firmest fixt, F. Q. I-9-17; firmely fix, F. Q. V-1-6; Dr. firmly fix'd, Leg. II. Mat. F.-30; firmly fixt, Pol. XII-122.

So fled she fast, (carre). F. Q. V-8-1; full fast, fled F. Q. I-3-12;
Sp. fled she fast, (rre). F. Q. V-8-1; full fast, fled, F. Q. I-3-12;
st away to flew. F. Q. IV S-10; fledd so fast, F. Q. III-1-15; fast she
       fledd, afrayd, F. Q. III-1-51;—C. 1 (6);—Dr. fled, followed
   , Pol. XII-157; Dan. fled, so fast, Q. A. 2173; fast, before fled,
  W. II-11.

Sp. fled afore, afraid, (feend). F. Q. III-1-17;—Dr. fled before, .B.
A. 2-1; before them, fly. B. A. 193;—Dan. (false) fled before, C. W.
II-1.

S. fled for feare. F. Q. V-6-35; flying from, feare. F. Q. I-2-12;
  fled to fly for feare. F. Q. V-1-22; for feare, fly, F. Q. II-12-3; fly, fly,
  care. F. Q. I-2-31; C. 1:—Dr. with fear, do fly, Pol. IV-105.

Sp. florish faire. F. Q. II-8-5; fayre it florish, M. VII-18;—Dan.
  flore. P. C. 21;flourisht with faire events, Mus. 853.

So flourish in flowers, S. C. V-204;—Dr. floures to flourish, Eclog.
  (sng. II), 1.

Sp. with, foe, fight. F. Q. III-11-23; fight with foe, F. Q. I-9-20;
against, foes, in field, flight, F. Q. III-3-29;—C. 1;—Dan. foe, with whom
we fought, L. B. W. 17.

Sp. follow'd fast, F. Q. II-11-23; ib. IV-7-37;—C. 1;—Dr. follow,
so fast. H. E. XXIV. G. D. J. G., 93; following on so fast. M. B. M.
II-231.

Sp. on foot, fight, F. Q. II-8-31; fight on foote, F. Q. V-11-9; fight-
g on foot. F. Q. VI-2-3;— Dr. on foot found fighting. B. A. 285; on
foot unto, fight, M. M. 212; fought on foot, Pol. XXIX-221.

So forced, to fly, F. Q. II-8-33; ib. VI-9-4; enforst my flight. F. Q.
II-1-32; Dr. forc'd to fly, M. M. 213; from her presence forc'd to fly,
M. C. 991; forced to flight. Pol. XXII-554; (friends) enforc'd to take,
  d. M. M. 73.

Sp. with, force, flies, F. Q. V-1-12; Dr. flies before, force. M. B.
M. I-191; before, force, flew, Pol. IX-221.

Sp. fortunate in fight. F. Q. VI-1-11;—Dr. fortunate in fight, M.
M. 245.

Sp. free from, feares. F. Q. III-9-1; (first) free from feare, F. Q.
VI-3-18; freed from fear. F. Q. IV-1-15; S. C. II-42; from feare free, F.
Q. IV-3-19; from feare and foule horror free, Epith. 322;—Dr.
  from, fear, B. W. VI-29; free him from his fears, M. B. M. II-
  Dan. free from feares, Phil. 2011; free me from my father's feare,
   free her fears, (O). C. R. 599.

Sp. freshly, at first, fight, F. Q. II-11-3; (fiercely) afresh to fight, F. Q. IV-3-35; Dr. freshly, the fight renew, Nym. 79.

Sp. full of feare, F. Q. III-12-11; ib. IV-7-21; C. C. II. 228; Dr. full of fear. M. B. M. II-135.

Sp. fall into the flood, F. Q. V-2-12 (vs. 6 and 7); Dr. to, flood, fall, Pol. XXVI-213; floods, that, fall, Pol. XIV-300.

Sp. fell upon, field, F. Q. V-5-11; in field before me fall, F. Q. V-11-53;—Dr. fell at this field, M. M. 96; falling back upon, field, B. A. 278.

Sp. forth to fight, F. Q. IV-4-27; forth into the field, F. Q. V-5-4; in field, fight, F. Q. I-3-38;—C. 4;—Dr. into the field, forth to fight, M. M. 120; forward to the field, Leg. I. R. X. 115.

Sp. fly like a flock, before, faulcon's (vew), F. Q. VI-8-49;— Dr. in flocks do fly, Pol. XXVII-310.

Sp. gain by giving, M. H. T. 350; Dr. given, to gain, Pol. III-357.

Sp. gainst, goe, F. Q. I-8-13; againe, go, H. L. 212;—Dan. goes againe, C. W. II-74; Cleo. 1182; gone againe, H. T. 1115.

Sp. gan againe, F. Q. III-12-6; ib. V-11-65; began againe, F. Q. V-5-30;—Dan. beginne, againe, C. R. 258; againe beginnes, C. W. VI-104.

Sp. garnisht, with guifts of high degree, Epith. 186;—Dr. (compare) in highest degree, grac'd, Pol. XXVIII-286.

Sp. together goe, F. Q. V-12-13;—Dr. together, go, X. F. 469; go together, M. C. 666.

Sp. goodly greeted in, guyse, F. Q. I-10-11; guize, goodly so to greet, F. Q. II-12-56; goodly greetes, F. Q. I-12-12; gooly, greet, F. Q. III-6-20; goodly gan to greete, F. Q. V-3-15;—Dr. (similar), gladly greet, H. E. II, II. E.-R. 144; (also) gently greet, Pol. XXII-42.

Sp. without golde, nothing, got M. H. T. 153; Dr. got, again for gold, Pol. II-299; got with gold, Leg. III. P. G. 6.

Sp. got agayne, F. Q. I-3-8;— Dan. got againe, C. W. IV-71; againe have got, Phil. 422.

Sp. greatly grieve, F. Q. IV-12-26;—Dr. greatly griev'd, Pol. III-271; with greater misery, grieve, B. W. V-63.

Sp. greater grew, F. Q. I-1-23; greater growe, S. C. VI.-92; R. R. 4; greatly grew (amazed), F. Q. I-5-21; in greater (number), grew, F. Q. VI-12-32; grew to great (impatience), F. Q. III-1-18; growen great, F. Q. I-7-10; ib. IV-1-25;—Dr. great doth grow, Pol. I-269; greater growes, Pol. XVIII-651; H. E. XI, C. O. T. 110; great, and greater grow, M. E. 1236; grow too great, M. M. 66; grown too great, Pol. V-

103 ...rew so great Pol. VIII-104; over-great were grown, B. W. **VI-45;** to greatness, grown, M. M. 204; in greatness grows, H. E. VII, E. A. 52, Den. growne so great, C. W. VI-135; grew more great, C. W. IV-21; growne too great, C. W. I-28; unto her greatest growne, Cleo. Sel.

Sp. grew out of the ground, F. Q. V-1-9 (1); growes, on, ground, F. Q. I-9-11; Dr. grown upon, ground, Pol. IX-163.

Sp. in hand, hath, F. Q. I-4-33; in hand, had, F. Q. III-12-16; have with, hand, F. Q. I-10-65; having in his hand, F. Q. VI-7-44; hath unto on s hands, F. Q. VI-8-1; had by, hand, F. Q. II-6-12:; hand in hand, F. Q. V-1-3; Dr. had in hand, Pol. XVI-244; from, hand, have M. E. 372; in hand, had Pol. XII-155;—Dan. had in hand, C. W. I-77; aving in, hands, C. W. IV-58.

Sp. in hand, held, F. Q. I-4-10; ib. VI-2-6;in, hand hould,F. Q. V-1-12; held in hugger mugger in, hand, M. H. T. 138; in her hand, hold, H. H. B. 28; C. 5, (7):—Dr. held in his huge hand, Pol. XX-85; a hermit's staff his, hand did hold, Leg. I. R. N. 121:—Dan. holdes in, hand, S. D. 12; in her hand doth hold, V. Gd. 118.

Sp. hard at hand, F. Q. II-12-18; ib. VI-9-16;—Dr. hard at hand, Pol. XVI-119.

Sp. in hands, upheld on hight, F. Q. I-12-6;—Dr. holdeth up so high, Pol. VII-30;—Dan. have upheld with holy hands, C. W. VII-68.

Sp. heaped hugely, F. Q. I-6-15; heaped with so huge misfortune, F. Q. I-7-39;—Dr. with huge ruine heapt, B. A. 262.

Sp. held in highest price. F. Q.V-1-1; held in high regard, F. Q. V-1-30; Dr. held in, high account, Pol. XIX-36.

Sp. highly honoured in haughtie (eye), F. Q. I-7-16;—Dr. highly honoured, Pol. XXII-46.

Sp. in, hollow caves, hid F. Q. III-9-15;—Dr. in hollow banks, hide, Pol. XX-119.

Sp. by, heeles, hung, F. Q. VI-7-27;—Dr. to, heels, hung, B. A. 237.

Sp labour under, lode, F. Q. III-6-12:—Dr. lab'ring with their loads, B. A. 295.

Sp. on, lap, lie, F. Q. V-7-9; lay in the lap, F. Q. VI-7-17;—Dr. in, land, M. M. 15; lying on her lap, M. B. M., I-137;—Dan. layd in lap, Ph'l. 311.

Sp. lately lost, F. Q. IV-4-15; lost of late, F. Q. VI-5-29; lost, late, F. Q. IV 9-21; late forlorne, F. Q. II-1-22:—Dr. lately lost, Pol. VIII-242; Dan. lately lost, C. W. VII-91; lose, at length, S. D. 14.

Sp. at last, when long. F. Q. IV-7-38; long in me lasted, R. T. 17; C. 2; Dr. (compare) last so long. M. E. 758; longer, last. M. B. M. II-236; long, lasted, M. M. 190; long it lasted, M. C. 677; Dan. lasts not long, C. R. 630; last not long, H. T. 613; last so long, Mus. 131; lasting longer, C. W. I-84; long, last, C. W. I-6.

Sp. at last relenting. F. Q. IV-11-8;—Dr. at length, let, relent, H. E. III, J. M. 177.

Sp. lay along. F. Q. I-5-31; lays, along, F. Q. VI-8-49; Dr. laid, along, Pol. XXIII-78.

Sp. led, along. F. Q. III-7-37; Dr. leads along. M. M. 189; along doth lead, Pol. XXVI-95; along, led, Owl, 784.

Sp. left her late. F. Q. I-6-9; left of late, F. Q. III-8-13; lately left, F. Q. III-5-4; ib. VI-9-4; late, left, F. Q. III-7-61; ib. VI-7-27; Dr. lately left, Pol. II-111; leaves me but late, Leg. IV, Crom. 114.

Sp. lefte at liberty. F. Q. III-7-38;—Dr. (similar) at liberty, let, B. W. VI-56; H. E. VII-E, A. 53.

Sp. left alive, F. Q. VI-6-24; (similar) left in living (sight), F. Q. III-10-56;—Dan. left with his life, C. W. VI-111.

Sp. let, live, as Lovers, F. Q. IV-12-10;—Dr. let me live, H. E. H. H. R. 66.

Sp. left, long F. Q. I-3-29; Dr. left too long, Pol. XXX-265; long since left, Elgs. G. S. 70;—Dan. so long that nought is left, C. W. VI-18.

Sp. (in, spoile) of life, delight F. Q. IV-12-6;—Dr. (compare) live in, delight, Eclog. VI-33.

Sp. lifted aloft, H. L. 10;—Dr. lifted, aloft, M. M. 204; lifts, aloft, Pol. VIII-51.

Sp. liv'd alone, F. Q. VI-6-4;—Dan. live alone, C. W. III-66.

Sp. long, lye, F. Q. III-7-51; long, lie, F. Q. IV-8-64; long, lay F. Q. V-7-17; long, lay F. Q. I-1-55; lay, long Am. 12;—Dr. long, do lie, Leg. IV, Crom. 56; long, to lye, M. M. 27; long had lain, B. W. III-28, Pol. XXII-1123; lain, long, H. E. H. H. R. 82; long, had lyen, Ids. 35; —Dan. long hath laine, Pan. 52; Mus. 271.

Sp. long he lov'd, F. Q. III-3-10;—C, 3;—Dr. long have lov'd, Ids. 45; lov'd so long, H. E. VIII, A. E. 108;—Dan. lov'd, long Q. A. 762.

Sp. long, laboured, F. Q. III-8-37; labourd long, F Q. VI-12-32;—Dr. long, had labour'd B. A. 246; labour'd long, Pol. XXIV-527.

Sp. lookt aloft, F. Q. VI-8-26; looke aloft, S. C. V-124; learne to looke alofte, S. C. VII-10;—Dr. look aloft, Pol. XXX-2; looking from aloft Pol. VII-3;—Dan. looking aloft, S. D. 17.

S[..] [..]oting, long, F. Q. IV-8-7; looked long, at last, F. Q. V-6-8; long, [....]d F. Q. IV-8-8;   Dr. long had looked, B. W. IV-17;—Dan. looke [...] long, II. T. 57; (prolog.); Cleo. 1445.

Sp. loo[k]ng lovely, F. Q. I-6-1; looke ever lovely, Am. 7; looke with love[l]y hew, Am. 7; looked on her lovely face, M. VI-31:—Dr. look in your lovely face, Elgs. L. L. L. 78.

So long del[a]yed, F. Q. VI-12-2;—Dr. longer, delay'd, Pol. XXII-[....]; delay no longer, M. M. 163; delay'd so long, Pol. IV-351.

So long forlose, F. Q. VI-12-12; lose so long, F. Q. V-5-18;—Dan long time lost, C. W. VII-63.

So alone, left, F. Q. V-11-38; leave alone F. Q. VI-6-16; left alone F. Q. VI-4-39; ib. I-6-33;—Dr. left alone, Pol. XXII-1637; Leg. II. Mat. F. 86;   Dan. leave me alone, Q. A. 1167; leaves m' alone, C. R. 633; left and all alone; C. W. II-5.

Sp. looke lowly, M. H. T. 498; lowly, looke Am. 13;—Dr. look so low, II. E. X., R-1-100; Pol. XXIV-213.

So loth to loose, F. Q. V-7-30;—Dr. (compare) loth, to leave. Pol. XXVI-17; loth to lose, Pol. XII-401.

Sp. louting low, F. Q. I-1-30; louting lowly, F. Q. II-3-13; louted lowly, F. Q. IV-3-5; lowly, louting, F. Q. IV-2-23; low to lout, F. Q. VI-10-16; low louted on the lay, F. Q. III-10-23;—Dr. lowting low, Pol. VIII-28; low louting, Leg. IV, Crom. 104.

Sp. with love, long time, languish, F. Q. I-2-24;—Dan. languish for love, S. D. 18.

Sp. lov'd alone, H. L. 36;—Dan. love alone, Q. A. 1591.

Sp. low dost lie, F. Q. III-9-33; low in ashes lay, R. T. 72; lying lowe. V. W. V. 2; lye on lowly land, F. Q. I-3-37; lower lay, ib. II-4-8; low, laid, ib. II-5-12; laid in lowest seat, F. Q. II-8-27:—Dr. low she lies. Eclog. VIII-23; lain full low, Leg. IV, Crom. 54; long ere this laid lower, M. M. 205; lies, low, Pol. XXIII-93;—Dan. layd full lowe, C. W. V-31.

Sp. large of limbe, F. Q. I-2-12:—Dr. large-limb'd, Owl. 1100; H. E. XX. C[.] B-M. 111.

Sp. lives so long, F. Q. I-1-31; lived, long. F. Q. II-8-28; liv'd, long, F. Q. IV-9-16;   Dr. livd'st long, Pol. 1-9; lived long. Pol. XVI-215; liv'd long ago. El. VIII, H. R. 12; liv'd but a little longer, El. VIII, H. R. 77; long, live. Ode IX. V. V. 7; long time liv'd, Pol. XIII-288; thus long, [..]d c[.] consolate. H. E. III, J.-M. 176;— Dan. live not long, Cleo. 1072; live so long, C. W. I-108; live no longer, H. T. 923; longer live, H. T. 15

(Ded.): long live, P. C. 21; longest live, Phil. 63; long. liv'd Q. A.2187; long enough hath liv'd, C. W. VI-87.

Sp. made of, mould, F. Q. V-1-12; made in one mould, F. Q. III-12-24; made out of one mould, H. B. 31; made, out of, mould, H. H. L. 17; Dr. made, in, mould, Leg. IV, Crom. 2; makes her mould (o), Pol. X-106.

Sp. match in might, F. Q. V-12-15;—Dr. match'd by men of might, Leg. III, P. G. 68; overmatcht his might (o), Pol. I-397.

Sp. amazed make, F. Q. I-8-26; Dr. amaz'd doth make, B. A. 236.

Sp. of, metall, made, F. Q. V-1-10; made of the metall, V. B. 3; made of the mettall most desired, R. T. 59;—Dr. of, metal made, Ids. 1.

Sp. met in middle space, F. Q. II-4-32; meeting, in the middle race, F. Q. V-10-34; ymett in middest (of the plaine), F. Q. VI-1-33; in, middle way, ymet, F. Q. V-4-38;—Dr. in the mid-way, are, met, M. M. 238; on mid-way, meet, Pol. XVI-121.

Sp. amongst, mightie men, mixt, F. Q. I-5-50; amongst, mingled, F. Q. VI-12-28;—Dr. intermixt among, B. W. I-10;—Dan. mixed among, Ep., I. T. E. 37; mixt among, C. W. II-110.

Sp. more augment, Am. 41; more and more augment, Ast. 4; much augmented, F. Q. IV-2-51; augment, more, F. Q. I-3-14; augmented more, F. Q. V-2-10; more augment with modest grace, F. Q. VI-9-9;—Dr. much augment, Pol. XXVIII-459; augmenting it the more, Pol. XXII-525.

Sp. much amazde, F. Q. I-1-26; much amaz'd, F. Q. IV-3-21; much amaze, F. Q. V-9-24; more amaz'd, F. Q. I-6-40; much amaze, H. H. B. 24;—Dr. much amazed, M. B. M. III-314; amaz'd much, M. M. 73.

Sp. much commend, F. Q. VII-2-2; C. C. H. 902; more commend, Am. 51; no more to, commend, T. M. 79;—Dr. much commend, Ods. IX. V. V. 12; Ids. 42; H. E. III, J-M. 102; commending much, M. E. 750.

Sp. much dismay, F. Q. I-5-30; ib. IV-8-20; much dismaid, F. Q. IV-8-7; in mind, much dismayd, F. Q. III-10-14; most dismay, F. Q. I-10-41;—Dr. much dismay'd, M. M. 249; dismay'd the more, Pol. XXIV-785.

Sp. much admyring, F. Q. IV-10-51; much admired, F. Q. IV-9-11; much the more admyr'd, M. H. T. 676; more admyr'd, F. Q. VI-2-13; most, admire, Am. 5;—Dr. much admir'd, H. E. XVIII, S-E. 16; most admir'd, Leg. II, Mat. F. 9; H. E. XVII, E-S. 6; most admir'd, Pol. X-135.

Sp. much, move, F. Q. IV-2-19; much was I moved, Daph. 11; moved much, F. Q. V-8-24; mov'd no more, F. Q. V-4-21; much enmove, F. Q. I-2-21; much enmoved, ib. I-9-18; much amoov'd, ib. I-8-21; much moved, in mind, F. Q. VI-2-11; most was moved, ib. IV-8-20;—Dr. most doth move, H. E. XVIII, S-E., 87;—Dan. more to move, O-M. A, 36; mov'd him most, C. W. VIII-16.

Sp. knowen by their names, F. Q. II-9-50; knowing by their names. F. Q IV-2-20; unknowne by name, F. Q. IV-6-6;—Dr. by name, known, Pol. XXI-17.

Sp. passen through, perilous (glade), F. Q. III-4-21;—Dr. through, perils past, M. M. 229; (similar) through peril, pressed, Leg. I. R. N. 117.

Sp. pine, in, paine, Daph. 63; pine for payne, S. C. VIII-18; pynen in payne, S. C. V-119; —Dr. pines in, pain, Eclog. II-19.

Sp. placest in a paradize, H. L. 11;—Dr. in paradise, placed, N. F. 118.

Sp. plainly, appeare H. H. B. 7; appeareth plaine F. Q. I-2-39; ap-peared plaine, F. Q. II-12-64; plaine appeares, F. Q. V-1-5 (1); appearing playne, ib. IV-11-1; appeared plain, ib. IV-11-47;—Dr. plainly doth ap-pear, Owl, 1115; plainly, appear, Pol. VI-176; Nym. 84;—Dan. plaine appeare, C. W. IV-85.

Sp. playing on pipes, apace, F. Q. VI-9-5; (also) pype, pype, apace, F. Q. VI-10-16;—Dr. upon, pipes, play, M. E. 1052; upon, pipe, play, Pol. XIII-62.

Sp. in person did appeare, F. Q. IV-9-10;—Dr. in person, appears, Pol. XXII-230.

Sp. privily he peeped, S. C. V-252; (similar) privily prolling, S. C. IX-160;—Dr. (similar) privily to pry, B. W. III-18.

Sp. oppressing, with power, M. VII-14; with, powre oppressing, F. Q. V-1-7; with, powre, oppresse, F. Q. V-12-24; by, powre oppressed, F. Q. V-10-30;—Dr. overprest with power.

Sp. in, prison, put, F. Q. IV-12-10; in prison, pent, F. Q. IV-5-34;—Dr. in prison put, Pol. XVII-129; H. E. XXIV, G. D.-J. G. 112; (into) M. E. 2010;—Dan. in prison pent, C. W. III-40.

Sp. puft up with proud (disdaine), F. Q. II-12-21; puffed up with pride, C. C. II. 759; puft up with pride, R. R. 11;—Dr. puft, up with praise, grew, proud Pol. IX-147.

Sp. enraung'd in ranks, F. Q. IV-10-25; enraunged on a rowe, M. VI-39; raunged in a rowe, S. C. IV-119; raunged in a ring, F. Q. VI-10-12; ranckt in, row, F. Q. III-6-35; in, rancks, enraunged, F. Q. III-6-35; raunged in a ring, F. Q. VI-10-11;—Dr. range, on a rank, Eclog. III-3.

Sp. read aright, F. Q. I-9-6; ared so right, F. Q. VI-4-28; areede up-reatly, S. C. VIII-130; rightly reed, F. Q. VI-3-31; rightfully aredd,

F. Q. I-10-17; rightfully aread, T. M. 9: rightly rad, F. Q. IV-7-16; —Dr. read aright, Owl. 105.

Sp. rent by the root, F. Q. VI-7-21;— C. 1; Dr. (compare) up by the roots, rive, Pol. XIII-120.

Sp. richly wrought, F. Q. II-9-19;—Dr. richly wrought, Pol. V-3; D| & G. 600; Pol. XVIII-27.

Sp. roard outrageously, F. Q. II-12-39; roaring, in rage, F. Q. I-6-25; (similar) raves in roring rage, F. Q. III-9-45 (vs. 3 & 4);—Dr. outrageously, roar, Pol. IX-401.

Sp. rov'd at random, F. Q. IV-10-19; at random, range, M. VII-21; at random ronne, F. Q. IV-4-38; runne at random, S. C. V-16; F. Q. V-8-19; at random, raunge, F. Q. III-8-20;—Dr. roving at random, Eclog. VII-17.

Sp. sadly set, F. Q. IV-7-35;—Dr. sadly I sit, Ids. 17; sadly sit, Ids. 45; sadly, sits, N. T. 416; M. B. M. II-102; sadly, sit, Eclog. VII-14; sat down sadly, H. E. XX, B. C-M. 59.

Sp. assayle on everie side, F. Q. II-2-22; F. Q. VI-11-18;—Dr. on, sides, assail'd, Pol. XXII-394.

Sp. set, aside F. Q. V-2-45; aside had set, F. Q. V-11-37;—Dr. set aside, M. M. 76.

Sp. seldome scene, F. Q. III-1-51; ib, VI-3-1; Mniop. 10, Daph. 17;— Dr. seldom seen, H. E. XVII, E-S. 152; M. M. 174; Owl. 301; M-C. 1239; —Dan. seldome, scene, H. T. 1930.

Sp. seeke for succour, F. Q. III-8-33; ib, V-10-6;—Dr. seeking succour (o), B. W. IV-35;—Dan. succour, sought Q. A. 344.

Sp. with, shaft, shot, F. Q. III-11-18;—Dan. flight shaftes to shoote C. W. VIII-15.

Sp. showed by, signs, F. Q. III-7-7; by signes, show, Proth. 117;—Dr. shewing by signs, M. B. M. I-516; by signs, shown, H. E. XIII-E-C-H. 148.

Sp. sing of sorrowe, S. C. XI-36; sings with, sorrowing, R. T. 46;— Dr. song is sorrow, M. M. 174; sorrow sing (o), H. E. IX, I-R, 2; for sorrow, forbear to sing, Eclog. VI-18.

Sp. sits in highest seate, R. T. 67; sit in, seat, H. H. L. 12; F. Q. V-1-10; sitt in second seat of soveraine (king), F. Q. III-9-41; sat on, seat, Pol. XI-299.

Sp. sitting, in secret shade, F. Q. II-7-3; sitting in, shade of arbors sweet, F. Q. IV-8-9; satte in secret shade, S. C. XII-5; set in secret shade, F. Q. VI-3-8;—Dr. sitting in silent shade, D. & G. 83; sit in, shade, H. E. XXI, H. H. L. Ger. 217; in shade they sit, M. E. 7082; Dan. under shade, sate, Q. A. 87, 8.

Sp. sitting, upon, shore, F. Q. III-4-7;—Dr. sitting is on shore, B. A. 83; set, upon, shore, Pol. XVI-68; sets, safely on, shore, Leg. III, P. G. 15.

Sp. sitting there beside, F. Q. IV-8-23; sitting, beside, C. C. II. 68; sate, side by side, V. B. XII; sate beside, F. Q. IV-8-6; sett beside F. Q. II-6-11; by her side there sate, F. Q. I-10-31; by, side, sitt, F. Q. II-2-37; on, side, in, consort, sate, F. Q. II-7-22; beside her set, F. Q. IV-4-9;—Dr. sitting by, side, B. A. 99; upon, side, sits, Pol. XXIII-36; on, side,so were set, M. M. 99;   Dan. sitting by his side, Q. A. 2068.

Sp. softly slid, F. Q. IV-11-35; soft sliding, V. B. 1; sliding softly, F. Q. I-1-51; sliding soft, F. Q. II-1-56;—Dr. softly, slide, Pol. XXIII-24.

Sp. soone shalt thou see, F. Q. II-8-22; soone, saw, F. Q. IV-6-10. soone as they see, F. Q. IV-10-45; soone as she saw, F. Q. V-4-40; oft-soones he saw, F. Q. VI-8-48;—Dr. soon, see B. A. 266; soon, saw, descend, D. & G. 707; soon, saw, Owl. 413;—Dan. sooner sees, Cleo. 1489, soone shall see, Phil. 431; sooner saw, C. R. 631; see how soone Mus. 677.

Sp. softly, sayd, F. Q. VI-12-19; softlie sayd, Daph. 9;—C. 1;—Dr. softly said, Pol. XVII-132.

Sp. sound he slept, F. Q. I-1-42; he slept soundly, F. Q. I-1-46; soundly slept, F. Q. III-4-58; sleeping soundly in, shade, F. Q. VI-11-38; sleeping sound, R. T. 78; F. Q. IV-7-4; sleepeth sound, M. H. T. 967;—Dr. soundly slept, Nym. 16; Eclog. X-9; soundly sleep, B. W. III-16;—Dan. sleepe so sound, Phil. 1227; sleepes unsound, C. W. III-63.

Sp. sought with, suit, F. Q. II-7-55; seeke with, suit, S. C. I-56;—Dan. with suite, sought, Q. A. 109.

Sp. upstanding, stifly stand, F. Q. V-7-20; (compare) stared still, F. Q. III-12-36;—Dan. stands he stiffe, C. W. VI-78.

Sp. standeth in, state, Daph. 62; in state, stands, F. Q. IV-10-35;—Dr. stands, in, state, M. E. 7019; standing in, state, Pol. VII-32; stood with, estate Pol. XI-111; gainst, state, stand, M. M. 61; in state, stood, Pol. XXIII-157;—Dan. what state stand these men in, C. W. V-90; in state stood sure, C. W. IV-15.

Sp. stately stood, F. Q. VI-10-6;—Dr. stately wood nymphs stand, Pol. XVII-369.

Sp. still, strove, F. Q. I-9-15, ib. V-5-28;—Dr. still we strive, H. E. XVIII-E-S. 153.

Sp. stalketh stately, M. H. T. 661;—Dr. stalks the stately crane (s), Pol. XXV-93.

Sp. astond stood, F. Q. I-2-3; astonisht, stood, Am. 16; stood all as-

tonied. M. VI-28; stand astonisht, C. C. II. 8; Epith. 11; standing aston-
ished, F. Q. VI-10-17.

Sp. astonied with, stroke, F. Q. I-2-15; astonisht with, stroke, S. C.
VII-227; stound with stroke, F. Q. V-11-29; with stroke astownd, F. Q.
III-1-17;—Dr. at, stroke, astound, B. A. 235.

Sp. stood as still as any stake, F. Q. V-3-31; stand ye still, Epith.
180; still to stand, F. Q. II-6-49; still did stand, V. G. 57; still he stood
as in a stound, F. Q. VI-3-30;—C. 3 (5);—Dr. still, to stand, II. E. XV.
W. Mar. 156; M. B. M. III-560; Pol. VIII-430; still durst stand, Pol.
XXII-873; still, stood, Pol. XXII-1111; stood still, B. A. 236; stood by,
still, M-C-19; stood as still, Nym. 82; Dan. still outlands, C. W. IV-
58; stood still, II. T. 1851; C. W. VI-85.

Sp. strongly strive, F. Q. III-2-16; strove with puissance strong, F.
Q. V-2-16;—Dr. striving, strongly lds. 58.

Sp. strong withstood, F. Q. II-1-11;—Dr. strongly stood, Pol. VIII-11;
Dan. stand against, strongest hand Ep. III, L. M. C. 71.

Sp. stoutly stond, F. Q. V-7-30; stoutly, withstood, F. Q. IV-9-29;
withstood with courage stout, F. Q. V-7-31;—Dr. stoutly stood, Pol.
XVIII-610; B. A. II-53; M. M. 95; stoutl'est withstood, Pol. VIII-297;
stood so stoutly, Pol. XXII-828.

Sp. strook with, astonishment, F. Q. III-7-3; stricken with, astonishment, F. Q. V-3-26;—Dr. with strong astonishment, strike, M. M. 16;
struck, with astounding fear, M. B. M. III-259.

Sp. restore unto, state, II. H. L. 20;—Dan. restor'd to an estate
Pan. 41.

Sp. suffer for my sake, F. Q. I-8-26; for his sake, suffer, F. Q. IV-12-7;
—Dr. suffer for your sake, N. F. 219; such to suffer for his sake, B. A.
87; suffering for his sake, Pol. V-187; suff'reth for her sake, Pol. X-56;
suffer'd for thy sake, II. E. XIX, M-C. B. 11.

Sp. sweetly, sound, F. Q. III-126; soundes so sweete, S. C. IV-3;—Dr.
sounds so sweet, Eclog. II-20.

Sp. sweetly sing F. Q. II-6-24; sweetly sung, M. VII-28; R. T. 81;
singing sweetly, F. Q. III-10-8; singen soote, S. C. IV-111; sing as soote
as swanne, S. C. X-90;—Dr. sirens sing sweetliest, Leg. II, M. F. 25;
sweetness of song, Pol. III-13.

Sp. swore by his sword, F. Q. VI-7-13;—Dan. upon, sword, sweare,
C. W. III-35.

Sp. scarcely, scene, F. Q. III-5-40; scarce could see, F. Q. IV-1-35;—
Dr. scarcely seen, Pol. VII-231.

Sp. take, tenderly, F. Q. II-11-49; taking, out of, tender hand, F. Q.

11-12-57; of, tender lamb' us- takest, S. C. XII-8;— Dan. take most tenderly, C. W. VIII-83.

Sp. in tempest tost, F. Q. VI-11-11; Dr. in, tempest, tost, M. M. 181; B. W. III-58; in, tempest, strangely tost, Leg. III, P. G. 37; in tempest long turmoil'd and tost, B. W. IV-37.

Sp. with teeth, teare, F. Q. III-7-20; to his teeth, tore, F. Q. I-8-16;— Dr. with teeth, tear, Pol. VII-283.

Sp. into tharldome throwne., F. Q. IV-7-19; into thralldome threw, H. H. L. 18; Dr. thrown into, thrall, Leg. I, R. N. 72.

So. thronging thicke, F. Q. IV-3-11;—Dr. thronging so thick, M. M. 218; thick'st to throng, M-C. 1166; thickly throng, N. F. 167.

Sp. thrusts into the thickest throng, F. Q. VI-8-19; thrust in, throng, S. C. XI-27; Dr. thrust, into, throng, B. A. 197; throws into throng, Pol. IV-15-2, 3; in, throng, thrown, B. A. 185; into thickest thrown, M. M. 116.

Sp. trembling, for terrour, F. Q. V-11-28;—Dan. trembles in terror, C. W. I-115.

Sp. truly taught, Ep. 10 (1); unto us taught, trew, H. H. L. 31;—Dr. by truth, taught, Leg. II, Mat. F. 1.

Sp. truly tryde in, extremest (state), F. Q. II-10-31; trew by tryall, F. Q. I-12-3; ib. IV-10-1;—Dr. for truth, try, M-C. 275;—Dan. true tried, Cleo. 1251.

Sp. true as, told, F. Q. V-8-12; M. VII-27;—C. 1:—Dr. truly tell, Pol. XXI-252; tell but truly, Ids. 17;—Dan. tell you true, C. W. VIII-70; tell me truly, Phil. 302; tels thee true, Des. B. 5; truly will tell, Q. A. 1651.

Sp. to avenge, vow'd, F. Q. II-8-11;—Dr. vow'd revenge, Pol. XXIX-361.

Sp. wander at will, S. C. IX-111; walk at will, and wandred, Muiop. 48; Dr. wandring at, will, Pol. XXVI-173.

Sp. wander in waste wildernesse, F. Q. II-1-22; through, worlds wyde wildernes, wander, F. Q. VI-7-37 (vs. 7 & 8);—Dr. wander in the wilderness, Elg. II, G. S. 56.

Sp. wandred in the wood, F. Q. VI-7-19; wandring in woods and forests, F. Q. I-2-9; Dr. wandring in the woods, Pol. V-225; wanoring in the wood, Q. C. 4.

So. wandred through the world, F. Q. I-10-9; wandred in, world, F. Q. III-6-11; wander through world, at, will, F. Q. III-7-54; wandring oad the world with wearie feet, F. Q. II-10-71; wander to the world end, M. H. T. 87;—Dr. wandr'd thro' the world, Pol. XXIV-

521; wander, wide world about. M. E. 3008; wandring in the world. Pol. 1-356.

Sp. waste in woe and wayfull miserye, F. Q. III-1-38; with wayling, wasted, S. C. 1-38;—Dr. (compare) in, woes, weares, H. E. X. R-1. 53.

Sp. walkt through the wood, F. Q. IV-5-4; (similar) walke the woodes, F. Q. III-8-11;—C. 1;—Dr. walking from the wood, X. T. 265.

Sp. on, way, went, F. Q. VI-5-10;—Dr. in, way, went, Pol. XI-255; (similar) windeth in her way. Pol. VII-195; went, away, Pol. XII-437;—Dan. way, went, Q. A. 1803.

Sp. wav'd, like water (free const.) F. Q. IV-11-15;—Dr. watring with, waves, Pol. XXII-1002.

Sp. well awakte, F. Q. III-8-22; well awake, Am. 70; waked well, F. Q. III-10-49;—Dr. well awake, M. E. 1708.

Sp. wexed wondrous glad, F. Q. 1-4-39; wexed wondrous proud, F. Q. II-3-7;—Dr. wax'd wondrous strong, X. F. 751; waxed wondrous neat, Eclog. IV-2; wax'd wondrous fair, Pol. XX-80.

Sp. (to his) will be wonne, F. Q. III-10-51; wonne unto her will, F. Q. V-1-30;—Dr. unto, will, won, Pol. IX-338;—Dan. win, from, will H. T. 1057.

Sp. wypt away, F. Q. IV-8-1; wipe cleane away, F. Q. II-1-35; away did wipe, F. Q. V-11-27; S. C. XII-108;—Dr. wipe away, Pol. II-406.

Sp. wise in workes, F. Q. II-2-17;—Dr. wisely worketh, M. B. M. III-625.

Sp. wondred at, wit, F. Q. 1-9-41; wondred at her wisedome, F. Q. 1-6-31;—Dr. (compare) wondrous wise, Pol. IV-37.

Sp. (in) woods, wonne, F. Q. VI-2-25;—Dr. within, woods, wonne, Pol. VII-33.

Sp. wore away, F. Q. IV-8-2; worne away, R. T. 72; weare away, Epith. 15; away to weare, F. Q. V-6-22; worne away, F. Q. II-4-4; worne away and wasted, S. C. XII-97;—Dr. in woes, away doe wear, Eclog. VI 12; worn, gave away, Elg. VI, L. P. C. 60.

Sp. woxan, wan, F. Q. IV-7-13; wexe, weake and wan, F. Q. II-7-65;—Dr. wax'd all so wan, Pol. XII-308; waxing wan, Owl. 1185.

Spencer and Chaucer.

Sp. drowned deepe, F. Q. 1-1-40; drown'd, deepe, Daph. 20; C. 1 (drenchen in, deepe):—Sp. dyde with dread, Daph. 37; dread to die, F. Q. III-7-24;—C. 1 (dye for drede):— Sp. fayre, befell, F. Q. 1-11-29;- C. 1 (falle, foule or faire);—Sp. falne into their fellowship, F. Q. IV-4-7;— C. 1;—Sp. in, field to fight, F. Q. III-3-29; fought, and in field, R. T.

16; C. 1; Sp. forth, to fare, C. C. II. 193; forward fare, F. Q. I-9-2; forth fared, F. Q. IV-5-46; C. 1; Sp. in hart, hate, F. Q. I-3-7; C. 1 (hertely hate); Sp. hent, in, hand, F. Q. III-7-61; S. C. II-195, hentest in hond, S. C. VII-37;—C. 3:—Sp. hid, in holes, F. Q. V-2-53, C. 1; Sp. high above his head, F. Q. I-11-38; on, head, hye, F. Q. I-7-16; high over his head, F. Q. V-9-26;—C. 1;—Sp. high in heaven, F. Q. I-4-14; C. 1; Sp. high on, hill, F. Q. I-1-23; high over billes, ib. III-10-55; C. 1; Sp. hye we homeward, S. C. XI-208; hie thee home, S. C. II-216; home to hye, S. C. V-317; (similar) haste us homeward, S. C. III-117; home, hasted, S. C. II-193;—C. 1:—Sp. (having) hang, on high, F. Q. III-6-18; on high, hang, F. Q. IV-1-22;—C.3:—Sp. piteously complayning, F. Q. IV-10-43; piteously complained, ib. IV-12-5;—C. 1; Sp. reckon right, F. Q. IV-11-53;—C. 2:—Sp. rich arayd, F. Q. II-2-11; richlier arayd, F. Q. III-11-51; C. 1;—Sp. rode upon, ready way, F. Q. V-6-18; unready, to ryde, ib. I-5-45;—C. (ready, ryde);—Sp. in, sea, sayld, F. Q. II-12-2;—C. 2 (4);—Sp. from shame to shield, F. Q. V-12-19; C. 1:—Sp. shone, sheene, F. Q. V-8-29;—C. 1:—Sp. sighing sore, F. Q. III-3-43; Daph. 27; sighing and sobbing sore, F. Q. IV-7-10; sigh full sore, F. Q. IV-8-64; sighed sore, Ast. 9; F. Q. VI-7-30;—C. 2 (7):—Sp. slombring soft, F. Q. I-9-13;—C. 2 (slepen soft);—Sp. smarting sore, F. Q. I-10-27;—C. 8 (11);—Sp. smite so sore, F. Q. III-3-49;—C. 2;—Sp. soft as silke, R. T. 78; silken soft, Muiop. 14;—C. 1;—Sp. soothly sayd, F. Q. VI-5-37;—C. 6 (9);—Sp. will, well, F. Q. I-7-40; F. Q. IV-8-29; M. H. T. 597; C. C. II. 84; Epith. 152; weened well, F. Q. I-10-58, ib. IV-9-7;—C. 1 (8);—Sp. well, wote, F. Q. I-12-31; S. C. XI-50; C. C. II. 919; well, wist II-3-17; ib. IV-9-18; well weeting, F. Q. II-9-39; well weete, ib. V-1-51; weet, well III-2-9; weete, well ib. III-10-40; well, wote, ib. III-6-29; C. 1 (19):— Sp. wearie wax, F. Q. II-10-30; wearie woxe, F. Q. VI-1-9; wexing weary, F. Q. VI-3-29; wexed weary, F. Q. V-1-17.

Drayton and Daniel.

Dr. brought, about, M. E. 1684; about to bring, M. E. 1928;—Dan. brought about, C. W. VI-13; bring about, C. W. VI-11.

Dr. never know, Pol. XII-101; never knew, H. E. VIII, E. C. II. 200, Dan. never knew, Cleo. 118; C. R. 497; never knowne, Q. A. 13.

SUBSTANTIVE AND VERB AS SUBJECT AND PREDICATE.

Sp. blast, overblowne, F. Q. IV-1-45; (vs. 5 & 6); blustring blast, F. Q. II-9-46 (vs. 8 & 9); Dr. blasts, that blew, Pol. IX-111.

Sp. no blemishe blotte, S. C. IV-51; blot (s), blemish, F. Q. V-6-2·
Dr. blemish blot, H. E. XVIII S-E. 89.

Sp. carefull (thoughts) creepe, S. C. V-190; carefull cold, creepe, F. Q.
I-7-39;—Dan. (compare), cares do creep, C. W. II-53.

Sp. cloud overcast, F. Q. V-5-38;—Dr. (compare) clouds that cover,
Leg. I, R. N. 17.

Sp. cloudie welkin cleareth, S. C. III-12; clouds, cleare, H. L. 40;—
Dan. (similar with objective const.) clear clouded world, S. D. 12; clereth
clouded air, S. D. 51; clouded brow she clears Cleo. 1190.

Sp. cocke, crowing cranck, S. C. IX-46 (cited already); crowing cocke,
F. Q. IV-5-41;—Dr. cock crew, with notes full clear, Mn. Mn. 536; cock
crows as he claps his wings, N. F. 895; chanty-clear, crowed crank, Eclog.
IV-41, (motto), cited in preceeding class).

Sp. day is doen, Epith. 298;—Dan. day is dunne S. D. 30.

Sp. death, doe, F. Q. II-6-44; death, doth, III-2-35;—Dan. death
doth, C. W. IV-92.

Sp. dread, dwells, F. Q. I-10-14;—Dr. (compare) darkness, seeks to
dwell, B. W. VI-17; (also) where damps, do dwell.

Sp. fame, flies (of, forraine foe) F. Q. III-5-9; flying fame, F. Q. I-7-
46;—Dr. fame, flie Leg. IV, Crom. 12; fame now flew, D. & G 190.

Sp. father fell, F. Q. V-10-11; father's fall, F. Q. II-1-37;—Dr. (similar) fathers fall, B. A. 133.

Sp. flashing, fire flies, F. Q. I-2-17; fire flies, Daph. 58; (similar) fire
did flash, F. Q. IV-3-15; fierie sparkles, flasht, F. Q. IV-3-25; Dan.
firie dragon, flye, C. W. I-414.

Sp. flockes, fully fed, F. Q. VI-9-13; flock is, fed, M. H. T. 142; flocks
doe feede, S. C. VI-106;—Dr. flocks as they did feed, H. E. XIII, E-D.
II. 134; how our flocks do fare, and how our herds do feed, Pol. IX-90.

Sp. floods, overflow, S. C. V-94; flouds, flow, perforce, S. C. XI-127;
Dr. famous floods, that, flow, Pol. XXIII-39.

Sp. fortune, befall, F. Q. VI-1-6; fortune, befall, F. Q. II-8-52; M
H. T. 618; fayrest fortune, befell, F. Q. III-1-17; V-3-29; fortunes, befell,
F. Q. VI-9-16;—Dr. fortune, fall, Leg. III. P. G. 11.

Sp. fortune, afford, F. Q. IV-8-18;—Dr. fortune here affords, B. A.
283;—Dan. fortune did afford, C. W. VII-26.

Sp. fortune frowne, F. Q. V-10-26; fortune felly frowned, F. Q. V-
5-36;—Dr. fortune, thou dost, frown, B. W. V-38; curse fortune if she
did not frown, M. M. 192.

Sp. fountaines that, freshly flowe, M. VI-39; Dr. flood, from fountain,
flow'd, Pol. XXVI-526.

Sp. fowles, flottering, I Q. II-12-35; C. 2. (fowles flee):—Dr. fowl that fly, Pol. I-72, fow., fly, B. A. 112.

Sp. God, gave, Ep. V.: Dr. God gives, Pol. XIX-53; God having , &c, Flg. III. W. B. 89; Dan. God give him grace, C. W. III-28; God gives, Phil. 1676; gods have given, (glory), Cleo. 312, 3.

S. God, forgiveth, F. Q. I-10-10:—Dr. God, forgive, M. B. M. II-444.

S. God, grace F. Q. I-10-61:—Dr. God, grac'd Pol. VIII-220; gods have grac'd M. E. 1920; God grac'd, M. B. M. III-765.

S. God, graunt, F. Q. I-10-42:—Dan. God grant, O.-M. A. 30; Q. A. 360; H. T. 381.

So. God to guide, F. Q. V-2-10; God, guided, S. C. V-113; God, guide, Muiop. 28; Dr. God, guide, M. F. 1271; God that guid'st, M. F. 1089.

So. good, that growes, F. Q. I-8-44:—Dr. good may grow, B. W. I-57.

Sp. goodly cedar grewe, W. W. V.-7; grew, goodly trees, F. Q. I-2-28; grew a goodly tree, F. Q. I-11-16:—Dr. goodliest flowers that, grew, M. B. M. I-691.

Sp. grace is given, F. Q. IV-10-2; grace were given, VI-6-43:—Dr. grace was, given, Pol. VII-119.

Sp. grasse did growe, V. W. V. 2:—Dr. grass that grows, Eclog. IV-26 (motto); the grass grows rank, Owl. 749.

Sp. griefe, grew, F. Q. I-1-53; griefe, greater grow, F. Q. I-7-41;—Dr. grief should grow, H. E. XI. C.-O. T. 77; griefs, grow, Ids. 3.

Sp. grove, growes, M. VI-41:—Dr. groves that grow, S. S. 47.

Sp. harvest hastened, S. C. XII-98:—Dr. harvest hast'ning, B. W. I-31.

So. heavens have, H. B. 17; how heavens had, F. Q. VI-12-16;—Dr. heaven hath, B. W. V-63;—Dan. heavens, have Cleo. 99.

Sp. he beheld, F. Q. VI-8-28;—Dan. he beheld, C. W. II-56.

Sp. land that lay, F. Q. II-6-11;—Dr. land, ly, Pol. XII-170.

Sp. l'fe, lye, (low), F. Q. I-9-8; life, lie, F. Q. V-5-31; life, was layd, F. Q. IV-12-28;— Dr. lives and fortunes lay, B. W. I-45;—Dan. on love, life, lyes, S. D. 15.

Sp. lasse, lye, F. Q. III-10-17;—Dan. lasse hath layd, P. S. 32.

Sp. lov doth lie, Epith. 65;—Dr. little love, lies, Eclog. II-1 (Elg.).

Sp. mightie Martial, most commend, F. Q. II-6-35;—Dan. (compare), Majestic commend, C. W. VI-60.

Sp. morne, my muse, S. C. XI-111:—Dan. matter for my muse to morne, C. R. 906.

So. none ever knew, F. Q. I-4-7;—Dan. none can know, Cleo. 772.

Sp. paine, apall, S. C. VIII-1.; Dr. ....; ... 6. H. 4 XXIV-12.

Sp. selfe to see, V. P. 3; Dan. self shall see, S. D. 11

Sp. shadow, shynes, H. B. 25; Dan. ...... promisse, ... C. W. 11-14.

Sp. sonne had sette, S. C. V-299; Dr. ..., ..., N. 1. 216; Dan. .... doth set, Past. 93; sunshine, sets, F. H. 06, ..., ... S. D. 30

Sp. sorrow, sad, soule asaid, F. Q. 1-2-21; Dr. .... assail, B. W. VI-92.

Sp. state, stands, S. C. V-95; state, .. de......, F. Q. V. 21; Dr. state stood, B. W. 1-56; Dan. state dol-tand C. W. VI-09, ... sure, Mus. 922; state stands-last, H. T. 2:

Sp. sunne, shine, F. Q. V-10-20; sunne, stores, S. C. VII-1..., ... shynd, F. Q. III-6-8;—C. 6;—Dr. sun dott ...., H. F. H. II-R. 13.; sun, shine, Pol. XXV-11; sun hath shone, Po. IV-22.; .... shone, Owl. 96.

Sp. tong can tell, F. Q. II-1-19; ...... N. ..., ... H. L. .., II. H. B. 30; tongues to tell, F. Q. IV-11-...; ..... 6, 29; Dr. .... tell, H. E. VII, E-C. 189; Dan. tongue .. ..., Po. 1565; F. D. 410; tongue, told, H. G. 866.

Sp. waters wexed (dull), F. Q. 1-1-5; Dr. .... Po. XV-285; wild waters are wax'd high, S. S. 49; waters ...... (.....), Pol. XXVIII 391.

Sp. waves, washt away, F. Q. 1-11-51; wa....., ... L. .... N. ....; Dr. waves, do wash, N. F. 684.

Sp. wo worth (the man), F. Q. II-4-32, wo worth the word, La. II-4; —C. 1;—Dan. wo worth the while, C. W. II-18

Sp. words, worke, F. Q. III-2-43; Dan. words ...., H. T. 950.

Spenser and Chaucer

Sp. life did last, F. Q. VI-11-31; life, last, Dan. ... ., ..., V. G. 8; C. 2

Sp. night doth ive, S. C. V-316, night ... ., La. ... F. ...... nighteth, S. C. VIII-196; C. 1, sh......., morning ...., F. Q. II-3-4, - C. 1; - Sp. ship shall saile, R. T. 22, ..., ... - C. 1.

Sp. wave, well, F. Q. 1-1-1, C. 1, 120; Dr. ...., ... —C. 2. — Dr. life was lost, B. W. V-68, - C. 2 (11)

4   VERB AND SUBSTANTIVE AS PREDICATE AND OBJECT.

Sp. bathe your brest, S. C. IV-38;—Dr. bathe their, breasts, Pol. IV-20.

Sp. batteill to abide, F. Q. III-7-11; bide him batteil, F. Q. III-8-16;—Dr. battle to abide, B. A. 112.

Sp. beare the bell, F. Q. IV-1-25; ib. VI-10-26;—Dr. beare away the bell, Pol. XXVII-22; for beauty, bear, the bell, Pol. XXVII-66.

Sp. beare blame, S. C. IX-101; C. 1;—Dan. beare some blame, C. W. 1-93; beares out blame, O. M. A. 12.

Sp. beare, blow, F. Q. I-8-18; blowes he bore, F. Q. V-5-7; beare off their blowes, F. Q. VI-5-18; blowes to beare, F. Q. IV-7-28;—Dr. bear their boist'rous blows, B. W. VI-66.

Sp. beare this burden on, backe, F. Q. VI-2-17; burden which, bore, F. Q. IV-11-26; burdens that, beare, S. C. V-110; burden, of brunt, beare F. Q. IV-8-12; beare the burden, F. Q. V-1-28;—C. 1;—Dr. bear, the burthen, Leg. II, Mat. F. 93; burthen bear, N. F. 350; bare Eclog. III-10; Mu. 281; bear Pol. XIV-278; burthen bear, M. B. M. III-112; burthen bears, M. B. M. I-171; burthens, borne, Ids. 59.

Sp. beate the bush, (byrdes), S. C. X-17; bush did beat, F. Q. V-9-17; —Dr. beat a bush Pol. XXIII-218; beating, branches, M. B. M. II-416.

Sp. blade about, blest, F. Q. I-8-22; burning blades, blesse, F. Q. I-5-6; Dr. (compare) blades are brandish'd, M. B. M. III-185.

Sp. blows, balefull breath, S. C. XII-119; (similar) breath, blast, F. Q. VI-4-22; blowen, bitter, blast, F. Q. III-9-11;—Dr. breath doth blow, B. W. II-32; breath that blows, H. E. XXII L. Ger.-II. II. 95; breath, blown, B. W. I-28.

Sp. braunch of laurell bore, F. Q. III-12-3; bay-braunches, beare, S. C. IV-101; of olive braunches beares, S. C. IV-123;—C. 1. (beare bowes);—Dr. branch of laurel, bear, Eclog. VIII-II. R. 112;—Dan. beare, olive bough, S. D. 4; beare olive-branches, C. W. VIII-14.

Sp. broke, bands, F. Q. II-11-33; broke his band, F. Q. III-7-61; break off bands, Daph. 3; breaking, bonds, F. Q. IV-3-11; bands, breake, C. C. II. 629; bandes had brast, F. Q. I-9-21; bonds broke, S. C. XI-165;—Dr. brake off, band, Leg. IV, Crom. 88; bounds, (that) brake, M. B. M. I-258; bonds, broke, B. W. I-21; Dan. broken out of bands, C. W. VII-21.

Sp. brought, backe, balefull body, F. Q. I-7-50;—Dr. body brought, Pol. XXIX-75.

Sp. bodie beare, F. Q. IV-12-35; ib. VI-8-16;—Dan. bodies beare, Mus. 70; are about the body, Cleo. 504.

Sp. bore a .... F. Q. II-1-... D. .... D. and G. 619

Sp. bow, beare F. Q. II-9-S. .... M. VII-... .... C. 1, (5);—Dr. born the ...... Pol. XIII-...

Sp. bow, bent F. Q. II-11-... .... Q. IV-... C. 5, (6); Dr. bows, ... t. B. V. 462.

Sp. build, bowre, F. Q. V-9-11, lords, ... bowre, S. C. J-42, how built, howres, M. VII-28, ... N. G. 1, ... V. G. 85; Dr. build, bowres, D. and G. 205, building, ... [v] 1162.

Sp. care, kept, F. Q. II-6-12; Dr. ....

Sp. cattell to keep, M. II. T-283. Dr. .... Pol. III-48 keeping, cattle, M. E. 851

Sp. keepen companee, F. Q. I-9-2... .... F. Q. II-9-... —Dr. company to keep, M. G. M. I-300

Sp. keepe, course, F. Q. II-12-... .... F. Q. V-1-... keepe his course, M. VII-18; (spider), ... F. Q. V-12-20 —Dr. keeps her course, Pol. XXI-..., ... B. V. Mer 152;—Dan. keepe, course, Luc. V. L. VC .... M 317.

Sp. chaunged, cheare, F. Q. III-2-40, ... Q. V-2-9 chang'd his cheare, M. VI-31, C. I. .... ;—Dr chang'd her cheer, N. F. 600.

Sp. (cupid) kept his court, F. Q. VI-..., ... F. Q. VI-10-9; Dr. court doth keep, H. I. XXI, II. H. I. 66-...

Sp. chawd the cud F. Q. III-1-18, ... F. Q. V-5-2; chawing the chud, F. Q. V. 6-19, Dr. .... N. F. 166, ... ends, Pol. XVIII-10; chews the cud, M. B. M. II-284

Sp. clove, crest, F. Q. II-6-... ...... Dr. .... B. V. 237; crown to cleave, Pol. XXII-1530

Sp. counsells call, M. II. T. 189, Dr. counsel quellis call, D. ...... G. 224; call a councel, B. V. 12-...; Dan. .... H. Mar. 1-9

Sp. crowne, kept, F. Q. II-10-20, kept the .... I-11; Dan kept the crowne, F. D. 290, kept their .... Pol. I-140

Sp. daunger darme, F. Q. VI-11-19; Dr. .... B. V. II-13.

Sp. did, reverence dew, F. Q. II-9-39, Dr. .... Leg. II. Mat. F. 40; do your due F. Q. VII-1-X-30, ... Pol. XXI-129

Sp. favour, found, F. Q. I-7-25; favor founidest, C. C. II. 461; favour, finde S. C. VII-138; finde favour, F. Q. V-555; S. C. IX-252; found favour, H. L. 36; found more favour, F. Q. IV-8-61;—Dr. favour, find, Leg. II. Mat. F. 2; Dan. finde, favour Cleo. 695-6; finde favour, Cleo. 356.

Sp. feare his force, F. Q. I-6-29; feare, no force, M. H. T. 1126;—D., fearing, the force, Leg. III P. G. 33.

Sp. feed, flocks, Daph. 15 (vs. 1 and 2); feede, flocks, in fields, S. C. VI-76; feede, flockes, S. C. VII-66; feeding, flocke, S. C. VII-51; flockes to feede, S. C. VII-166;—Dr. feeds his flocks, Pol. XXVIII-380; flocks to feed, M. B. M. II-111; flocks, feed, Pol. IX-172; fair flocks he fed, Eclog. VI-17.

Sp. (for to) feed, fierie eye, F. Q. I-6-4;—Dr. fires to feed, Pol. VIII-300; (similar) feeds, flames, M. B. M. I-671.

Sp. fill the fields, F. Q. I-8-11; (also) forest, fill, F. Q. III-10-43;—Dr. field, to fill, B. W. IV-42.

Sp. finde, faithfull frend, F. Q. IV-8-57; found a new friend, F. Q. I-2-27; finde friends, F. Q. I-12-28;—C. 3, (4);—Dr. finding one friend, Leg. II. Mat. F. 2; found her friends, M. M. 119.

Sp. (occasion) fittest found, F. Q. VI-11-42; fit (occasion), finde, F. Q. I-12-15;—Dr. finding fitting roomth, Pol. IV-123.

Sp. fruitfull (issue) afford, Proth. 6;—Dr. fruit afford, B. W. IV-54.

Sp. gave, grace, F. Q. II-12-68; graces, give, Am. 71; great grace, given, F. Q. I-10-17; grace, give R. T. 37; grace, God, give M. H. T. 402;—C. 2;—Dr. gives, grace, H. E. XVIII, S. E. 90;—Dan. gave him grace, C. W. VII-92; gives his grace, Pan. 26; gives you grace, Ep. II, H. II. 18.

Sp. gave a grone, F. Q. II-1-38;—Dr. gave a groan, Eclog. X-17;—Dan. give out groning sounds, C. W. I-115.

Sp. glories gaine, F. Q. III-9-37; glory, gayned, Am. 36;—Dr. glory (that doth) gain, Pol. XXX-15; glory gain'd, S. S. 14; gaind, glorious gole, Pol. XVII-112;—Dan. gaind a glorious end, C. W. VI-97.

Sp. glory, give F. Q. II-8-51;—Dan. glory give, Ep. IV, L. L. 96; C. W. IV-38.

Sp. glorie gotten, F. Q. V-3-22; glory can be got, Am. 57;—Dr. glory, get, B. W. I-46.

Sp. graunt, grace, Am. 57; gifts of grace do graunt, F. Q. VI-10-15; graunt, grace, F. Q. IV-6-32; graunt them grace, C. C. II. 881;—Dr. grace, grant, Pol. XI-337.

Sp. greatest grace, gaine, F. Q. VI-2-2; greater gifts for guerdeon, ayne, S. C. XI-15;—Dr. great experience, gain'd, Leg. IV. Crom. 2 ; Dan. greatest trophy, game, Cleo. 717.

Sp. hand, heav'd, F. Q. VI-8-15; heavie hand he heaved, ib. VI-C. I. Q. I-7-14; hand, heav'd on hie, F. Q. IV-6-18; (standart ... not so across, F. Q. I-4-17; high, hand enhaunst, F. Q. II-6-31;—Dr. to be gd't, hand on heav'd, M. M. 211; the hand that heav'd him up ... thell low come down, M. M. 218.

Sp. hand, held, F. Q. I-1-33; ib. IV-10-55; hasty hand, hold, F. Q. I-3-38; hands to hold, F. Q. V-8-12; head, band, F. Q. IV-7-36; vpheld, hand, F. Q. IV-6-23; holding no, hands, F. Q. V-11-44; holding, hand upon, hart, F. Q. IV-10-51; held, hand upon, hart, F. Q. II-6-26;—C. I.

Sp. had, hap, F. Q. IV-2-15;—Dr. had his hap, B. W. III-21; Dr. hold, hand, B. W. II-17; hold thy hand, Nun. 29; hold off, erthallow'd hands, B. W. V-36; held, hand, Pol. VII-295; her hands raised to heaven held up her hands, B. W. III-20.

Sp. hand withhold, F. Q. II-5-42; hand withhold, F. Q. III-12-32; Dr. his hand, withheld, Leg. I. R. N. 108.

Sp. hang, head, F. Q. III-11-11; hang their heads, S. C. XI-131; hanging, head with heavie cheare, F. Q. V-11-65; hung the head, F. Q. V-12-13;—C. 2, (5):—Dr. hang their heads, M. F. 33; hanging down the head, Eclog. X-17; hung the head, M-C. 1217; Q. C. 11; hung, head, M. E. 1902.

Sp. hart, heale, Am. 50;—Dr. heart that beats, Pol. XVIII. 669.

Sp. hath, hart to hit, F. Q. III-2-35; had, hart not hardiment, F. Q. III-7-16; heart, had, F. Q. IV-8-2; Dan. hav her heart, Q. A. 95; have my heart, Q. A. 1608; hast a heart, Q. A. 1817; have our harts, C. W. VII-5; hath our hearts, Ep. I. T. L. 212; had a heart, Phd. 2151; had my heart, Cleo. 631; heart hast, O.-M. V. 30.

Sp. heare, heavenly notes, H. H. B. 38;—Dr. heavenly voice, heari, Eclog. IX-5 (Sng.).

Sp. heapen hills, S. C. VII-202;—Dr. heap'd hills on hills, Leg. IV. Crom. 53.

Sp. uphold his heavie hedd, F. Q. I-4-19; noble up, heavie head, S. C. X-1; head upheld, S. C. V. 205;—Dr. hold up thy head, Ids. 26; hold her head aloft, Pol. XIX-29; Dan. holds up their heads, H. L. 1808; held up his head, Q. A. 2128; head well held, Cleo. 1708; hold up thy head, H. T. 1155.

Sp. hide thy head, F. Q. I-2-18; hide their heads, F. Q. IV-6-32; hide, head, T. M. 46; head, hidd, V. B. XV;—Dr. head doth hide, Pol. IX-118; high, heads, do hide, Pol. V-311.

Sp. (for) hope which in, helpe, had. F. Q. I-1-2: harvest-hope I have, S. C. XII-121: have, hope, F. Q. III-2-11:—Dan. have no hopes, H. T. 551: have, hopes, bye, F. D. 37.

Sp. hunt, hartlesse hare, S. C. XII-28:—Dr. hunt, harmless hare, Eclog VII-6: Dan. hunts, hares, Q. A. 1592.

Sp. to lerne, a lesson, F. Q. V-5-46 (vs. 3 and 4); learnde a lesson S. C. XI-156: Dan. learne his lesson, C. W. III-57; learne this lesson, Q A. 491.

Sp. leave the love, F. Q. V-11-63; leave, love alone, Epith. 17; left his love, F. Q. V-8-3; left his lowe, III-8-18; ladies love to leave, F. Q.I-10-62:—Dr. leave his loved nymph, Pol. XXI-60: love, left, H. E. I., H. E. R. 50:—Dan. (similar) leave his lemman, Owl. 919; leave his love, Col. III-332: leave her love, S. D. 18.

Sp. left your lord, F. Q. I-7-48; leaving his lordes (task), S. C. V-53;—Dr. leaving his lord (to lead), Leg. I, R. N. 121.

Sp. lend, reliefe, F. Q. III-1-53;—Dr. lend relief, M. B. M. 1-195.

Sp. lent, light, F. Q. II-6-43; lend, light, Epith. 23; H. L. 11; lendeth light, Daph. 59:—Dr. lends us light, Mn. Mn. 40.

Sp. let out loved life, F. Q. VI-8-48; life, let, F. Q. IV-3-11;—C. 3;—Dan. let out life, C. W. VI-90; Cleo. 1161.

Sp. life, ladd, F. Q. III-12-46; life doth lead, F. Q. IV-7-11; life here led, F. Q. VI-5-35; leading a life, F. Q. VI-9-19; ledd, long life. F. Q. IV-3-52; lead, life V. G. 16;—C. 7 (15);—Dr. life he leads, M. B. M. 1-681; life, leads, Leg. I, R. N. 120: life I lead, M. E. 1559; life, lead, Pol. XXIV-831; life I led, Leg. IV, Crom. 33; life he led, Pol. II-268; life they led, M-C. 1333; leads, life M. E. 1750; led, life, H. E. XVIII, S-E-9:—Dan. leads a life, S. D. 26: life I led, C. R. 824.

Sp. life, left, F. Q. VI-6-32; life hath left, H. H. L. 27: life not leave, F. Q. II-1-17; leave this life, Daph. 64;—C. 1 (2):—Dr. leave their lives, B. A. 28; left his life, Pol. XXIV-330; left, life, B. W. IV-22:—Dan. left his owne life, Q. A. 1878.

Sp. little, lacke, F. Q. I-11-11: little lacketh, S. C. VIII-126;—Dr. little lackt, M. M. 189; little lack'd, M. M. 63.

Sp. life doth loath, C. C. H. 201; life does loath, Daph. 13;—Dan. loath this life, (lesse) Cleo. 518; life seems to love and loath, C. W. VIII-21.

Sp. lode, layd, F. Q. II-11-29; lode, did lay, F. Q. VI-6-28; lay on load, F. Q. IV-9-33; laying on, lode, F. Q. IV-4-23; laid on load, F. Q. IV-9-22: Dr. lay on load, H. E. XVI, M-W. 102: laid a heavy load, B. W. V-50.

Sp. lost his labour, F. Q. II-7-61; lose thy labour, M. H. T 656.—Dr. lost his labour, M.-C. 635; labour, lost, Leg. I. R. N. 35.

Sp. loseth, light, Epith. 15; light hath lost, Ep. 2 (II); C. 4; D. light, loseth, light Leg. II. Mat. F. 31.

Sp. love have lost, F. Q. IV-9-38; love to lose, loth, F. Q. IV-1-10; Dan. lost my love, S. D. 11; loving loose your loves, O.-M. A. 23.

Sp. life forlore, F. Q. IV-10-10; life to losse, forlent, F. Q. IV-3-6;— Dr. life, lose, Pol. XXII-1617; Ods. VIII, S. C. 1; lives, lose, B. A. 213; lose, life, B. W. VI-64; lost, life, M. M. 31;—Dan. life, lose Cleo. 1606; lives do lose, C. W. VI-9.

Sp. made, musick, F. Q. I-12-7; make them musick, S. C. VI-29; making your musick, of, mone, T. M. 1; musicke, which I made, C. C. II. 70; musick which, make, Am. 38;—Dr. make, music, M. M. 13; make him such musick, M. B. M. 1-699; musick, make, M. E. 1670; (merrily), to musick that I make, M. E. 1707; musick made, M. E. 1525; by, musick, make, N. F. 900.

Sp. many, make, F. Q. III-12-23; many, made, F. Q. II-7-55; many (wounds), made, F. Q. V-12-19; maken, many, S. C. A -92; madest many (harts), II. L. 2;—Dr. many (beauties) make, II. E. VII, E.-A. 18;—Dan. makes, many lawes, Ods. U. S. 52; made as many rights as men. Q. A. 2246.

Sp. Mayster, might, F. Q. III-2-16; maistered his might, F. Q. III-12-32;—Dan. mastering the mightie, C. W. 1-9.

Sp. make, mone, III-7-15 (vs. 3 and 4); S. C. XII-6; II. L. 19; makes, mone, F. Q. III-1-38; making, mone, F. Q. II-1-13; makes, mone, F. Q VI-4-32; made, mone, F. Q. III-1-35; made great mone, F. Q VI-1-12; made, mourning, F. Q. VI-1-31; mournfull plaint to make, F. Q. IV-8-9, makes, mone S. C. IV-89; made, mourning F. Q. VI-1-31; mone, made, Ast. 29; made, mone, T. M. 31;—C. 2;—Dr. make her moan, M. M. 257. moan, maketh, Ods. VI;—C. 5.

Sp. amends to make F. Q. IV-8-60; make, amendment, F. Q. II-1-90. made amends, C. C. II. 924; make amends, II. H. L. 21; C. 2;—Dr. make amends, Pol. XXII-530; amends shall make, Leg. II Mat. F 96; amends must make, II. E. XIX. M-C. B. 110; amends, make, M. M. 202, B. A. 205; Pol. XVII-201;—Dan.make amends, Q. A. 1917; make her amends, II. T. 761.

Sp. mariage make, F. Q. II-1-21; matrimony make, Epith. 12;—Dr. make a marriage, B. W. VI-8;—Dan. make a marriage, Q. A. 2192.

Sp. match, make, F. Q. III-11-33; made a matchless paragon, F. Q.

VI-1-1: Dr. match to make, M. M. 11;—Dan. make up a match, H. T. 318.

Sp. measure doth make, F. Q. I-2-9;—Dr. means to make, B. W. VI-16.

Sp. measur'd many miles, F. Q. II-9-9;—Dr. measure, many miles, Pol. XXVIII-309.

Sp. admyr'd his might, F. Q. V-1-8;—Dr. admire his might, M. M. 5.

Sp. mirrour make, Epith. 4;—Dr. make a mirror, Eclog. V-28; made the mirror of a man, H. E. IX, I-R. 32.

Sp. misse his mark, F. Q. VI-1-7; missing the marke, F. Q. I-8-8;—Dr. miss his mark, M. E. 2015.

Sp. miserie bemone, F. Q. IV-12-12;—Dr. bemoan, miserable case, M. E. 7007; bemoan, miserable plight, B. W. V-24.

Sp. mollify your mind, F. Q. III-2-13;—Dr. mollify his mind, Leg. 1, R. N. 76.

Sp. motion made, Muiop. 50;—Dr. motion, make, Mn. Mn. 310; make it move, Leg. III, P. G. 12.

Sp. mustering, men, C. C. II. 769;—Dr. muster'd men (adj.), B. W. IV-17.

Sp. musick mard, S. C. VIII-12;—Dan. musicke mar'd, Mus. 163.

Sp. for passage pay, F. Q. VI-1-13;—Dr. for his pass must pay, Pol. XXVI-318.

Sp. pay the price, F. Q. I-5-26; S. C. II-49; H. H. L. 19; price, payd, F. Q. V-8-23;—Dan. pay the price, Cleo. 579; pay backe the, price, Cleo. 541; paid, price, F. D. 173.

Sp. perilles past, F. Q. III-9-11; pathes and perils, past F. Q. VI-9-2; past that perill, F. Q. VI-3-34; perill, which he, past, F. Q. III-5-3;—Dr. perils, past, Leg. IV, Crom. 39; H. E. XV, W-Mor. 71; peril, past, Leg. II Mat. F. 16;—Dan. on the perill they have passt, Phil. 933.

Sp. pitie they plight, S. C. III-103; prayd to pitty, plight, F. Q. VI-6-20; plight I pitty, F. Q. IV-7-19;—Dr. the princely eagle pitying, his plight, Owl. 1294;—Dan. pittie him that pitties our sad plight, C. W. II-76.

Sp. supply, place, F. Q. VI-4-35; S. C. VIII-163; place supplyde, F. Q. II-10-51;—Dr. place, supply, Pol. XXII-584; place, supplying, M. E. 1152.

Sp. powers repaire, F. Q. I-8-50;—Dr. powers, repair'd, Pol. XII-84; repairs his powers, Pol. I-162.

Sp. powrse, applied, F. Q. IV-4-24; powrse, apply, F. Q. V-8-18;—Dr. to purpos'd end, powers, apply, Pol. IX-333.

Sp. powres, employ, F. Q. VI-5-14; –Dr. employing powers, Pol. XXIV-355.

Sp. prove your powre, F. Q. VI-5-30; Am. 25;—Dr. prove, power, B. W. I-16;—Dan. the powre, to prove, O. M. A. 36.

Sp. prune his plumes, T. M. 68; –Dr. pruning his plumage, N. F. 865; prune, plumes upon, pleasant sich, Pol. XVI-308.

Sp. putting his puissance, F. Q. VI-12-30; –Dr. puissant hand, put, Pol. XII-94.

Sp. parts impaire, F. Q. V-2-32;– Dan. impaire, part, F. D. 122.

Sp. play, part, M. H. T. 234; play my part, Am. 18, playing, part, F. Q. IV-10-21; plaid, part, F. Q. II-1-14; playes, partes, F. Q. III-6-49; —Dr. play his part, Ids. 29; playing manly parts, Ods. XVII, Bal. A 10; playd, part, B. W. V-24; parts, play'd, Leg. IV, Crom. 95; II. E. XI, C-O. T. 14; –Dan. play, their parts, Phil. 10 8-9; plays, part, Ids. 7.

Sp. red her riddle, F. Q. V-11-25;– Dr. reading riddles, Eclog. VI-3; (similar) in riddles to bewray, H. E. XXII-171.

Sp. wreake her wrong, F. Q. II-1-12; wrong to wreake, F. Q. V-8-11; wrongs to wreak, F. Q. I-6-42;– Dr. wrongs to wreak, Pol. XXIX-322; – Dan. wreake her wrong, C. R. 580; wreck my wrong, S. D. 38.

Sp. ronne, race, F. Q. I-5-14; (renne) S. C. VII-60; runne, a race, M. H. T. 744; run her, race, Epith. 9; race, runne, F. Q. V-7-4; race, run, Ep. 12;—Dr. run their race, Pol. IX-111;—Dan. run, race II. T. 108.

Sp. seest, secret, F. Q. III-10-4; Dr. into secrets, have seeing Leg. I. R. N. 30.

Sp. seeing such, F. Q. I-3-26; ib. VI-12-17; such, see, F. Q. VI-1-9; Dan. seeing such, F. D. 198.

Sp. see the, sunne, F. Q. VI-12-35; –Dr. see the sun, Pol. IX-81; see, sun, B. W. I-47; saw the sun, M. M. 156; saw no sun, Leg. I. R. N. 128. sooner saw my sun, Ids. 56; as sun, shining see, M. B. M. II 182; sun n'er saw, Pol. XII-79.

Sp. seeke some succour, Am. 2;– C. 1; –Dr for, succour seek, H. F XXI, II. II.-L. Ger. 83.

Sp. itselfe, save, F. Q. II-6-5; herselfe, save, F. Q. II-2-24; himselfe to save, F. Q. IV-3-32; save himselfe, F. Q. V-11-13; –Dr. save themselves, Pol. XXII-1025; M. M. 135; scarce shifts to save himselfe, Pol. XXII-1343; save himself such shifts, M. M. 225, save themselves from, shower M. M. 223;–Dan. save my selfe, Q. A. 705

Sp. selfe, seemes to see, F. Q. I-6 16; selfe (subj.), see F. Q. II-12 23; Am. 45; safe himselfe, see, F. Q. III-10-53; myselfe in safety, see, F. Q. III-1-10; seeing herselfe descryde, F. Q. III-3-20; seeing, herselfe forsaken so, F. Q. V-4-10;--Dr. itself doth see, II. E. VII, E-A, 33; see our-selves, C. R. 537;--Dan. himselfe, you see, Phil. 584; see, himselfe, C. W. VIII-30; see thyselfe C. W. I-91; seeing herselfe, C. R. 591; seeing himselfe, Cleo. 985.

Sp. sell myselfe, F. Q. VI-9-24; Itselfe hath sold, F. Q. IV-11-22; him-selfe unto, service sold, F. Q. III-9-8; sold thyselfe to serve, F. Q. I-9-46;-- Dan. sell yourselves, Mus. 758; sell myselfe to lust my soul to sinn, C. R. 307.

Sp. set himselfe, F. Q. V-6-14; himselfe she set, F. Q. III-6-10; him-selfe, set, F. Q. IV-3-6;--Dr. themselves safely, set, N. F. 692;--Dan. set ourselves, Q. A. 2225; set myselfe to speake, II. T. 862; sets himselfe C. W. VII-64; seeing themselves, set, Phil. 829.

Sp. himselfe, shew, F. Q. III-1-45; side itselfe did, show, F. Q. V-5-9;-- Dan. for shame shew not yourselfe so weakly set, II. T. 1182.

Sp. himselfe, slew, F. Q. II-10-55; sacred selfe to slay, F. Q. V-8-19;--Dr. self he slew, Pol. IV-316; slain himself, M. M. 240.

Sp. seized, sence (with sorrow sore), F. Q. III-6-10;--Dr. soon each sense, seize, B. W. III-15.

Sp. shade, saw F. Q. III-7-1; scene the shadowes, F. Q. II-2-44;--Dr. see thy shadow, II. E. II, II, E-R. 151;--Dan. shadowes that we see, T. F. 311.

Sp. shaft, send, F. Q. I-11-19:--Dr. shafts, send, B. A. 97.

Sp. shame, shonne, F. Q. I-8-8:--Dr. shun not sin, (shame) B. W. III-10.

Sp. shewd herselfe, F. Q. III-9-26; shewd himselfe, F. Q. IV-1-37; shewing himselfe, F. Q. IV-4-17; shew itselfe in sunny beams, F. Q. VI-3-45; herselfe, shew'd, F. Q. V-8-23;--Dr. shew themselves, Mn. Mn. 261; shew herself, B. W. III-33; shew itself near, seat, Eclog. IX-8 (bat.); show, herself M. B. M. I-351; scarce, shewd himself upon, southern shore, Pol. VIII-226; shew herself, Pol. XXI-111; herself, show, M. E. 7058; as themselves, show'd, B. A. 74;--Dan. shew'st thyselfe C. W. IV-52; shew yourselfe a savage, II. T. 705-6.

Sp. signe did send, F. Q. III-7-5:--Dr. sign, sent Pol. IX-388.

Sp. signes he shewed, F. Q. IV-12-35; shewing forth signes, F. Q. IV-2-16; shewed signe, F. Q. VI-5-9;-- Dr. signs to show themselves M.-C. 151;--Dan. certaine signes, shew, Q. A. 103. .

Sp. cities, sacke, F. Q. III-3-34; cities sackt, F. Q. V-10-23;--Dan. ransacke the cittie, C. W. IV-6.

Sp. sonet song, S. C. XII-15;--Dan. sing me sonnets, II. T. 1400.

Sp. soules to save, F. Q. I-9-19; C. 18, (17);- Dr. sent. souls, to save. Pol. XXIV-569; sinful soul to save, Pol. XXIV-408.

Sp. stay the steppe, F. Q. I-1-13; stayed step, F. Q. V-11-3; stayed (adj.) steps, S. C. VI-38; steps to stay, F. Q. IV-10-11; on, staffe, steps to stay, F. Q. I-10-5; steps upstayd, F. Q. III-12-24; steps, stayed still, F. Q. M. VII-31;— Dr. staff, steps to stay, Pol. XII-252.

Sp. succor, send, F. Q. III-8-29; send her succour, F. Q. VI-4-10; - C. 1;—Dr. succour sends, M. M. 157; succour, send, Pol. XIX-404.

Sp. summons soules Daph. 39; Dr. soul summoning to sit, Leg. IV, Crom. 57.

Sp. assure yourselfe, F. Q. I-1-51; ib. V-11-13;—Dr. herself assure, M. M. 192; himself, assur'd, B. W. IV-10.

Sp. taske to take, F. Q. IV-9-10; taske, take, T. M. 36;—Dr. tass to undertake, Pol. VII-79; task, undertake, Eclog. IV-9; Elg. VIII-II. R. 82; task which, he undertooke, B. W. I-18;—Dan. take this taske, C. R. 34.

Sp. thrillant darts, threw, F. Q. II-4-46; throw, thrilling shricks, F. Q. I-6-6;—Dr. thrilling darts, throw, Pol. VIII-193.

Sp. thing, (that) think, F. Q. II-1-20; thoght one thing, F. Q. IV-1-27; thought it thing, F. Q. VI-2-17;- Dr. a thing he thought, Nym. 15; thought, thing, H. E. II II. E.-R. 51;—thought it for a thing B. A. 299; thought to be a, thing, Leg. III, P. G. 80.

Sp. tigers, tame II. L. 7;- Dr. tigers, tame, ----

Sp. traine, tender youth, F. Q. II-3-2;—Dr. (similar), teach, tender young, Owl. 536.

Sp. tread, trace, F. Q. VI-1-6;—Dr. (compare) tracts, tread, Pol. V-215.

Sp. tressed locks, teare, S. C. IV-12;—Dr. torn his tressed locks, Eclog. II-20;—Dan. untressed locks, torn rent haire, Cleo. 727.

Sp. waile his woes, S. C. VI-85; wail, woe, S. C. VIII-165; waile, woefull waste, of worke, S. C. XI-64; bewayle, wofull tune, S. C. XI-14; - Dr. woe bewail, B. W. VI-92.

Sp. washing, wall, F. Q. IV-11-33; wash, ground-work, of, wall, V. B. 8;—Dr. from well, wash, walls, Pol. X-124.

Sp. way, wend, S. C. IX-211; went, way, F. Q. III-10-38; went, way, F. Q. VI-5-41; way to wend, F. Q. III-10-40; wend, way, Am. 16; way, went, F. Q. VI-7-12; - C. 2 (weyt, wend,) 4, (6) (wenten, way);—Dr. wend through way, Pol. XXX-62; way, went, M. M. 66; Dan. way it went, II. T. 104.

Sp. weave, web of wicked (guyle), F. Q. II-1-8; weaves, webbes S. C. X-102:   Dr. wove, webs in, wings, Owl. 559.

Sp. weld, weapon, F. Q. II-7-40, (vs. 8 and 9); weapon, weld, F. Q. IV-3-21:   Dr. weapons, wield, D. & G. 620; B. A. 278; M. M. 133.

Sp. win his wish, H. L. 31; winne, wished rest, F. Q. IV-12-8; win, wished (victory), F. Q. III-7-33; (compare also) winneth way, F. Q. VI-12-1; waiting, to win, wished sight, F. Q. I-4-6;—Dr. wished way to win, Pol. IV-210.

Sp. worketh, way, F. Q. I-11-10;—Dr. working, way, Pol. XXX-278;—Dan. to worke a way, C. W. I-84.

Sp. workes her will, F. Q. II-1-52; workes, wilfull smart, F. Q. II-2-29;—Dr. work thy will, Leg. I, R. N. 124; work his will, Leg. II, Mat. F. 71; work their wills, B. W. III-37; work his will, Pol. XX-280·—Dan. work the world unto, will, C. W. VI-52.

Sp. worke, woe, F. Q. I-12-34; working, woe, F. Q. V-8-20;—C. 2;—Dr. work our much woes, Leg. IV-Crom. 120.

Sp. weigh, words, F. Q. VI-3-36; weigh but one word, F. Q. V-2-43;—Dr. (comapre) words whose weight, Pol. IV-267; words want weight B. W. V-65.

SPENSER AND CHAUCER.

Sp. bones, brake, F. Q. VI-7-11;—C. 2 counsell can, S. C. II-77;—C. 1 (knew counseil)) dreading death, F. Q. I-3-6; death to dread, F. Q. II-12-9;- C. 4. drunk an, draught, F. Q. IV-3-48;—C. 5 gave her gold, F. Q. I-7-46; give her gold, ib. I-3-18;—C. 1 gave, good, F. Q. II-10-69; God giveth good, S. C. V. 173;—C. 3 (8) barrow'd hell, F. Q. I-10-40;—C. 2. helmets hewen, F. Q. I-5-7; helmes did hew, F. Q. IV-2-17; hewing, helmets, F. Q. IV-1-14; hew'd their helmes, F. Q. VI-1-37;—C. 2. love as life, F. Q. I-6-17; as life, liefe, F. Q. IV-3-52;—C. 5 (6), many minstrels maken melody, F. Q. I-5-3; makes, melodie, S. C. X-78;—C. 4 (5); mention may be made, F. Q. VI-10-28; mention should make, T. M. 76;—C. 7 (12); myrth, made, S. C. XI-57; myrth in May, meetest to make, S. C. XI-11   C. 4; needeth, none F. Q. IV-10-11;—C. (needeth nought) 9 (14); slake, sorow, S. C. III-6; sorrow slaked was, F. Q. I-7-28;   C. 1 (3); sorrowes suffer, for, sake, F. Q. I-11-1; sorrowes suffered, F. Q. V-3-1;   C. 2 (4); speeches, spend, F. Q. I-10-15; speeches spent, F. Q. III-9-52; VI-5-21;   C. 4 (2); (spilte speche) stint, strife, F. Q. I-9-29; 1 nt all strife, F. Q. IV-2-18; stinted, strife, F. Q. IV-3-18; strife, stinted, M. II. T. 1092; stint of strife, F. Q. V-8-21; tell, tidings, F. Q. III-7-28; telling, tidings, F. Q. II-7-23; tydings tell, F. Q. I-1-30; ib. IV-1-16;—C. 3. (4).

Dr. counsel, keep. Leg. I. R. N. 22;— C. 3:—Dan. keepe my counsell, Phil. 210; Dan. keeps the keis, Cleo. 257;—C. 1.

Dr. giving up the ghost, Ids. 15; C. 1;—Dr. strokes, withstood, Nym. 29;—C. 1.

Words connected by other grammatical relation, such as subject and predicate, substantive and modifying prepositional phrase, frequently alliterate, but the relation is not sufficiently emphatic to create a class of formal alliteration; there is, however, another method of alliterating, so extensively employed by the three poets that it deserves notice; a word, usually as substantive, is repeated and the two words are connected by a co-ordinate connective or a preposition. This method of alliteration was also employed by Chaucer. ((See McClumpha, p. 30.)

Sp. arme in arme, F. Q. I-10-12:—Dr. arme in arme, Nym. 41.

Sp. from bed to bed, Muiop. 22; from bough to bough, S. C. III-92. from beame to beame, M. II. T. 1375; by and by, F. Q. II-6-5; ib. IV-12-25; ib. VI-7-35; M. II. T. 1092;—Dr. by and by, M. B. M. 592.

Sp. brest to brest, F. Q. V-2-12:—Dr. breast, on, breast, M. E. 5503; breast to breast Pol. XXIX-351.

Sp. brother unto brother, M. VII-14:—Dr. brother like to brother, M. M. 84.

Sp. day by day, F. Q. IV-2-13; T. M. 11; Daph. 53; from day to day, R. R. Q. 27; F. Q. IV-8-52:—Dr. day by day Eclog. VII-3; Ode XVII-2; B. W. II-50; D. & G. 305; S. S. 122; M. M. 110; from day to day, M. M. 233.

Sp. deeper and deeper, S. C. IX-133; cheeke by cheeke, F. Q. V-2-49; from coste to coste, S. C. VI-15:—Dr. from coast to coast, M. M. 39; Pol. XXVIII-126.

Sp. cuff with cuff, F. Q. I-2-17:—Dr. cuff for cuff, II. E. XXI-175.

Sp. crime to crime, F. Q. VI-6-31; each to each, M. VII-11; face to face, F. Q. VI-5-20:—Dr. face to face, Pol. XII-399.

Sp. fate for fate, V. G. 51; foot to foot, F. Q. III-1-66; foot by foot, F. Q. VI-6-28:—Dr. foot to foot, Pol. XVIII-502; Pol. XII-399.

Sp. frend with frend:—Dr. friend to friend, Pol. XIV-75.

Sp. from hand to hand, F. Q. V-11-7; hand (to joyne) in hand, F. Q. IV-10-33:—Dr. from hand to hand, Pol. XXIX-296;hand to hand, Pol.

XVIII-109; hand in hand, Pol. XVIII-504; Leg. I, R. N. 9; B. A. 176; Eclog. III-4:—Dan. hand in hand, H. T. 1837.

Sp. from hill to hill, F. Q. V-9-15; like and like, F. Q. IV-11-47; lyke with his lyke, M. H. T. 48; more and more, F. Q. III-2-39; ib. VI-5-6; S. C. III-100; ib. VIII-104; V. G. 33; Muiop. 50; Ast. 4; V. B. 7;—Dr. more and more, M. M. 236; B. W. I-16; Leg. III; P. G. 34; H. E. XVII; Mor. W. 133; Pol. XXVI-91; Q. C. 45:—Dan. more and more, C. W. IV-84.

Sp. one by one, F. Q. V-10-13; one on th' one, ib. V-9-37;—Dr. one by one, Pol. IV-242; S. S. 348;—Dan. one by one, C. W. III-31.

Sp. oft and oft, F. Q. II-2-3.

Sp. from place to place, F. Q. III-6-25; ib. V-8-36; Am. 78;—Dr. from place to place, B. W. II-28;Pol. XXI-158; D. & G. 303; M. C. 1098.

Sp. from poynt to poynt, F. Q. I-12-15:—Dr. from point to point, Leg. II, Mat. F. 67; Nym. 69.

Sp. part to part, F. Q. III-6-44; (per) ib. VI-2-6;.

Sp. from roome to roome, F. Q. VI-6-29; (rowme) M. H. T. 1375;—Dr. from room to room, Pol. XXVI-83.

Sp. from shore to shore, F. Q. III-9-41;—Dr. from shore to shore, Pol. XVI-104;Leg. II, Mat. 758.

Sp. from sea to sea, F. Q. II-10-63;—Dr. from sea to sea, Pol. XXIX-350; from sea again to sea, Pol. XVI-98.

Sp. from side to side, F. Q. V-8-41; side by side, V. B. 12; syde to syde, F. Q. III-1-66:—Dr. side to side, B. A. 196; Pol. XII-328; M. C. 175.

Sp. so and so, F. Q. IV-7-2; stroke on stroke, R. R. 13; from tree to tree, F. Q. V-9-17;—Dr. betwixt tree and tree, N. F. 324.

Sp. from time to time, F. Q. III-6-3; ib. V-5-31;—Dr. from time to time, Pol. XVI-66.

Sp. worse and worse, F. Q. II-4-61; wourse and wourse, F. Q. V-1-19;—Dr. worse and worse, Leg. III, P. G. 67; back and back, M-C. 1355; from creek to creek, Pol. XXVII-9; drop by drop H. E. XIX, M.-C. B. 152.

ALLITERATION IN SPENSER'S POETRY

DISCUSSED AND COMPARED WITH THE ALLITERATION AS
EMPLOYED BY DRAYTON AND DANIEL.

———————

A DISSERTATION PRESENTED TO THE PHILOSOPHICAL FACULTY
(I. SEET.) OF THE UNIVERSITY OF ZURICH, FOR THE
ACQUISITION OF THE DEGREE OF DOCTOR
OF PHILOSOPHY.

———————

PART II.

—BY—

VIRGINIA EVILINE SPENCER.

APPROVED BY PROF. TH. VETTER.

— — —

1898.

ALLITERATION IN SPENSER'S POETRY

Discussed and Compared with the Alliteration as
Employed by Drayton and Daniel.

A Dissertation Presented to the Philosophical Faculty
(I. Sect.) of the University of Zurich, for the
Acquisition of the Degree of Doctor
of Philosophy.

PART II.

BY

VIRGINIA EVILINE SPENCER.

APPROVED BY PROF. TH. VETTER.

1898.

(1, 2, 3, 5)   Whilst still the battle strongly doth abide, B. W. II-39.

1, 2, 1, 5)   May cure the sore, but never close the scar B. W. I-18.

(1, 3, 1, 5)   When Fame began my beauty first to blaze, Leg. II. Mat. F. 13.

formula a b b a:

(1, 2, 3, 1)   And tortures me in most extremity Ids. 20.

(1, 2, 3, 5)   A monster both in body and in mind, II. E. I R. II. 161.

(1, 2, 4, 5)   Darkness so long upon the land doth dwell, M. B. M. II-510.

(1, 3, 4, 5)   Pauses, ere it the deluge down will pour, N. F. 195.

(2, 3, 4, 5)   Did make a night of day, a day of night, II. E. VI, M. 1. 16.

Five alliterating words and rhyming letters: a a a b b:

If such a ship can such a burden bear, N. F. 530.

(a a b a b)

They dar'd to do what none should dare to name, N. F. 97.

(a a b b a)

In mossy mantles sadly seem'd to mourn, Eclog. X-1.

(a b a b a)

That many a purpose many a plot hat marrd, B. W. III-60.

Alexandrine: four alliterating words and two rhyming letters: a a b b:

(a a b b)

(1, 2, 3, 6)   Most full most fair most sweet and most dilicious source Pol. XXVI-165.

(1, 2, 4, 5)   So blyth and bonny now the lads and lasses are, Pol. XXVII-248.

(1, 2, 5, 6)   The worst that war can do on either side she showes, Pol. XXII-1153.

(1, 3, 4, 5)   The Sylvans in their song their mirthful meetings tell, Pol. II-189.

(1, 3, 4, 6)   But beaten down with bills, with pole-axes and pikes, Pol. XXII-1321.

(1, 3, 4, 6)   And nearer to the north the wandring seaman set, Pol. XIX-289.

(2, 3, 5, 6)   To trip from wood to wood, and scud from grove to grove, Pol. XXVI-116.

(a b a b).

(1, 2, 4, 6)   And oft embracing her she oft again embraces, Pol. XXVII-196.

(1,3, 4, 6) In many a bloody field in many a doubtful fight Pol.
XXVII-237.

(2, 3, 4, 5) Who with a puissant force prepared forth to set, Pol.
XXVII-1126.

(a b b a)

(1, 2, 3, 1) His hopes so faint before so happily reviv'd, Pol. XXII-
1408.

(2, 3, 1, 5) This said, the forrest rubb'd her rugged front the while,
Pol. XXX-74.

Five alliterating words and two rhyming letters: a a a b b:

(1, 2, 3, 4, 5) The bourns, the brooks, the becks; the rills the rivulets, Pol. I-78.

(1, 2, 3, 4, 5, 6) Each moor each marsh each mead, preparing rich
array, Pol. IX-53.

(a a b a b)

(2, 3, 4, 5, 6) At Barnets fatal fight, both life and fortune lost, Pol.
XXII-1274.

(a b b a a)

(1, 2, 3, 4, 6) My future strength and state; then forward I do flow.
Pol. XXIX-56.

(1, 2, 3, 5, 6) Of more abundance boasts as of those mighty mines,
Pol. XXX-249.

(1, 3, 4, 5, 6) At length attains those lands that south of Severn lie,
Pol. XIV-174.

(a a b b a)

(1, 2, 3, 4, 6) Of God's first garden plot th' imparadised ground Pol.
XXX-70.

(a a b b b)

Whose swains in shepherd's gray and girls in Lincoln green, Pol.
XXV-262.

Heroic Verse: four alliterating words:

My brow his book my bosom was his bed, Leg. III, P. G. 22.

The Moorland maiden so admired of men Eclog. XX-16.

Then since th' assay our good success assures, B. W. III-55.

Back to the tents retire and take the spoil, D. and G. 810.

Whilst we in woes the time away do wear ,Eclog. VI-42.

Who spares to speak, doth spare to speed, Ids. 59.

Alexandrine:

Amongst us evermore remembered shall remain, Pol. XI-252.

Alliteration of Non=Emphatic Words

V.

Spenser's alliteration is not, by any means, confined to the emphatic words in the sentence; the non-emphatic words, such as exclamatory words, auxiliary verbs, pronouns, and prepositions, when receiving the metrical accent frequently alliterate. But such words have no power to alliterate when they fall in the thesis. This feature of alliteration is not sufficiently important to form a distinct characteristic of style, but is considered here simply to show to what an extent alliteration was employed: verbs: did disdayne F. Q. I-1-10; did redresse F. Q. I-5-36; he upbrought, F. Q. I-9-3.

Exclamatory: but loe; my Lord, my Liege, whose warlike name F. Q. II-3-35.

Personal pronouns: At her abhorred face, so filthy and so foule F. Q. I-5-30 Theat heaped on him so many wrathful wreakes F. Q. I-12-16.

The alliteration of the personal pronoun by Drayton and Daniel is essentially the same as in Spenser, except some set combinations as thee and thine Cleo. 1011; C. W. V-62; me and mine Cleo. 1081.

Prepositions: And burning blades about their heads doe blesse F. Q. I-5-6. The wood-borne people fall before her flat F. Q. I-6-16.

In the poems of Drayton and Daniel, the alliteration of the prepositions does not differ essentially from that in Spenser's poems; examples:

Dr. which for her fatning fens, her fish, her fowl may have Pol. XXIII-113.—Dan. Before her feete too slow for her swift feare Q. A. 2099.

The close structural relation as the most usual, as: Dr. by the brim; by a fountain brim; about the brim; about the border; about my body; for the field; for their faith; for defence; for a fashion; behind the hedge; along the lawn; amongst the mountains; amidst his men; into a trance;

Dan. both by your birth; for the few; out from the fields; from affection; to the tombe; into the toyle; with our wounds.

VOWEL ALLITERATION.

Vowel alliteration occurs frequently in Spenser's poems, but with the exception of a few instances, when there are several terms in one verse, or when the terms are made prominent by position or logical relation, the form of alliteration is not employed for special emphasis, but rather helps to make up the main bulk of alliteration, and lends variety to the general alliterating tone; examples:

That he in ods of arms was conquered, F. Q. II-5-14, glistring in armes and warlike armament, F. Q. II-11-24; and wondred at his endlesse exercise F. Q. II-9-59.

For the vowel alliteration by Drayton and Daniel, there is nothing new to be added. The reciprocal phrase, each other, each the other etc., is used repeatedly by Spenser, and appears also both by Drayton and Daniel: within, without, in and out, etc are common to all three, but appears especially frequent by Drayton in his Poly-Olbion.

Alliteration of Proper Names.

VI.

The alliteration of proper nouns is employed by Spenser so extensively and under such varied relations, that it reveals a conscious use on the part of the poet, and may well be considered a distinct feature of his alliteration. A very frequent use is a substantive with modifying adjective, as: Barnaby, bright, Epith. 15; Bellodant the bold, F. Q. V-4-30; blamelesse; Britomart, F. Q. IV-5-31; boastfull Blandomour, F. Q. IV-2-13.

Proper names frequently alliterate with a dependent genitive, or with another name connected by a preposition, or by repetition, as: Colin, Colin S. C. VIII-190; Cuddie, Cuddie S. C. VIII-192; Daphnes death C. C. II. 386; Phoebus flame M. VI-39; Hobbin ah Hobbin S. C. IX-56; mother of, Marinell F. Q. IV-12-3; messenger of Morpheus, F. Q. I-1-36; Proteus, with prophecy, F. Q. III-4-25;

The names of the personified characters sometimes alliterate as:

The maister Cooke was cald Concoction;

A carefull man, and full of comely guyse.

The kitchen Clerke, that hight Digestion, F. Q. II-9-31.

The other cleped Cruelty by name, F. Q. III-12-19.

The hideous Chaos keepees, their dreadfull dwelling is, F. Q. IV-2-17.

Behind him was Reproch, Repentance, Shame;

Reproch the first, Shame next, Repent behind, F. Q. III-12 21.
Emongst them was sterne Strife; and Anger stout;
Lewd Losse of Time; and Sorrow seeming dead;
Inconstant Change, F. Q. III-12-25

Sometimes the names alliterate for themselves as:
Thereto the Blatnat Beast, by them set on, F. Q. V-12-11.
The names of places may alliterate in the same way, as:
Whereas the Bowre of Blisse was situate, F. Q. II-12-12.
Returnd to stately Pallace of Dame Pryde, F. Q. I-5-15.
In peace may passen over Lethe lake, F. Q. I-3-36.
Long fostred in the filth of Lerna lake, F. Q. I-7-17.

A proper name may alliterate with a verb as subject and predicate, as:
Boreas, blow, bitter bleake, F. Q. I-2-33; Boreas, bluster F. Q. V-11-58;
Britany, burne, (bright) F. Q. III-3-52; Britomart, beare F. Q. IV-4-16; Cupid, kindled, F. Q. III-1-39; Calidore, cry, F. Q. VI-11-29.
Or as predicate and object, as: called Cornwaile F. Q. II-10-12; chas-ing, Calepine F. Q. VI-1- 2; challenge Calidore F. Q. VI-9-13; encloseth Corke, F. Q. IV-11-14; affrighted, fairest Florimell F. Q. III-5-23; love-ly Lasse hight Lucida, C. C. II. 456.
In a few instances a proper noun alliterates with another word as sub-ject and object, as:
And stouping Phoebus steepes his face, S. C. III-116.
Through which, when Paris brought his famous prise F. Q. IV-11-19.
A proper name alliterating with a verb or adjective with which it is connected by a phrasal construction, as: brought for Braggadochio F. Q. II-8-19; Braggadochio, with bloody launce, F. Q. III-8-18; unto, Bel-gard, brought, F. Q. VI-12-3; borne in Britaine land F. Q. VI-12-39; Cupid with, killing bow F. Q. IV-10-55; cared, for Colins carolings F. Q. VI-9-35.
Proper names may alliterate in a coordinate construction, and also frequently alliterate independent of any close grammatical relation; as:
. Brutus, nor. Britons F. Q. II-10-36; Bellamour and Claribell F. Q. VI-12-13; Boyne, Ban F. Q. IV-11-11; Churne and Charwell F. Q. IV-11-25; Canacee and Cambine F. Q. IV-2-31; Camphora, and Calarnint F. Q. III-2-19; Cuddy, Colin C. C. II. 260; Chrysaor, and Caicus F. Q. IV-11-14; Cantium, Kent, F. Q. II-10-12; Cador, Cornish king F. Q. III-3-27.

Not unfrequently, does a proper name alliterate with another less important word, and independent of a close structural relation, as:

The second Brute, the second both in name, F. Q. II-10-23.

Which when Malbicco saw, out of a bush, F. Q. III-10-47.

The alliteration of proper names is usually made in accordance with the rules of accent; there are however some irregularities which deserve notice; the most frequent of these is a modifying adjective falling in the thesis, as: base Braggadochio, F. Q. III-5-27; bold Britonesse, F. Q. III-12-2; bold Britomart F. Q. III-12-29; brave Briton (Knight) F. Q. V-11-1; faire Phoebe, M. VI-21; faire Florimell F. Q. III-5-8; faire Philomele T. M. 40; great Ganges F. Q. IV-11-21; great Gloriane F. Q. V-12-3; great Godmer F. Q. II-10-11; great Gorgen F. Q. I-1-37; great Gormond F. Q. III-3-33.

Occasionally the accent does not fall upon the alliterating syllable, as:

With bright Chrysaor in his cruell hand, F. Q. V-2-18;

From that day forth Duessa was his deare F. Q. I-7-16.

A few proper names of more than two syllables alliterate with different words according to the alliterating syllable, as:

Tho when as Artigall did Arthure view F. Q. V-8-12;

How bright that Amazon, sayd Artegall F. Q. V-4-33.

but with the last syllable:

And thereat greatly grudged Artegall F. Q. IV-5-9.

All being guided by Sir Artegall F. Q. IV-6-39,

and another word:

The which this famous Britomart did beare F. Q. IV-4-46.

Then Britomart unto a bowre was brought F. Q. V-6-23;

but with the last syllable:

The whiles faire Britomart whose constant mind F. Q. III-1-19;

There all that night remained Britomart F. Q. V-6-24.

It will be seen from the above classification that proper names alliterate in all their various constructions; that this form of alliteration is employed most extensively in the Faery Queen, and is applied most frequently to the names of the characters. The alliteration of proper names in Daniel's poetry occurs only occasionally, and is not of sufficient importance to require further notice. Not so with Drayton's poetry, for here is it not only more extensively employed than in Spenser's poetry, but the most important uses are strikingly similar to the latter. The representatives of the formal alliteration of the two poets are confined to a few terms, and even then it is oftener the same term, with varied combinations, than identical expressions; of these terms Phoebus and Cynthia, Florimell and Flora are the most frequent; it is the manner of the alliteration of the two poets that is important.

As has been said Spenser alliterates most frequently the names of his characters. The number of charatcers in the Faery Queen, and the frequent recurrence of the more important ones, give ample opportunity for this method of alliteration. Florimell is one of the poets favorite names for alliterating, and some examples of its use will illustrate very well this manner of alliterating and its importance.

And is ycleped Florimell the fayre.
Faire Florimell belov'd of many Kings F. Q. III-5-8.
For that rich girdle of faire Florimell F. Q. IV-4-5.
So Florimell with Ate forth was brought F. Q. IV-4-10.
And Florimell him fowly gan revile F. Q. IV-4-11.
Shall fall the girdle of faire Florimell F. Q. IV-5-2.
Yet all were glad there Florimell to see;
Yet thought that Florimell was not so faire as shee F. Q. IV-5-14.
But Florimell exceedingly did fret, F. Q. IV-5 19.
These foure were they from who false Florimel F. Q. IV-9-20.
But chiefly of the fairest Florimell F. Q. V-2-2.
And then to him came fayrest Florimell F. Q. V-3-15.
Then forth he brought his snowy Florimele F. Q. V-3-17.

The alliteration of proper names in the Faery Queen is on the whole, very equally distributed. It fits very naturally and unobtrusively into the general alliteration as can be readily seen from the varied constructions which are not different from those of other alliterating words. But in the second book and tenth canto, where "A Chronicle of Briton Kings from Brute to Uther's rayne, and Rolls of Elfin Emperours, till the time of Gloriane," are laid open before Sir Guyon, proper names become quite a prominent feature; it is an enumeration which of itself is important, as different from the general style of the poem. The fact that it is an enumeration gives a certain artificial character to the whole, and which also marks the alliteration of the names as the following references show: F. Q. II-10-12; 10-25; 10-36; 10-40; 10-65; 10-67.

As the names of the characters in the Faery Queen alliterate, so alliterate the names of the personages, parties, and places in Drayton's descriptive and narrative poems. The Battle Agincourt, The Baron's Wars, The Heroic Epistles, The Miseries of Queen Margaret, and the Polyolbion; a marked example of the recurrence of one term, in various construction is "France (French and Frenchmen), in The Battle of Agincourt.

The name of one character would naturally not occur as frequently and throughout an entire poem as the example just cited, be that character never so important; but repetition is often sufficiently frequent to give special importance to the term and a distinct characteristic to the style; in this the poet resembles Spenser more closely than in the extreme instances, as a few examples will show:

To Lancaster deliver'd at thy death B. W. I-14.

Great Lancaster was lord of all the North, B. W. I-52

By Lancaster and valiant Hartford led B. W. II-12

When Thomas Earl of Lancaster, that late B. W. II-64

The way to death where Lancaster had led, B. W. II-66

Brave Mortimer, that ever matchless man B. W. I-19.

The Mortimers being men of greatest might B. W. I-50.

The Mortimers were masters of the West, B. W. I-52.

This she her most lov'd Mortimer bespake B. W. III-50.

O Mortimer, sweet Mortimer, quoth she B. W. III-51.

With Mortimer, that mighty malcontent B. W. IV-19.

But Mortimer commended his desire B. W. VI-61.

In the poem, Queen Margaret's Miseries, which contains 2080 lines, the name Warwick alliterates at least six times, and Margaret seventeen times. Drayton employs the alliteration of proper names very extensively and examples might be given in great abundance, but they could only confirm what has already been cited in Spenser's poems, for the manner of application is the same, but great variety in terms.

As in Spenser's poetry repetitions occur so even in a more marked degree are they employed by Drayton, as:

There Dutton Dutton kills; a Done doth kill a Done;

A Booth, a Booth; and Leigh by Leigh is overthrown;

A Venables, against a Venables doth stand;

A Troutbeck fighteth with a Troutbeck hand to hand;

There Molineux doth make a Molineux to die;

And Egerton, the strength of Egerton doth try. Pol. XXII-638-42.

The alliteration of proper names, even where most extensively employed by Spenser, is hardly of sufficient importance to admit of an estimate by percentage. In the second book and tenth canto of the Faery

Queen, the number of lines containing such alliteration do not exceed three per cent. In Drayton's Polyolbion, which contains more alliteration of proper names than any of his other poems, the percentage rises as high as eight per cent. In addition to the alliteration of the names of persons and places, the names of rivers are a prominent feature, and form a component part of the alliteration through the entire thirty songs. It is especially interesting to find just here, a direct connection between this important feature of Drayton's alliteration and a similar use in the Faery Queen. In the fourth book and eleventh canto, the poet sings the Marriage of the Medway with the Thames, to which Drayton in the eighteenth song of the Polyolbion, lines 105-8, refers as following:

And but that Medway then of Thames obtained such grace:
Except her country nympths, that none should be in place:
More rivers from each part, had instantly been there:
Than at their marriage, first, by Spenser numbered were.

In this canto where the different rivers are named, it must necessarily be done more or less in the manner of an enumeration. A few verses will illustrate the manner of alliteration, for it is not greatly varied.

The churne and Charwell, two small streames which pained F. Q. IV-11-25.
Still Ure, swift Werfe, and Oze the most of might.
High Swale, unquiet Nide, and troublous Skell F. Q. IV-11-37.
The Ouze, whom men doe Isis rightly name ib. 24.
Then was the Liffy rolling downe the lea:
The sandy Slane; the stony Aubrian.
The spacious Shenan spreading like a sea:
The pleasant Boyne; the fishy fruitfull Ban:
Swift Awniduff, which of the English man
Is calde Blackdwater: and the Liffar deep:
Sad Trowis, that once his peoples over-ran:
Strong Allo tombling from Slewlogher steep:
And Mulla mine, whose waves I whilom taught to weep. F. Q. IV-11-41.

A few examples from Drayton's poem will suffice to show the similarity of manner, which is a striking one.

Then Bradon gently brings forth Avon from her source Pol. III-188.
First Blackmoor crownss her bank, as Pensham with her pride, Pol. III-191.
Then came the lusty Froom, the first of floods that met

Fair Avon entring into fruitful Somerset,
With her attending brooks; and her to Bath doth bring Pol. III-222-24
To noble Avon, next, clear Chute as kindly came,
To Bristol her to bear, the fairest seat of Fame; Pol. III-226-27.

In giving the description of the rivers and their location Spenser sometimes alliterates the names of places and regions, as:

And Twede, the limit betwixt Logris land
And Albany; and Eden, though but small. F. Q. IV-11-36
The spreading Lee that, like an Island fayre,
Encloseth Corke with his divided flood; F. Q. IV-11-44.

This use is very frequent in Drayton's Polyolbion, as:
Where she of ancient time had parted, as a mound,
The Monumethian fields and Glamorganian ground,
Intreats the Taff along, as gray as any glass:
With whom clear Cunno comes, a lusty Cambrian lass: Pol. IV-157-61
From Brecknok forth doth break; then Dulas and Cledaugh,
By Morgany do drive her through her watry saugh; Pol. IV-167-8.

Such examples are numerous for the alliteration is not less varied
than are names of all the different rivers, places, and location of all
England. There is another style of combination in this class of alliteration, which is even more striking than what has already been noticed.
An etymological connection between the name of the river and its surroundings, sometimes joins the alliterating terms, some examples of
which have already been cited in another connection, F. Q. II-10-12;
other examples are:

And, meeting Plim, to Plimmouth thence declines, F. Q. IV-11-31.
And after came the stony shallow Lone
That to old Loncaster his name doth lend F. Q. IV-11-39.

This manner of combination by Drayton, as by Spenser, is naturally
much less frequent, than other combinations, because of its marked character; but the former employs it much oftener (comparatively speaking)
than the latter, and with as great a variety of application as the form will
admit, as the following examples show:

For Luncaster, so nam'd the fort upon the Lun.
And Lancashire the name from Lancaster begun Pol. XXX-43, 4.
For Cumberland, to which the Cumri gave the name Pol. XXIX-13
As Kellop coming in from Kellopp-Law her sire. Pol. XXIX-51.
My other North-nam'd Tyne, thro' Tyndale maketh in, Pol. XXIX-
111.

Till Rother, whence the name of Rotheram first begun Pol. XXVIII-31.

Their fountain's find in me, the Ryedale naming Rye, Pol. XXVIII-274

First Roch a dainty rill, from Roch-dale her dear dame, Pol. XXVII-19.

In Drayton's poem The Owl, where birds take the place of persons, their names alliterate in much the same way as the personages of his other poems; the names alliterate with a modifying adjective as: bald Buzzard, 860; black-ey'd Bat, 502; cruell Kite, 201; jolly Jay, 603; Peacock, proud, 947; witless Wood-cock, 942.

For other constructions a few examples will suffice, as there is nothing in the manner of alliterating different from what has already been remarked.

The Kite, the Crow, and all the birds of prey, 313.

The Lark, the Linnet, and the gentler sort, 217.

When the sweet Merle, and warbling Mavis bee, 114.

This form of alliteration is carried even further by Drayton in his poem, Noah's Flood, for there not only the names of the birds, but also of the animals which are gathered into the ark are often joined through alliteration. In The Owl the birds are the characters of the poem, and hence their names stand quite prominent. In Noah's Flood, however the relation is different, and this form of alliteration does not extend through the whole poem, but is confined almost entirely to the passages which describe the assembling of the fowls and animals into the ark, and their rejoicing, when the dove's return announces that the flood is past. Examples for the name with modifying adjective, are:

brisly boar, 275; crook-backd camel, 295; crowned cock, 387; carrion crow, 401; iron-eating ostrich, 385; skipping squirrel 323; swift-wingd swallow, 391; prating parrot, 421.

Examples for other constructions:

The hart with his dear hind, the buck the doe, 281

The clambring goat, and coney, us'd to keep, 284

The merl and mavis on the highest spray, 417.

The bull doth bellow, and the horse doth nigh,

The stag, the buck, and shag-haired goat do bray 881-2.

Verses Connected by Alliteration.

VII.

In Spenser's poetry, the general alliterating effect is greatly emphasized by carrying over the rhyming letter from verse to verse. This method is most extensively employed in The Faery Queen, and hence can be best illustrated by examples from this poem. The repetition of the rhyming letter connects and intensifies, and is often so employed, as to increase the amount of alliteration, which in estimating a percentage of verses containing alliteration can not be counted. For instance one verse may contain alliteration, a, a, and the following verse a, as:

To stay his hand, and of a truce to treat
In milder tearmes, as list them to devise F. Q. IV-9-35
and another example with different positon:

And garnisht all with gold upon the blade
In goodly wise, whereof it tooke his name F. Q. V-1-10.

The repetition may be made in connection with other alliterating letters, with the formula a a, for first line, b, a, b, for second, as:

Yet that his guilt the greater may appeare
And more my gratious mercie by this wize F. Q. V-5-18;
or for first line a, a, a; for second b, a, b, as:

Not farre away, but little wide by West
His dwelling was, to which he him addrest. F. Q. V-6-22

Several lines may be connected with one letter, as:
Else how could one with equall might with most
Against so many no lesse mightie met
Once thinke to match three such on equall cost,
Three such as able were to match a puissant host? F. Q. IV-3-21.
and with a different arrangement, according to the formula, a; a a a; a a; a, as;

Is not (I wager) Florimell at all;
But some fayre Franion, fit for such a fere,
That by misfortune in his hand did fall."
For proofe whereof he had them Florimell forth call. F. Q. V-3-22
or with the formula, a a; a a; a; a; a; a a; a

With bowed backe, by reason of the lode
And auncient heavy burden which he bore
Of that faire City, wherein make abode

So many learned impes, that shoote abrode.
And with the braunches spred all Britany,
No lesse than do her elder Sisters broode.
Joy to you Both, ye double Noursey, F. Q. IV-11-26

Such a repetition may be so combined with other letters, as to form a connecting link, so to speak, between the different alliterating words, and still be a prominent feature in the alliteration of the lines so combined, as:

And causelesse crimes continually to frame,
With which her guiltlesse persons may accuse,
And steale away the crowne of her good name;
Ne ever knight so bold, ne ever Dame
So chaste and loyall liv'd, but she would strive
With forged cause them falsely to defame:
Ne ever thing so well was doen alive,
But she with blame would blot, and of due praise deprive, F. Q. IV-8-25.

A formula for the last example shows plainly the connecting by the repetion: a a b; a; a; c d c; a e e; b a b b; c e; d d f, f.

The formulas of other instances, from the fourth book will illustrate the variety in combination, and show something of the frequency with which they occur.

F. Q. IV-3-30, (ls. 5-8) a, a; a, a; a, b b; a.— IV-3-32 (ls. 1-4), a, a, a; a, a; a, a b; b, b, a.—IV-3-33. (st.) a, b, c; c, c, d, b; d, c. c; f, f; f; f, f, f; c, c; f.—IV-4-27- (st.) a, a; b, b,a; c; c, c; a, a; d, d, d; c, d. b; b, b; c, c.—IV-4-35 (ls. 4-9) 8th excepted). a, b, b; a, c, c; c, a, d; d, d;—, d, d, d.—IV-6-8. (ls. 1-3) a, a, b; b, b; b, a.—IV-6-17 (ls. 5-9) a, a, b; b, b; b, b; c, c, b; c.—IV-8-26 (st.) a, a, b; c, b, b; d, c; d, b; d, d, d; c, c; a. e, e; e; a, c, a, c.—IV-9-8 (ls. 3-7); a, b; a, b, b; a; b, b, a; a.

The alliteration is often carried over from one stanza to another thus forming a connecting link; this is frequently done by repetition, as:

But, finding no fit seat, the lifelesse corse it left.
It left; but that same soule which therein dwelt, F. Q. IV-3-21 22.
And brought with her from thence that goodly Belt away
That goodly Belt was Cestus hight by name, F. Q. IV-5-5 6.

Other examples: IV-5-30 and 31; IV-6-14 and 15; IV-8-13 and 14; V-4-13 and 14.

In the fifth book, sixth canto, stanzas 25 and 26 are one of the most marked instances of the interweaving of alliterating in all of Spenser's poetry:

"Ye guilty eyes, (sayd she) "the which with guyle
My heart at first betrayd, will ye betray
My life now too, for which a little whyle
Ye will not watch? false watches, wellaway!
I wote when ye did watch both night and day
Unto your losse; and now needes will ye sleepe?
Now ye have made my heart to wake alway,
Now will ye sleepe? ah! wake, and rather weepe
To think of your nights want, that should yee waking keepe,"

Thus did she watch, and weare the weary night
In wayfull plaints, that none was to appease;
Now walking soft, now sitting still upright
As sundry chaunge her seemed best to ease.
Ne lesse did Talus suffer sleepe to seaze
His eye-lids sad, but watcht continually,
Lying without her dore in great disease:
Like to a Spaniell wayting carefully
Least any should betray his Lady treacherously, F. Q. V-6-25 ,d 6,
  (Formula) (25) a a; b b; c d c d; d d d d d; d d; c d e; d d; d e; d d;
d e d d; (26) d d d; d f f; d e e e; e e; c e e e; c d, c e; c d; c e b c b.

The repetiton of the rhyming letter, as in the above examples, is seldom employed by both Daniel and Drayton, and is never carried farther than two or three lines.

Repetitions in the Verse.

VIII.

Words and expressions frequently alliterate by repetition in the verse. Such repetitions are often employed by Spenser and in a great variety of combinations and constructions; the simplest method, and the one most extensively employed, is the repetition of a word or phrase in identical construction, as an adjective, a verb, or substantive; repetition of adj.:

For no, no usuall fire, no usuall rage F. Q. III-2-37.
And some had wings, and some had clawes to teare, F. Q. II-11-8.
And every Knight, and every gentle Squire, F. Q. III-1-56.
Through many a wood and many an uncouth way, F. Q. III-10-34.

REPETITION OF SUBSTANTIVE.

This hand her wonne, this hand shall her defend, F. Q. IV-2-14

He had three sonnes, all three like fathers sonnes, F. Q. V-6-33.
And that bright sword, the sword of Justice lent, F. Q. V-12-10.
And he her suppliant hands, those hands of gold,
And eke her feete, those feete of silver trye, F. Q. V-2-26.

REPETITION OF VERB.

And built Cairleill, and built Cairleon strong F. Q. II-10-25
Some fell to daunce; some fell to hazardy F. Q. III-1-57.
And sett her by to watch, and sett her by to weepe, F. Q. III-2-47

Such words are also repeated in other constructions as:
The wretched sonne of wretched mother borne, F. Q. III-1-36.
Of errant Knights, to seek her errant Knight F. Q. V-6-6.
Then she was fayre alone, when none was faire in place, F. Q. I-2-38.
Though faire as ever living wight was fayre, F. Q. I-3-2.
Another method of repetition, much more marked, and hence by far
less frequent than the above, is to connect two terms, either by alternating or coordinating the repeated terms; as:
For life must life, and blood must blood repay, F. Q. I-9-43;
Thus heaping crime on crime, and griefe on griefe, F. Q. II-4-31
Ay joyning foot to foot, and syde to syde, F. Q. III-1-66.
(Similar verse from Drayton),
Foot goes with foot, and side is join'd to side. B. A. 230.
Right now is Wrong, and Wrong that was is Right, F. Q. V-1-4 (I).
That dying lives, and living still does dye, Daphn. 62.
Drayton—
The fire seem'd to be water, water flame, B. W. VI-10.
As darkness light, and light but darkness were. B. W. VI-51.

Drayton employes this method of representing rapid motion more
frequently than Spenser, as:
And skip from bank to bank, from valley trip to valley, Pol. XIV-232.
To trip from wood to wood, and scud from grove to grove. Pol. XXVI-116.
From hill again to vale, from vale to hill it went, Pol. XXVII-253.
And skip from crag to crag, and leap from rock to rock. Pol. XXX-136

Repetitions which express amount, extent or intensity, emphatically,
as in the second example from Spenser, cited above, are employed by
Drayton, especially in his descriptions of battle; as:

Where strength still answered strength, on courage courage grew. Pol. XII-293.

Care draws on care, woe comforts woe again, H. E. XXI, H. H. L. Ger. 87.

Ensign beards ensign sword 'gainst sword doth shake, B. W. II-54
Drum brawls with drum, as rank doth rank oppose,
Friend by his friend, as foe by foe, does fall, B. W. II-54 (v. 8)

Alliterations are occasionaly made by Spenser by repetition of words in parenthetical expressions in the verse; as:

My crime, (if crime it be,) I will not reed, F. Q. II-2-37.
And verses vaine, (yet verses are not vaine), Ast. 12.
They stopt his wound, (too late to stop it was) Ast. 26.
Love is lifes end; (an end but never ending), B. I. II-8.

Spenser, in repeating, frequently combines different forms of the same word as in the last example: for such alliterations see etymological division of the classification; in this method of repetition different verb forms are most extensively used; as:

Ne which of them did winne, ne which were wonne, F. Q. IV-3-36.
Sometimes pursewing, and sometimes pursewed, F. Q. IV-6-18.

Much less frequent, are other word-forms as:

And washt away his guilt with guilty potion, F. Q. II-4-30
So huge their numbers, and so numberlesse their nation, F. Q. IV-12-1.
A messenger with letters, which his message said, F. Q. I-12-24.

Such repetitions are ocassionally made with two terms in the verse; as:

The crowned often slaine, the slayer cround. F. Q. II-7-13.
And learne to love by learning lovers paines to rew, F. Q. IV-12-13.

Percentage of Verses Containing Alliteration.

IX.

In making out the following table, all irregularities have been excluded; the purpose is to show approximately, the amount of alliteration whose variety is beyond dispute. The first number gives the per cent (of each poem respectively) of verses containing alliteration, the second number the per cent of verses that have only two rhyming letters:

17 -

SPENCER			DRAYTON			DANIEL		
F. Q								
I....	42	74	B. A.	30	95	S. D.	30	90
II....	39	83	B. W.	33	92	C. R.	24	8
III.	42	82	**Ave	32	93	Pan.	18	89
IV.	43	81	M. M.	32	93	F. D.	18	93
V.	43	88	Nym	12		Eps		
VI.	42	81	M. C.	23	91	****Av	30	89
M. VI and VII.	39	85	)**Leg	30	93	Mus.	21	90
*Ave	41	82	)***Av			Ode &	20	(95 vs
C. C. H.	44	80	Pol	39	81	Past.		
V. G.	53	85	Eleg	22	91	Des. B	27	
Eclog I	52	56	Ida.	21	87	P. S	23	
II.	57	77	Mn. Mu.	27		U. S	19	
III.	37	84	Owl	30	92			
IV.	42	80	Ods	10				
V.	40	78	Eelog I	46	80			
VI.	58	74	II.	31	90			
VII.	48	83	III.	33	90			
VIII	44	78	IV.	31	88			
IX.	43	82	V.	31	91			
X.	72	64	VI.	40	84			
XI.	60	80	VII.	33	89			
XII.	66	62	VIII	39	91			
II. L.	52	84	IX	28	43			
H. B.	46	82	X	29	80			
II. H. L.	51	84						
II. H. B.	42	88	M. E.	7	90			
V. B.	35	86	N. F.	38	90			
V. P.	42	90	M. B. M.	21	92			
V W. V.	47	82	D. G.	25	95			
Ave	44	86						
M. H. T.	36	87						
Proth	36	79						
Epith	40	87						
Am.	50	81						
Daph	43	87						
Asth	52	81						
T. M	43	83						
R. R.	36	87						
R T.	49	85						
Muiop.	33	88						
B. I	30	87						

*Average for six books. **First five and last five epistles; 1893 verses. * **Average I. III. IV. V. XIX, XX. XXII. XXIII; 4636 vs.

Accent.

X.

In studying the alliteration of Spenser's poetry in its relation to the accents of the verse, it must be borne in mind that the change which had come about in the use of this old element of Germanic poetry, had brought with it a new use, so to speak, or at least the old use was so freed from its former limitations that it became quite a new feature in poetry, and was employed with altogether a different purpose by the poet. When alliteration ceased to be a prime element in verse-structure, a development already quite marked in King Horn, (see Schipper's Englische Metrik, Bd. I, s. 196, Sec 85) it changed from a stern, formal element of rule, to an extravagant, florid adornment, to be used with a sparing or a lavish hand, by the poet, who recognized no restrictions except those enjoined by the nature of his subject and the manner of his treatment of

d. In this new relation, alliteration naturally retained its position in regard to its connections with metrical accents, for that gave it prominence. But as it was not bound, as formerly by rule, it did not long confine itself to this placing. Already by Chaucer was this freedom in the use of alliteration marked. Ten Brink, in Chaucer's Sprache und Verskunst, Sec. 341, says:

"Chaucer gehoert nicht zu den Dichtern, die Alliteration und Endreim in ihren Versen consequent verbinden. So reich seine Sprache an alliterirenden Formeln ist und so manche alliterirende Verse seiner Feder entfliessen, so ist doch von einer den Stabreim betreffenden Regel, der er sich geugt haette, Nichts zu entdecken. In Folge dessen ist es nicht leicht zu sagen, wo bei ihm die Alliteration beginnt und wo sie aufhoert." To set limitation to Spenser's Alliteration is even more than a difficult task; I regard it as altogether impossible; so the following discussion lays no claim to finality. Only those instances have been considered, where repetition, either of form, or manner of application, usually the latter, point definitely to an intentional use on the part of the poet. We have first to consider alliterating syllables which fall in the thesis. For words in the unaccented positions of the verse, the lack of emphasis may be somewhat compensated by their direct and close connection through structural relations with the accented syllables. This is distinctly shown by Spenser's extensive application of alliteration in such instances. The most frequent construction is the adjective and the noun, where the attributive adjective falling in the thesis, modifies the following substantive which receives the accent. The following classification shows something of the extent of such alliteration, but not the amount, for repetitions can not be dealt with here. (All examples from F. Q. marked simply by number of book, canto and verse).

blacke houre S. C. IX-97; black booke Am. X; blinde bard R. T. 62. old Brere S. C. II-139; borne brethren IV-1-24; brave beasts. M. H. T. 629; bright beames H. H. B. 18; (beams) Am. 7; broad Beacons I-11-14; broad braunches II-7-56; brute beasts IV-4-47; dead Dragon I-1-29; deare Daughter I-5-25; dear dred Am. 33; deepe darknesse H. L. 2; dread daunger V-5-8; dredd dartes III-3-3; dredd darknesse I-5-44; dredd Dragon, I-11-17; dull drops M. VII-31; fayre face I-5-27; faire 91. VI-2-10; fayre fields S. C. XI-188; fayre flocke S. C. VIII-118; a 11 floure S. C. IV-111; faire forest M. VI-54; faire forhead III-11-13; faire arrowes (end) V-3-40; false faytour I-4-47; false foe V-6-4; false 11-11-10; false Fortune VI- 8-34; false footman I-12-34; false

Foxe S. C. V-279; fast friendship II-2-31; fiers fate II-1-11; fell force III-5-19; fierce fight V. G. 61; fierce furie IV-3-26; fine fingers, (fowle) II-12-56; first folly V-5-48; fond favorites II-12-69; fond flies S. C. II-39; fond favours IV-2-9; fowle falshood IV-1-17; foule fiend VI-4-31; fowle force III-10-27; fowle footings (trade) T. M. 40; fraile flesh II-11-1; fresh flowrets, (defaced) S. C. II-182; good garments M. H. T. 168; good glee S. C. V-282; good gold IV-5-15; good grace IV-1-17; good gentlemen M. H. T. 525; great gardin II-7-56; great glee I-5-16; great glory II-1-19; great God II-8-10; great goddesse H. B. 3; great good I-9-2, great graces II-8-55; great grandsire M. VII-16; great gravitie, II-6-17; great griefe I-4-11; great grudge III-1-61; great guerdon II-9-6; greene gras III-10-45; hard handling H. L. 21; hard hap III-4-54; hard hart Am. 18; hard help II-1-53; hard hold S. C. V-99; high heavens (grace) V-9-12; high headland C. C. H. 249; high hilles, M. VI-39; high house I-5-19; huge heavinesse I-6-40; huge havocke VI-11-16; huge heapes I-4-21; huge hight M. VI-10; huge hills III-3-11; huge hostes III-3-12; late love Daph. 12 (st.); least lamb, Daph. 18 (st.) lewd layes H. H. L. 2; lewd life II-8-45; lewd lover III-7-20; liege Lady V-8-21; liege lord, (life) S. C. II-150; long labours I-4-1; long languour, III-2-52; long languishment Am. 60; long locks, V-6-14; lost labour (believe) R. T. 13; lost Lover's (name), III-6-29; mad man II-4-44; mad mastiffes, IV-2-17; mad moode VI-4-6; meete majestic, F. Q. V-12-25; meet modestie II-2-15; moist moores V. G. 29; myld modestie, I-8-26 poore prisoners I-10-40; poore passengers, C. C. H. 203; pure pitie Daph. 56 (st); proud port, Am. 13; red roses Epith. 13; rent robes F. Q. IV-1-21; rough rockes II-2-24; rough rynd I-2-31; rude rablement F. Q. I-12-9; rude rout V-11-44; sad semblant IV-10-49; sad shadowes III-11-55; sad sights V. W. V. 12; sad sorrowes I-6-31; sad sufferaunce Daph. 73 (st.) same season S. C. V-7; same soule IV-3-22; same song S. C.; sharpe sword V-5-13; sly skill Am. 37; slie shiftes V-6-32; soft soundings V. P. 4; sole cities (strength) R. R. 8; sole service Ast. 12; soft Silence F. Q. IV-10-51; sterne stounds M. VI-37; strong stound Daph. 80; sweete selfe II-6-44; sweete sleepe V. G. 18; sweet smyling II-12-78; sweete smile Daph. 44; sweete sympathie H. B. 30; tall trees II-12-12; true tragidies, T. M. 28; vile villany III-12-35; vile vassals M. H. T. 156; vaine votaries C. C. H. 766; waste wildernesse V. G. 17; waste wordes, I-1-42; weake wemens (hearts) I-4-26; weake wench II-6-8; weake wings H. L. 26; wide waters II-12-11; wide way II-8-11; wide wings III-11-34; wide wonders R. R. 29; wide woods V. G. 1; wide world V. G. 19;

wide wound III-1-11; wilde wood V-8-48; wylde wolves Epith. 4; wise words IV-2-2.

Such alliteration, although affecting but a small portion of the verse, retains for itself a distinct characteristic. By the aid of the logical, and the verse accent, a culminating effect in sound is produced. The unaccented adjective introduces the sound, which glides up to the accented substantive, with emphasis, increased because of such an introduction, just as in music, the emphatic tone is most effective, when preceded by an unaccented one, which is so related, that it leads up to the accented tone. That the poet was conscious of such an effect, is clearly shown by the fact, that only in a very few instances, the first word receives the metrical accent, and the substantive falls n the thesis. Such an arangement produces an entirely different effect, as the following verse shows.

A wyde way made to let forth living breath F. Q. I-9-30.

The same effect is produced by joining an adverb to a more emphatic word. Such a use, although not employed as frequently nor in such varied combinations, is not seldom. A few examples will be sufficient to illustrate the method of application.

close crouched III-1-62; close covered V-3-20; farre fled R. T. 21; fast fixed III-10- 11; fast flying III-7-37; first fed R. R. 20; forth fiercely V-11-31; forth fled Muiop. 55; foorth flowd R. T.; forth freshly Am. 62; fresh flowring V. W. V. 2; full fayne V-12-9; full faire VI-3-20; full fast VI-8-17; full fiercely V-8-4; full fit Muiop. 38; long languishing IV-10-13; long lingring III-4-60; long listning IV-7-10; more meete VI-2-18; more mindfull I-11-39; most meet Muiop. 23; much more V-9-21; still standing III-12-5; sweete slumbring V. G. 11; soft sliding V. B. 1; well weened III-8-19; well worthie C. C. H. 502.

The adverb when logically emphatic, may receive the accent and in such instances it usually follows the verb, as:

fell fast M. H. T. 1135; fled fast M. H. T. 1349; flew first IV-10-1; looke lovely Am. 13; looke lowly M. H. T. 498; stood still IV-3-20.

Very seldom indeed, does the first word of such combinations fall in the arsis; such instances are so few and the alliterating effect so obscured, that conscious use on the part of the poet seems out of the question, as one or two examples will show:

Unto the earth, and lay long while in senselesse swowne F. Q. IV-8-42. They fled farre off, where none might them surprize M. H. T. 576.

Occasionally two adjectives, which modify an unalliterating noun are bined; such combinations are not as effective, because the second tive word is less emphatic in the sentence and the thought admits of no pause until the substantive is reached, but they are distinctly alliterative as the following examples show:

And with faire fearefull humblesse towards him she came F. Q. I-3-26.

Ordained have, how can-fraile fleshly wight Muiop. 29.

The close relation between the two alliterating words is sometimes made more emphatic by joining them into a compound word, as:

dead-doing (might) Am. 1; derdoing (armes); II-7-10; fine-fingred (workman) Muiop. 33; long-lacked (flood) Am. 1; love-learned (song) Epith. 5; woe-working (Jarre) II-5-16.

The word-accent is naturally strong in such combinations. When the first part of the combination receives the word-accent, it attracts to itself the verse-accent also and the second part falls in the thesis, as:

base-borne II. L. 25; live-long (day) Epith. 11; love-lads S. C. V-2; selfe-same (price) II. II. L. 25; tell-tale (sunne) B. I. II-3.

Such alliteration is most emphatic, for itself, when standing alone in the verse, but it is very frequently joined with other alliterating terms whch are more prominent and then its individual characteristic is lost in the whole; yet what is lost for itself is gained for the general alliterating effect. In such service it is not less important, for by such use, Spenser deepens and intensifies the effect of the regular alliteration throughout all of his poems. Its importance may be clearly seen by the following examples:

fayre Framion fit for such a fire V-3-22; fast flying through this forest from her fo' III-5-6; from that first flaw defended V-5-6; but with fierce fury and with force infest. VI-4-5; fled fast away afeard VI-8-31; fraile fancy fed with full delight Am. 72; full fast she fled I-3-12; fresh flowring fields I-4-37; full faint and feeble IV-3-28.

There may occur two such combinations in the same verse as:

And with fine fingers cropt full feateously Proth. 2.

The alliterating adjective sometimes falls in the thesis even when the structural relations are not so close. This occurs often when a second non-alliterating adjective is placed between the alliterating adjective and the noun, as:

brode snowy breasts IV-11-51; bright shining brides M. H. T. 176; brave warlike brood R. R. 31; faire blushing face V-3-23; faire goodly fields C. C. II. 216; long loose yellow locks. Epith. 9.

The alliterating portion of a compound modifier may fall in the thesis as: new-budded beard S. C. V-211; cole-black blood I-1-24; bright-shining baudricke V-1-11; fire-spitting forge, II-7-3; fire at her faire-burning eyes II-27; light-foote Fairies T. M. 6; gore-bloudy gere VI-12-28;

hart-swelling hate Muiop. 1; hart-burning Hate II-7-22; lamp-burning light II-9-7; life-giving light C. C. II. 861; light-giving lampe Epith. 2; long-wished light I-12-21; olde-said sawe S. C. VII-98.

In combinations where the grammatical or logical connection is very close for the whole expression, the adjective may fall in the thesis and still alliterate with a word which it does not modify. Such expressions are most usually connected by co-ordinates or prepositons; as: that base service of her band V-4-32; bountie and brave mynd C. C. II. 496; due thankes and dutifull respect VI-1-45; faintnesse and foule cowardize VI-6-35; faithfull service of faire Cynthia C. C. II. 381; Gods that gave good ease M. VI-28; goddesse of great powre V-7-3.

An adjective which falls in the thesis frequently alliterates with a verb when connected with it in a subject, object, or qualifying phrase, as: base love hath blynded V-5-40; from all brave knights be banisht, V-3-38; fayre light defaced T. M. 45; fayre bosome, fraught Am. 76; faynes to weave false tales V-12-36; fed, with the faire sight VI-2-39; follow that faire Mayd, VI-10-1; grudging his good house, II-9-39, dissemble her sad thoughts V-5-44; sing my loves sweet praise Am. 80; thundred his thicke blowes V-12-17.

The verb may sometimes fall in the thesis when closely joined in construction to the words with which it alliterates, as: brought forth on beare R. T. 28; feare not her force R. R. 12; hold up thy heavie head S. C. X-1; at last laid forth T. M. 27; left all alone VI-9-16; left to his losse M. H. T. 311; let in a little thought Epith. 13; made of the mettall most desired R. T. 59; puffed up with pryde and vaine pleasaunce S. C. II-222; sent for his sake R. T. 56; sowne in the sacred sand R. R. 10.

In compound words the non alliterating portion may receive the accent without destroying the alliterating effect as: in his bras-plated body to embosse I-11-20; strife and debate bloodshed and bitternesse II-7-12; bleding out his hart-blood neare III-5-32; brother by birth-right M. VI-37; chaffred chayres in which churchmen were set M. H. T. 1159; follow out those false footsteps V-9-6; to heaven the high-way S. C. IX-90; like a mil-wheele in midst of miserie Daph. 62; day-spring he espyde III-10-52; the greene-wood long did walke and wander wide III-10-36.

Compound words and words of more than one syllable may alliterate to different words according as the accent falls upon the different syllables; as:

Of that displeasure, broke his bag-pipe quite VI-10-18.
How can bag-pype or joynts be well apayde S. C. VIII-6
So up he rose, and forth streightway in did pass VI-5-36.

Other exaples in which, through the influence of the metrical accent, a syllable alliterates contrary to the word accent, are: A comley knight all arm'd in complete wize III-2-21; Fraunce a forlorne Dame II-10-23; infinite shapes of creatures men doe fynd III-6-8.   Yet thought it was not love, but some melancholy III-2-27; with bitter rayling and foule revilement F. Q. II-4-12.

On the other hand, the word accents sometimes enables a syllable to retain its power of alliterating, although the metrical accent falls upon another syllable, as: Another gay girland Epith. 3; feare of all falshedd V. G. 31; lust and loose living II-5-28; telling sad tidings II-7-23; with torment and turmoyle Am. 11.

Such conflict of accent is frequent, especially with present participal as: And with her breast breaking the fomy wave II-2-21; dropping like honney dew II-5-33; in that wide lake looking for plenteous praise R. T. 22; piteous beast pleading her plaintive cause V-4-40; and lawlesnes reigning with riotize M. H. T. 1310.   It does occur, although seldom, with the past participle, as: And perfectly practized in womans craft IV-2-10; His locks, faded leaves fallen to ground III-5-29.

In a few intsances when the words are closely joined in construction, the alliterating effect is not lost, although one syllable is placed quite independent of word and metrical accent; as: melodious measures F. M. 93; most magnificke V-9-22; what more miraculous thing may be told, Am. 30; pavilion be pight V-7-26; paynted and purloynd III-12-14; prostrated on the plaine V-12-23; penurious paine V-5-46.

A word may occupy an accented and an unaccented position in the same line.   In such cases, whether the word adds to the alliteration or not, depends upon its position and surroundings.   When the two words are widely separated and have no other alliterating words near, they themselves are non-alliterating, as:

And car'st for one that for himselfe cares nought, Daph. 11

When I doe praise her say I doe but flatter Am. 84; but when placed in alliterating surroundings ,they add to the effect of the line as a whole in something of the same manner as the examples already considered, as:

Most wise most holy most almightie spright H. H. L. 6.

When single much much more when mixt. B. I. II-2

Mine ah! not mine amisse I mine did say Daph. 34.

A word of more than one syllable may receive the accent upon different syllables and still be alliterating, as:

Both wise and hardie (too hardie alas) Ast. 12

And cryde, "Mercie, Sir Knight, and mercie Lord." F. Q. II-1-27.

The verse very frequently begins with an alliterating word. Such placing is usually made with special reference to emphasis, and such prominence is thereby given to the word that it not unfrequently attracts the metrical accent, either partially or wholly to itself, and even when that is not the case, it hardly ever falls in so obscurely as to lose its part in the alliteration. One of the mose emphatic placings is where the alliterating words begin and close half of the verse independent of the other half; such instances are frequent and usually occur in the first half of the verse; as:

Badde is the best; (this English is flat), S. C. IX-105.
Cattle to keep, or ground to oversee M. H. T. 283.
Dark is my day, whyles her fayre light I mis, Am. 88.
Fast in their foldes he did them lock S. C. IX-205.
Good is no good, but if it be spent S. C. V-72.
Light of thy lampe; which, shining in thy face H. B. 9.
"Name have I none," (quoth she) "nor any being" R. T. 5.
Wide is the world I wote, and everie streete M. H. T. 90.

Occasionally such dividing-off of the half-verse is applied to both parts of the verse, as:

Grewe in this gardin, fetcht from farre away Muiop. 26.

A similar placing and with similar effect is where the alliterating words begin and close the verse, as:

Bearing a trusse of trifles at his backe T. C. V-2-39.
Rude ditties, tund to shepheardes Oaten reede S. C. XII-14.
Tolde of a strange adventure that betided M. H. T. 37.
Drudge in the world, and for their living droyle M. H. T. 157.

In imperative and exhortative expressions, the verse frequently begins with an alliterating word, as:

Bid me, O bid me quicklie come to thee R. T. 44 (v. 6).
Crowne ye god Bachus with a coronall Epith. 14.
Feede ye henceforth on bitter Astrofell, Daph. 50.
Let never Ladie to his love assent, F. Q. IV-5-18.

On account of the emphatic nature of such placing, verb-forms are most frequently employed; the present participle is a special favorite for ch arangements. There is necessarily but little variety in the alliterating effect; as:

Blasting his splendient face and all his beauty swarted B. I. VI-9.
Cooling againe his former kindled heat R. R. 11.
Feeding the Ct of him forward to die R. T. 81.
Swimming, the whilome seemed to have been R. T. 82.

Rolling in rymes of shamelesse ribandrie T. M. 36.

Tossing huge tempests through the troubled sky. R. R. 16.

Other verb forms: bent hollow beetle browes, 11-9-52; basted with bonds V-5-3; beare off the burden V-5-16; carried in clouds. M. H. T. 540; clothed with cold S. C. 11-79; drew out a deadly bow F. Q. III-1-61; graunt him your grace IV-6-32; looke up at last V-5-36. powdered with pearle IV-10-31; seemed she saw S. C. V-211.

An alliterating adjective or adverb is often placed at the beginning of a verse, as:

Fearlesse and free a faire young lionesse Daph. 16.

Safe then, and safest were my sillie sheepe, Dap. 20.

Long though it be at last I see it gloome, Epith. 16.

Rudely thou wrongest my deare harts desire. Am. 5.

Wildly to wander in the worlds eye M. H. T. 185.

In a few instances an alliterating substantive is placed at the beginning of a verse, as:

Reason with sudden rage did overgoe Muiop. 17;

Shepheards kept sheep, was not like mourning seen Ast. 35.

Position of Alliterating Words in the Verse.

XI.

VERSES OF TWO ACCENTS

Verses of two acents are employed by Spenser only in the Shepherd's Calender, and in but two poems, April and November. In the first it occurs as the second, fourth, seventh and eighth verses in the song of Fair Elisa, which is composed of thirteen stanzas of nine verses each. In November the death of Dido is lamented in a song of fifteen stanzas, and each stanza contains ten verses. The stanza closes with a refrain of three verses, of which the first and last have two accents; the seventh and eighth lines of stanza seven, and the seventh line of stanza eleven in the song for April have three accents, so there are but seventy-nine verses of two acents, in all of Spenser's poetry. In the song for November of the Calender, the first verse of the refrain varies only from "O heavie herse," to "O happie herse." The closng verse of the refrain does not alliterate. In April, eleven of the forty-nine verses alliterate. The following examples illustrate the different constructions and combinations of the alliterating words:

In princely plight S. C. IV-2; like Phoebe fayre 1; The pritie Paunce 12; In royall aray 13; Doe bathe your brest 1.

VERSES WITH THREE ACCENTS.

This verse form is employed more extensively than the preceding one, but it is never used except in combination with other forms. It occurs in Prothalamion and Epithalamion and in the third, seventh and eighth songs of the Shepherds Calender. It affords but little opportunity for variation in the combining and placing of the alliterating words; a few examples will suffice to illustrate the variations in constructions and combinations:

Two alliterating words:

(1 and 2)   To feede their flockes at will S. C. VII-66.

(1 and 2)   The trode is not so tickle S. C. VII-14.

(2 and 3)   I heard a busie bustling S. C. III-68.

(1, 2, 3)   Simple as simple sheepe S. C. VII-130.

VERSES WITH FOUR ACCENTS:

The verse of four accents in combination with the verse of three accents is employed in the third and seventh song of the Shepherds Calender. It occurs also in connection with other forms in some stanza formations, and in the second and fifth songs of the Shepherds Calendar, it is used independent of other forms. Although it allows greater variation in alliteration than the verse of three accents, yet the limits are so soon reached that repetition is necessary. But this lack of variety caused by the verse structure is somewhat compensated by a greater freedom in the use of unaccented syllables, than is permissable in the heroic verse. Allitteration varies from two to four words in a verse, from the least to the greatest number possible, and it is applied in all the different constructions and combinations which the form will permit.

VERSES WITH TWO ALLITERATING WORDS.

(1 and 2)   Youngthes folke now flocken in every where S. C. V-9.

(1 and 3)   Your carefull heards with cold bene annoyed S. C. II-18.

(1 and 4)   There grewe an aged tree on the greene S. C. II-103.

(2 and 3)   Now thyselfe hath lost both lopp and topp S. C. II-57.

(2 and 4)   To gather May buskets and smelling brire S. C. V-10.

(3 and 4)   Must not the worlde wend in his common course S. C. II-11.

VERSES WITH ALLITERATING WORDS.

(1, 2, 3)   Whose witte is weakenesse, whose wage is death S. C. II-88.
(1, 2, 4)   What fallen the flocke so they han the fleece S. C. V-49.
(1, 3, 4)   "Kiddie, (quoth she) thou kenst the great care S. C. V-215.
(2, 3, 4)   For if he mislive in lewdnesse and lust S. C. V-87.

VERSE WITH FOUR ALLITERATING WORDS.

His harmefull hatchet he bent in hand, S. C. II-195.
Verses with four alliterating words and two rhyming letters: Formula a a b b:
I wone her with a girdle of gelt, S. C. II-65.
Formula a b b a:
Bearing a trusse of trifles at hi sbacke S. C. V-239.

HEROIC VERSE, WITH TWO ALLITERATING WORDS.

(1 and 2)   Breedes dreadful doubts; oft fire is without smoke. F. Q. I-1-12.
(1 and 3)   Deformed monsters, fowle and blacke as inke. F. Q. I-1-22.
(1 and 4)   The deare remembrance of his dying Lord F. Q. I-1-2.
(1 and 5)   And dead, as living, ever him ador'd, F. Q. I-1-2.
(2 and 3)   The cruel markes of many a bloody fielde, F. Q. I-1-1.
(2 and 4)   Upon his foe, and his new force to learne, F. Q. I-1-3.
(2 and 5)   Upon his shield the like was also scor'd, F. Q. I-1-2.
(3 and 4)   All suddenly about his body wound, F. Q. I-1-18.
(3 and 5)   A gentle knight was pricking on the plaine F Q. I-1-1.
(4 and 5)   Who, nought aghast, his mightie hand enhannst F. Q. I-1-17.
Verses containing three alliterating words:
(1, 2 and 3)   And like to lead the labyrinth about F. Q. I-1-11.
(1, 2 and 4)   Her father fierce of treason false accused, F. Q. I-5-37.
(1, 2 and 5)   His forces faile, ne can no longer fight F. Q. I-1-22.
(1, 3 and 5)   A litle glooming light, much like a shade F. Q. I-1-11.
(1, 3 and 5)   Much daunted with that dint her sence was dazd F. Q. I-1-18.
(1, 4 and 5)   Unweeting of the perillous wandring wayes F. Q. I-5-18.
(2, 3 and 4)   Till that infernall feend with foule uprore, F. Q. I-1-5.
(2, 3 and 5)   And on his brest a bloodie crosse he bore, F. Q. I-1-2.

(3, 4 and 5) But of his cheere did seem too solemne sad F. Q. I-1-2.

Verses containing four alliterating words:

(1, 2, 3 and 4) Greeting his grave: his grudging ghost did strive F. Q. I-2-19.

(1, 2, 3 and 5) And burning blades about their heades do blesse F. Q. I-5-6.

(1, 2, 4 and 5) But fame now flies, that of a forreine foe F. Q. III-5-9.

(1, 3, 4 and 5) Where Boreas doth blow full bitter bleake F. Q. I-2-33.

(2, 3, 4 and 5) In which my Lord, my Liege, doth lucklesse ly F. Q. I-8-2.

Verses containing five alliterating words:

No foote to foe: the flashing fier flies F. Q. I-2-17.

By traynes into new troubles to have toste F. Q. I-3-24.

Verses containing four alliterating words with two rhyming letters, formula, a a b b:

(1, 2 and 3, 4) He was, to weete, a stout and sturdy thiefe F. Q. I-3-17.

(1, 2 and 3, 5) Thy soone consent: so forth with her they fare F. Q. II-2-33.

(1, 2 and 4, 5) Who well it wards, and quyteth cuff with cuff F. Q. I-2-17.

(1, 3 and 4, 5) No measure in her mood, no rule of right F. Q. II-2-36.

(2, 3 and 4, 5) And with fresh clay did close the wooden wound F. Q. I-2-44.

Formula, a b a b:

(1, 2 and 3, 4) And foorth they passe, with pleasure forward led, F. Q. I-1-8.

(1, 2 and 3, 5) Now like a foxe, now like a dragon fell, F. Q. I-2-10.

(1, 2 and 3, 5) And doubled strokes, like dreaded thunders threat, F. Q. I-5-7.

Formula, a b b a:

(1, 2, 3, 4) The rolling billowes beate the ragged shore, F. Q. I-11-21.

(1, 2, 3, 5) Then forth I went his woefull corse to find F. Q. I-2-24.

(1, 2, 3, 5) Hurles forth his thundring dart with deadly food, F. Q.

(2, 3, 4, 5) And to augment her painefull penaunce more. F. Q. 1-3-14.

Verses containing five alliterating words with two rhyming letters; formula, a a b b b:

Both stricken stryke, and beaten both doe beat. F. Q. 1-5-7.

Speed thee to spred abroad thy beames bright F. Q. III-4-60.

Formula, a b a b b:

And trembling Feare still to and fro did fly, F. Q. II-17-22.

Or thrild with point of thorough-piercing paine. F. Q. II-1-38.

Formula a b b a a:

A song of bale and bitter sorrow sings F. Q. II-7-23.

Formula a a a b b:

And robd of roiall robes and purple pall F. Q. 1-8-16.

Position of alliterating words in verses of six accents:

(1 and 2) And right and wrong ylike in equall ballaunce waide F. Q. 1-4-27.

(1 and 3) He led a wretched life, unto himself unknowne F. Q. 1-1-28.

(1 and 5) And him encombred sore, but could not hurt at all F. Q. 1-1-22.

(1 and 6) The red bloud trickling staind the way as he did ride F. Q. 1-2-14.

(2 and 3) In drowsie fit he findes; of nothing he takes keepe F. Q. 1-1-40.

(2 and 4) And ever false Duessa seemde as faire as shee F. Q. 1-2-37.

(2 and 5) His fair enchaunted steed and eke his charmed launce F. Q. 1-3-25.

(3 and 4) And match his brother proud in battailius aray F. Q. II-8-22.

(3 and 6) And in her many troubles did most pleasure take F. Q. 1-2-9.

(4 and 5) So left her, where she now is turnd to treen mould F. Q. 1-2-39.

(4 and 6) The carver Holme; the Maple sceldom inward sound. F. Q. 1-1-9.

(5 and 6) And with that sudden horror could no member move. F. Q. 1-2-31.

Three alliterating words:

(1, 2 and 3) But she, or such as she, that is so chaste a wight, F. Q. III-7-52.

(1, 2 and 1) That hardest heart would bleede to hear their piteous mone, F. Q. I-8-36.

(1, 2 and 5) He left him lying so, ne would no longer stay, F. Q. I-3-39.

(1, 2 and 6) Their backward bent knees teach her humbly to obey F. Q. I-6-11.

(1, 3 and 1) Consum'd but did himselfe to safety retyre, F. Q. III-9-10.

(1, 3 and 5) The groveling fell, all gored in his gushing wound, F. Q. II-8-32.

(1, 3 and 6) Old loves, and warres for ladies doen by many a Lord, F. Q. I-5-3.

(1, 4 and 5) With fire not made to burne but fayrely for to shyne, F. Q. I-4-9.

(1, 4 and 6) And doth transfixe the soule with deathes eternall dart F. Q. III-10-59.

(1, 5, 6) And fiercely each assayling gan afresh to fight F. Q. IV-3-35.

(2, 3, 4) Yet wist her life at last must lincke in that same knot, F. Q. III-2-23.

(2, 3, 5) The yron walles to ward their blowes are weak and fraile. F. Q. I-5-6.

(2, 3, 6) Do kisse her feete, and fawn on her with count'nance fayne F. Q. I-6-12.

(2, 4, 5) He cast about it, and searcht his baleful bokes againe, F. Q. I-2-2.

(2, 4, 6) But ready passage to her pleasure did prepaire M. VI-7.

(2, 5, 6) She did it fayre dispred and let it florish fayre F. Q. III-5-51.

(3, 4, 5) Them on her bulwarke beares and bids them nought availe F. Q. II-8-35.

(3, 5, 6) And by her, in a line, a milke-white lambe she lad F. Q. I 1-4.

(4, 5, 6) My last left comfort is my woes to weepe and waile F. Q. I-7-39.

Verses with four alliterating words:

(1, 2, 3, 4) In westerne waves his weary wagon did recure F. Q. I-1-1.

(1, 2, 3, 5) Was fledd afore, affraid of him as feend of hell F. Q. III-1-17.

(1, 2, 3, 6)   Yet were her words but wynd, and all her tears but water F. Q. VI-6-12.

(1, 2, 4, 5)   And much admyr'd the Beast, but more admyr'd the Knight F. Q. VI-12-37.

(1, 2, 4, 6)   Himselfe to save; but he there slew him at the skreene F. Q. V-10-37.

(1, 2, 5, 6)   Dying each day with inward wounds of dolours dart F. Q. III-12-16.

(1, 3, 5, 6)   Or made them both one masse withouten more remorse F. Q. V-8-32.

(1, 4, 5, 6)   Whose bridle rung with golden bels and bosses brave F. Q. I-2-13.

(2, 3, 4, 5)   And twixt them both was born the bloudy bold Sansloy F. Q. I-2-25.

(2, 4, 5, 6)   A thousand feares that love-sicke fancies faine to fynde F. Q. V-6-3.

(3, 4, 5, 6)   And by his side his hunters horne he hanging had F. Q. VI-2-5.

Verse with five alliterating words:

(1, 2, 3, 4, 5)   And mov'd amisse with massy mucks unmeet regard F. Q. III-10-31.

Verse with six alliterating words:

The feeble flocks in field refuse their former food. S. C. XI-133.

Verses with four alliterating words and two rhyming:

letters: formula a a b b:

(1, 2, 3, 4)   Doe backe rebutte, and ech to other yealdeth land, F. Q. I-2-15.

(1, 2, 3, 5)   But after all his warre to rest his wearie knife. F. Q. III-4-24.

(1, 2, 3, 6)   That fayrest Florimell was present there in place. F. Q. IV-2-22.

(1, 2, 4, 6)   And hewen helmets deepe shew marks of eithers might, F. Q. I-5-7.

(1, 2, 5, 6)   For both to be and seeme to him was labor lich F. Q. III-7-29.

(1, 3, 4, 5)   The hidden powre of herbes, and might of Magick spel. F. Q. I-2-10.

(1, 4, 5, 6)   Till, scorned of God and man, a shamefull death he dide, F. Q. I-5-48.

(2, 3, 4, 5) He brusheth oft, and oft doth mar their murmurings F. Q. I-1-23.

(2, 3, 4, 6) In shape and life more like a monster then a man F. Q. I-1-22.

(3, 4, 5, 6) For though they bodies seem, yet substance from them fades F. Q. II-9-15.

Formula a b a b:

(1, 2, 3, 4) Chaunged thy lively cheare, and living made thee dead, F. Q. III-2-30.

(1, 2, 3, 6) Chaufing and foming choler each against his fo, F. Q. IV-1-29.

(1, 2, 4, 5) Ne evil thing she feard ne evill thing she ment, F. Q. III-1-19.

(1, 2, 5, 6) Was ment to her that never evill ment in hart, F. Q. V-6-31.

(1, 3, 4, 5) For life she him envyde, and long'd revenge to see, F. Q. III-12-34.

(1, 3, 5, 6) How many of their friends were slaine, how many fone, F. Q. VI-11-20.

(2, 3, 4, 5) He took his leave of her, there left in heavinesse F. Q. V-12-27.

(2, 3, 5, 6) He hath his shield redeemd; and forth his swerd he drawes, F. Q. I-3-41.

(2, 4, 5, 6) Along the fomy waves driving his finny drove, F. Q. III-8-29.

Formula a b b a:

(1, 2, 3, 4) And ever more and more her owne affliction wrought, F. Q. VI-5-6.

(1, 3, 5, 6) She seem'd to passe. So forged things do fairest shew, F. Q. IV-5-15.

(2, 4, 5, 6) Of secrete foes that him shall make in mischiefe fall, F. Q. III-3-28.

(3, 4, 5, 6) Gay girlonds from the sun their forheads fayr to shade, F. Q. III-1-29.

Verses with five alliterating words and two rhyming letters: Formula a a b b b:

(1, 2, 3, 4, 6) At her abhorred face, so filthy and so fowle, F. Q. I-5-30

(2, 3, 4, 5, 6) The wasted had much way, and measured many miles, F. Q. II-9-9.

(2, 3, 1, 5, 6) And yet was loth to let her purpose plaine appeare, F.Q. III-3-17.

formula, a b a b b:

(1, 2, 3, 4, 5) She wandred many a wood, and measurd many a vale F. Q. I-7-28.

formula, a b b a b:

(1, 3, 4, 5, 6) Who flying still did ward, and warding fly away F. Q. VI-6-28.

formula, a b b b a:

(1, 2, 3, 5, 6) And knighthood fowle defaced by a faithlesse Knight F. Q. III-9-1.

formula, a b b a a:

(2, 3, 4, 5, 6) Nought but her lovely face she for his looking left F. Q. II-12-67.

formula, a b a b a:

(1, 2, 4, 5, 6) And Idoles serves: so let his Idols serve the Elfe! F. Q. V-8-19.

formula, a a b a b:

(1, 2, 3, 5, 6) When she herselfe did bathe, that he might secret bee M. VI-43.

(1, 3, 4, 5, 6) Which from a sacred fountaine welled forth alway F. Q. I-1-34.

formula, a a a b b:

(1, 2, 3, 5, 6) Then gins her grieved ghost thus to lament and mourne F. Q. I-7-21.

(1, 2, 3, 4, 6) That her enhaunced hand she downe can soft withdraw F. Q. IV-6-26.

(1, 2, 4, 5, 6) But soone he shall be fownd, and shortly doen be dedd F. Q. III-10-32.

(1, 3, 4, 5, 6) Well warned to beware with whom he dar'd to dallie F. Q. IV-1-36.

Verses with six alliterating words and two rhyming letters; formula a a a b b b:

From Limbo lake him late escaped sure would say F. Q. III-10-54.

formula a b b a b b:

And eke too loose of life, and eke of love too light F. Q. IV-8-19.

Verses with six alliterating words and three rhyming letters:

formula, a b c a b c:

Yet every one her likte, and every one her lov'd F. Q. III-9-24.

And whether he did woo, or whether he were woo'd F. Q. V-6-15.

Drayton Compared With Spenser.

When the number of alliterating words of a verse does not exceed three, the great variety of positions, and the limited variety of combinations possible, would hardly reveal, in the works of any two poets, features sufficiently marked as to show their relation to each other; but when the number exceeds three, the manner of placing and combining becomes so distinctly characteristic, that it can well be taken as a basis for comparison. The examples given above, show that Spenser employed four and five alliterating words, both in the heroic verse and in the long line; that a favorite method was to combine two rhyming letters, and that he frequently employed even three. There is a striking similarity in the manner in which Drayton makes the same combinations. With him as with Spenser, when there are four alliterating words, two rhyming letters are most frequently employed, and the favorite method of grouping is the parallel one (a a b b); the other combinations, a b a b, and a b b a, appear frequently. When there are five alliterating words, he usually employs two rhyming letters, with the same grouping as given above. He also occasionally employs three rhyming letters. Four alliterating words with one rhyming letter, are not unfrequent, although much more seldom used, than with two rhyming letters. Five alliterating words with one rhyming letter are, as with Spenser not frequent and it is rather a strange coincidence, that of the few instances of such alliteration two have the same rhyming letter (f) as similar instances with Spenser. Drayton employs five alliterating words with two rhyming letters more extensively than Spenser; this is especially true in his poem, Polyolbion, and is no doubt due to the verse-form which affords opportunity for such grouping, without monotony. The following examples show plainly the similarity of the method of the two poets.

Four alliterating words with two rhyming letters; heroic verse: formula a a b b:

(1, 2, 3, 4) To make his midday great and glorious thus B. W. 1-17.

(1, 2, 3, 5) Those follow Fame whose weeds are nearly worn Leg. 1. R. N. 24.

(1, 2, 4, 5) Roving at random with his feather'd flight Eclog. VII-13.

(2, 3, 4, 5) As through the pores its passage fitly finds M. B. M. 11-395.

(1, 3, 4, 5) He feels the crown even from his temples torn M. M. 173.
formula a a b b:

(1, 2, 3, 4) A thousand bills, a thousand bows among, B. A. 214.

When many men were maim'd and many slain outright. Pol. XXII 539.

Who Seymoree sent by land, and Dudley sent by sea. Pol. XXIX 233.

Till victuals waxed weak and winter waxed strong, Pol. XXIX-232.

Five alliterating words; heroic:

Friend by his friend, as foe by foe, doth fall. B. W. II-54.

Down from his full hand flung that forceful fire, M. B. M. III-383.

Alexandrine; six alliterating words and two letters: a b b a b a:

His father's kingly court was for a crosier fled Pol. XXIII-650.

Six alliterating words and three rhyming letters: a a b c c b:

Some less but lively rills with waters waxing rank. Pol. XXVIII-384.

Wave woundeth wave again and billow, billow gores. Pol. II-157.

(a a b b c c)

And from this fall the Can still keeping in our eye. Pol. XXX-38.

Distribution of Alliteration.

XII.

The amount of the alliteration of Spenser's different poems does not vary greatly, with the exception of two or three of the songs in the Shepherd's Calendar, so it is not the amount, but rather the distribution or grouping of the alliteration which show distinct characteristics for at least some of the different poems, such as Colin Clout, Mother Hubberd's Tale, The Hymnes, and The Faery Queen. The effect of the alliteration is varied, according to whether the alliterating verses occur with more or less regularity, or whether they are gathered into distinct groups, of which each group forms its own little picture, separated from the others by verses which contain no alliteration; and also according to the number of alliterating words in several successive verses. Spenser's general tendency is to group the alliteration, but as his poetry is seldom entirely without alliteration, a certain regularity of recurring sound is sustained in a kind of undertone, so to speak, even where the grouping is most marked, as it is in The Faery Queen. Colin Clout is comparatively free from such grouping. Each verse seems to alliterate for itself, or when directly conected with other verses, to fit into the whole as a coordinate factor; for example, see vs. 126-137.

Regularity is sustained not only where alliteration occurs frequently as in the above passage, but also where there are comparatively few al-

li-erating verses; in this poem we find longer pasages with fewer alliterating verses, than in any other poem of Spenser:(see vs. 185-524). This
passage is important because it shows a distinct characteristic of the one
poem, and also furnishes an example in which a minimum of alliteration
for Spenser is given.

In the Hymnes there is something of the same regularity in the distribution of the alliteration as in Colin Clout; but the proportion of the
alliterating verses is greater, and the number of alliterating words for the
verse, on the whole, greater, so that the poems contain a great deal of
alliteration but have, at the same time, a certain stateliness well b fit-ing
Hymnes.

In Mother Hubbards Tale, there is a greater tendency to grouping
than in the two poems just discussed; the grouping effect does not
depend so much on the number of rhyming letters, as it does upon the
separation, through non-alliterating verses, from the preceding and following, and a completion of the thought, to a certain etxent, which lends
an individual and distinct character to the passage; the following is one
of the most marked passoges in Mother Hubbards Tale, where such an
arrangement is employed: (The two preceeding verses contain no alliteration):

He fed his cubs with fat of all the soyle,
And with the sweete of others sweating toyle;
He crammed them with crumbs of Benefices,
And fild their mouthes with meedes of malefices:
He cloathed them with all colours save white,
And loded them with Lordships and with might,
So much as they were able well to beare, (1151-57).

But it is in the Faery Queen that we find the grouping most extensively employed. There are very few stanzas that contain no alliteration; examples, see F. Q. II-10-53; IV-1-12. With such a constant flow
of alliteration there is naturally a certain regularity in the recurring
sounds, forming as it were, the main tide that sweeps along with the
rythm of the poem, but it is the groupings that mark the ebb and flow.

The knight of the Red Crosse, when him he spide, 1.
Spurring so hote with rage dispiteous, 2.
Gan fairely couch his speare, and towards ride; 1.
Soone meete they both, both fell and furious, 2.
That, daunted with their force hideous, 1.
Their steeds doe stagger, and amazed stand; 3.
And eke themselves, too rudely rigorous, 2.

Astonid with the stroke of their owne hand. 2.
Doe backe rebutte, and ech to other yealdeth land. F. Q. 1-2-15-2-2.

The Sarazin, sore daunted with the buffe.
Snatcheth his sword, and fiercely to him flies; 2-2.
Who well it wards, and quyteth cuff with cuff; 2-2.
Each other equall puissaunce envies. 2.
And through their iron sides with cruelties.
Does seeke to perce; repining courage yields. 2.
No foote to foe; the flashing fier flies. 5.
As from a forge, out of their burning shields; 2.
And streams of purple bloud new die the verdant fields. F. Q. 1-2-17.

His blessed body, spoild of lively breath, 3.
Was afterward, I know not how, convaid,
And fro me hid; of whose most innocent death
When tidings came to mee, unhappy maid. 2.
O, how great sorrow my sad soule assaid! 3.
Then forth I went his woefull corse to find. 2.
And many yeares throughout the world I straid
A virgin widow; whose deepe-wounded mind 2.
With love long time did languish, as the striken hind F. Q. 1-2-21.

Drayton's metrical forms are much more varied than Spenser's, and
we find a correspondingly varied application and distribution of alliteration.   In his poems, The Battle of Agincourt, The Baron's Wars, The
Heroic Epistles, and Polyolbion the amount of alliteration is very
constant, as the percentage shows, and does not vary greatly from
Spenser's poems, but in the poems where the shorter verse-form is employed, as in Nymphidia, and Muses Elysium, alliteration ceases to play
an important role.   In Nymphidia the verse is light and airy with just a
tinkling here and there of recurring sound, but the movement is so
dainty that the rhyme furnishes ample repetition, for the accent is quite
centered upon that.

It is in the Alexandrine verse that Drayton employs most allitteration,
as may be seen from the percentage of the Polyolbion.   The Muses Elysium contains only a few passages where the Alexandrine is used; those
passages are descriptive very much in the same way as the Polyolbion, and
it is interesting to note that the amount of alliteration increases accord-
ingly; in the poem, which represents as a whole the minimum, we find
these passages representing the maximum.   The forester, fisher, and

shepherd, each pleads his cause in Alexandrines and a short quotation will be sufficient to show the importance of alliteration in the lively descriptions:

Forrester: (Silvius):

For my profession then, and for the life I lead,
All others to excel, thus for myself I plead:
I am the prince of sports, the forest is my fee,
He's not upon the earth, for pleasure lives like me;
The morn no sooner puts her rosy mantle on,
But from my quiet lodge I instantly am gone,
When the melodious birds in every bush and brier
Of the wild spacious wastes, make a continual choir,
The mottled meadows then, new varnish'd with the sun,
Shoot up their spicy sweets upon the winds that run
In easy ambling gales, and softly seem to pace,
That it the longer might their lusciousness embrace.   (M. E. 1559-70).

The frisky fairy oft, when horned Cynthia shines,
Before me as I walk dance wanton matachines;
The numerous feather'd flocks, that the wild forests haunt,
Their silvan songs to me, in chearful ditties chaunt;
The shades like ample shields, defend me from the sun,
Through which me to refresh the gentle rivulets run;
No little bubling brook from any spring that falls,
But on the pebbles plays me pretty madrigals. (1595-1602).

The fisher closes his plea with the following verses:
And for my pleasure more, the rougher gods of seas
From Neptune's court send in the blue Neriades,
Which from his bracky realm upon the billows ride,
And bear the rivers back with every streaming tide.
These billows 'gainst my boat, borne with delightful gales,
Oft seeming as I row to tell me pretty tales,
Whilst loads of liquid pearl still load my labouring oars,
As streth'd upon the stream they strike me to the shores:
The silent meadows seem delighted with my lays,
And sitting in my boat I sing my lass's praise.
Then let them that like, the forester up-cry,
Your noble fisher is your only man say I.   (167-82).

Repetitions of Various Alliterating Combinations.

XIII.

The repetition of formal alliterating phrases is, comparatively speaking, not very frequent in Spenser's poetry, for here as in the other relations the formal element is lost in the different and varied combinations in which the repetitions are made. The following are some of the formal expressions which occur most frequently in the Faery Queen:

might and maine (mayne); F. Q. I-11-13; III-1-20; ib. 5-21; IV-4-41; ib. 8-45; V-9-19; ib. 12-23; ib. 10-32; ib. 3-12; VI-6-23; ib. 1-39; ib. 4-7; maine and might, VI-12-23.

well, weete (weet, wist, weeting, wote); I-10-28; ib. 65; III-2-9; ib. 4-57; ib. 10-40; IV-1-6; ib. 7; ib. 9-18; ib. 11-53; ib. 12-15; ib. 12-21; IV-6-25; V-4-5; ib. 5-38; ib. 8-15; ib. 10-1; ib. 19; VI-3-46; ib. 5-15; ib. 6-43.

well, weene, (weened,); weeneth, (weened) well; I-7-10; ib. 10-58; II-1-8; ib. 11-35; III-6-1; ib. 6-54; ib. 8-19; ib. 10-21; IV-8-29; 9-7; V-11-42; VI-1-33.

was to weet (weete) III-6-54; ib. 7-30; IV-2-4; ib. 4-8; ib. 4-40; ib. 7-5; VI-5-11.

lightly leaping, (leape, lept, leaped); leaping light; I-8-7; ib. 8-24; II-7-6; ib. 8-49; ib. 11-36; III-1-62; ib. 7-25; ib. 7-33; ib. 12-32; IV-4-31; V-4-40; VI-5-25.

The repetition of the thought is more frequently made by employing different combination. A few examples will show the use:

But he was warie, and it warded well, F. Q. II-11-21.

Yet warily he watcheth every way, ib. III-10-3.

But I them warded all with wary government ib. I-9-10.

Kept watch and ward about her warily ib. III-2-28.

And had she not it warded warily, ib. V-4-11.

His first assault full warily did ward, ib. VI-4-5.

But the most frequent repetitions are those of the word. From the very nature of the subject matter, as in the Faery Queen, certain terms are used repeatedly, and some of these, Spenser seldom employs without alliteration. Such are love, lady, lord, knight, friend, foe, fight, feare, flight, pity, plight, dread, daunger, darkness, death, etc. Of all these love (loving, loved, beloved, lover,) occurs most frequently. One hundred and fifty verses in the Faery Queen have been noted in which some form of this word is used in alliteration. For the word lady (ladies) eighty-eight verses were noted; foe and friends (foe; friend; foe or friend etc),

fight, and fear (fearing, feared, fearfull, fearlesse) alliterate in more than
fifty verses. This manner of repetition is too varied to admit of illustra-
tion by example. It is however important because it shows the great
freedom with which the poet employs alliteration and at the same time
points out significantly some of his favorite terms for alliteration. In
the first term, love, we find the all important subject of the poem. In
the terms lord, lady, knight, foe, friend etc., we recognize the agents,
and in fight, flight, fly, fled, one of the most important features of the
action of the poem. Dread, daunger, darkness, death, perils, punishment, and paine, are the obstacles with which these agents meet, and
feare and pity are the principal emotions. The list might be increased
and we would find alliteration in proportion to the importance of the
terms.

Comparison of Spenser's Shepherd's Calendar With Drayton's Eclogues.

XIV.

Spenser's influence upon Drayton was so direct that he well deserves
the title of "master" for such he was in some respects for the younger
poet. In Poets and Poesy, Drayton praises him above all poets since
Homer, he says:

"Grave moral Spenser after these came on,
Than whom I am persuaded there was none
Since the blind Bard his Iliade up did make,
Fitter a task like that to undertake,
To set down boldly, bravely to invent,
In all high knowledge, surely excellent." (Elg. VIII Vs. 79-84).

He again expresses his admiration in the letter "To the Reader of his
Pastorals," where he calls Spenser "The prime Pastoralist of England."
Of the Shepherd's Calendar, he says: "Master Edmund Spenser had
done enough for the immortality of his name, had he only given us his
Shepherd's Calendar, a master-piece if any." It was as Pastoralist especially that Drayton made Spenser his master, as a comparison of the
Eclogues with the Shepherd's Calendar shows. It does not lie within
the scope of this treatise to discuss in full, this question; but a short comparison of these two poems would show more clearly than has yet been
done, the relation of the two poets, and would prove beyond doubt, that
many striking similarities already pointed out are to be attributed to

a direct influence. There is great similarity in structure; the closing of several of the poems are strikingly similar, and different passages, which it does not lie within the scope of this treatise to discuss, point clearly to a direct influence.

Should this comparison be carried out it would be remarked that in almost every instance. Drayton takes up Spenser's thought and enlarges upon it. In Spenser's poetry we find terse, vivid descriptions, narrations. comparisons etc., which form little pictures all for themselves. This very terseness lends to such passages a ditinct individuality and a strong poetic force. which are one of the great charms of our Poet of the Faery Queen. But when Drayton attempts to follow his master, he loses himself in detail. He heaps up and enlarges until the distinct outlines of the picture are destroyed and the individuality and force are lost.

Such enlarging is the characterizing feature of the relation of the two poets. It is to be found not only in the arrangement and development of the thought, but also in the manner of expression, and it is in the latter, that the influence is most extensive. After a careful comparison of the works of the two poets I have no hesitancy in saying that the influence is most marked in the formal element, or method, and that the alliteration is the prime factor of that element.

The purpose of this investigation so far as the comparison of Spenser and Drayton is concerned, has been to set forth clearly the influence of the one upon the other, and in the pursuance of this purpose, but one side of the question has been discussed, which is by far the less important side, where the question is considered as a whole. Spenser's influence, distinct as it appears in certain respects, was comparatively small. Drayton is a poet for himself with an individuality too marked, and a scope of poetic activity too extensive to be at any time a copyist, or even simply an imitator. In a busy life of forty years he wrote something near a hundred thousand verses. He is above all a writer of historical poems, but we have only to read his fairy poem Nymphidia. his satirical poems, The Moon-Calf. and The Owl, to realize how skilfully he handles the different subjects. He is a vivid writer, but the fine poetic essence of Spenser eludes his every attempt to embody it, and herein lies Spenser's influence. When Drayton, standing on the tip-top of his art reaches up to pluck some delicate blossom from the sweetest of poets, then it is that this influence becomes marked, but his is a rough hand that destroys the beauty in trying to make it his own.

Use of Alliteration.

XV.

We may with truth say, that in Spenser's poetry alliteration is never lacking. In the whole of the Faery Queen, there are no two successive stanzas free from alliteration. In all his other poems written in stanza form (with a varying length of stanzas from four to fourteen verses), there is not a single stanza that does not contain alliteration and of the other poems, Colin Clout has the longest non-alliterating passages (see quotation p.——). Alliteration is so interwoven into the very texture of Spensers poetry that it is impossible to draw a dividing line. The sounds often echo and reecho, and finally die away, so imperceptibly giving place to other sounds that the time of change is not noticed. Yet no where does alliteration become a prime structural factor. As with the poets of the fourteenth and fifteenth centuries, (see Schipper, Englische Metrik, vol. I, p. 223), the use is simply a decorative one. Where then are we to find a guiding principal that will reveal to us the rules or purposes of the poet? We could as well expect from the artist, a rule for his lights and shades, or from the musician a definite and fixed principle for his accentuation and tone-colorings.

Mr. Saintsbury, in his Elizabethian Literature, p. 86., says of The Shepherd's Calendar "Already we can see in it that double command at once of the pictorial and the musical elements in which no English poet is Spenser's superior if any is his equal." It is in the vivid pictures and in the sweet strains of Spenser's poetry that alliteration is most extensively employed. In the rise and swell of the music, in the rush and hurry of the action, and in the sobs and sighs of the lamentations of his music, alliteration is ever present. As we have already seen, the poets favorite method of distribution is the grouping; these groups mark the pictures, the strains. They are not the pictures, nor do they form the pictures, but they are always to be found in the brightest lights or in the darkest shadows. To attempt to illustrate such uses fully would lead us too much into detail, but I cannot forbear giving a few examples, such as the first stanza in Canto 2, Bk. I:

"By this the northern wagoner had set .
His sevenfold teme behind the stedfast starre
That was in ocean waves yet never wet,
But firme is fixt, and sendeth light from farre
To all that in the wide deepe wandring arre;

And chearefull Chaunticlere with his note shrill
Had warned once, that Phoebus fiery carre
In hast was climbing up the easterne hill,
Full envious that night so long his roome did fill."

The following is a vivid little strain:
"It was in freshest flowre of youthly yeares,
When corage first does creepe in manly chest,
Then first that cole of kindly heat appeares
To kindle love in every living breast. (I-9-9).

In the thirteenth stanza is a broader sweep:
Forwearied of my sportes, I did alight
From loftie steed, and downe to sleepe me layd:
The verdant gras my couch did goodly dight,
And pillow was my helmett fayre displayed:
Whiles every sence the humour sweet embayd,
And slombring soft my hart did steale away,
Me seemed, by my side a royall Mayd
Her dainty limbes full softly downe did lay;
So fayre a creature yet saw never sunny day."

The description of a fight is an occasion upon which the poet uses
alliteration with a bold hand. The contest between the knight of the
Redcrosse and the Sarazin furnish good examples. In the fifteenth
stanza (Bk. I-2) the conflict begins:
"The Knight of the Redcrosse, when him he spide
Spurring so hote with rage dispiteous,
Gan fairely couch his speare, and towards ride;
Soone meete they both, both fell and furious,
That, daunted with their forces hideous,
Their steeds doe stagger and amazed stand:
And eke themselves, too rudely rigorous,
Astonied with the stroke of their owne hand,
Doe backe rebutte, and ech to other yealdeth land."

In the seventeenth stanza it continues thus:
"'The Sarazin, sore daunted with the buffe,
Snatcheth his sword, and fiercely to him flies;
Who well it wards, and quyeth cuff with cuff:
Each others equall puissaunce envies,
And through their iron sides with cruellties
Does seeke to perce; repining courage yields

No foote to foe; the flashing fier flies.
As from a forge, out of their burning shields;
And streams of purple bloud new die the verdant fields.

The nineteenth stanza gives the conflict a vivid close:
Who, thereat wondrous wroth, the sleeping spark
Of native vertue gan eftsoones revive;
And, at his haughty helmet making mark,
So hugely stroke, that it the steele did rive,
And cleft his head. He, tumbling downe alive,
With bloudy mouth his mother earth did kis,
Greeting his grave: his grudging ghost did strive
With the fraile flesh; at last it flitted is,
Whither the soules doe fly of men, that live amis."
The portrayal of fear and flight are often by the use of alliteration,
given a breathlessness surprisingly vivid, as:
"So as they traveild, lo! they gan espy
An armed knight towards them gallop fast.
That seemed from some feared foe to fly,
Or other griesly thing, that him aghast.
Still, as he fledd, his eye was backward cast,
As if his feare still followed him behynd;
As flew his steed, as he his bandes had brast,
And with his winged heeles did tread the wynd,
As he had been a fole of Pegasus his kynd." (F. Q. 1-9-21.)
From the strong and bustling tone of battle and of flight, the poet
sometimes modulates his verse to a low sweet strain befitting night, and
sleep, and there also alliteration plays its part:
"The drouping night thus creepeth on them fast;
And the sad humour loading their eyeliddes,
As messenger of Morpheus, on them cast
Sweet slumbering deaw, the which to sleepe them biddes. (F. Q. I-1-36).
And again in the same canto, stanza 41:
"And more to lulle him in in his slumber soft,
A trickling streame from high rock tumbling downe.
And ever-drizling raine upon the loft,
Mixt with a murmuring winde, much like the sowne
Of swarming bees, did cast him in a swowne."
In contrast to the flurried haste of flight, we find descriptions of a soft
ing motion that has not a ripple of agitation:

"Eftsoones her shallow ship away did slide.
More swift than swallow sheres the liquid skye,
Withouten oare or Pilot it to guide,
Or winged canvas with the wind to fly:
Onely she turnd a pin, and by and by
It cut away upon the yeilding wave,
(Ne cared she her course for to apply)
For it was taught the way which it should have,
And both from rocks and flats it selfe could wisely save." (F. Q. II-6-5.)

The quality of the rhyming letters should be noted in the above quotations for they are significant. st is preeminently the rhyming letter for strong conflict, sturdy opposition etc., f and w occur in descriptions of flight, and m and s are the letters for such descriptions as the last few quotations. Such a use of letters in general can be traced throughout Spenser's poetry; d sustains the doleful note of doubt, dread, and danger in all their varied relations; r represents the roaring, rugged, raging element, as c, k, the unkempt, uncurled, etc. In the broad lines of such a use, it seems to me, may be discovered something of the poets personal feeling for the adornment he has used so lavishly. It was at the altar of the Beautiful that Spenser worshipped, and in that worship he sang his sweetest strains, for which as has been shown alliteration was considered a fitting adornment. But in descriptions of disagreable objects, alliteration is frequently almost entirely lacking, as for example the description of the dragon in the closing lines of eight and first lines of ninth stanzas, Bk. 1-11:

"Approaching nigh, he reared high afore
His body monstrous, horrible, and vaste;
Which, to increase his wondrous greatnes more,
Was swolen with wrath and poyson, and with bloody gore:
And over all with brasen scales was armd,
Like plated cote of steele, so crouched neare
That nought mote perce."

For otheer examples see description of a witch, 1-8-17-18; III-7-2 (monster); III-12-11 (Daunger); V-12-30 and 31 (hag).

In conclusion then, we have seen that alliteration is used throughout Spenser's poetry, that is is employed to vivify and intensify the scenes, and that it is the poets favorite adornment for his brightest colored pictures and for his sweetest harmonies. Drayton employs alliteration profusely in many of his poems, but not with a masterful touch. It frequently adds to the jingle but not to the sweetness of his numbers. We find in his poetry but little trace of that finer feeling for music, which alone can guide in a good use of alliteration. Daniel with his sparing use of alliteration, forms a strong contrast to Spenser and Drayton, and furnishes a good means of estimating and comparing the extent to which alliteration has been employed by the other two poets.

VITA.

I, Virginia Eviline Spencer, was born near Pleasanton, Linn Co., Kansas, U. S. A. in 1861. My early education was procured in the public school. Later I attended a private school at Paola, Kansas, conducted by Mr. Wherrell, and completed the course given there in 1884. In the autumn of '86 I entered upon college course in the Kansas State University at Lawrence. I received the degree of B. A. and B. C. from that institution in '91. A part of the next year I spent studying and travelling in Germany. In the spring of '93 I began work in Germanic Philology at the University in Zurich, spending one year there and then returning to America. A part of the following year I spent in London and received the degree of M. A. from the Kansas State University. In '95 I returned to Zurich and resumed my work there and received the degree of Ph. D. from that University in 1897.